Hayballs

Hayballs

Peter Tinniswood

Hutchinson
London Sydney Auckland Johannesburg

First published in Great Britain in 1989 by Hutchinson
Ltd, an imprint of Century Hutchinson Ltd, Brookmount
House, 62–65 Chandos Place, London WC2N 4NW

Century Hutchinson Australia (Pty) Ltd
89–91 Albion Street, Surry Hills, NSW 2010

Century Hutchinson New Zealand Limited
PO Box 40–086, Glenfield, Auckland 10, New Zealand

Century Hutchinson South Africa (Pty) Ltd
PO Box 337, Bergvlei, 2012 South Africa

Set in Linotype Ehrhardt by Input Typesetting Ltd, London

Printed and bound in Great Britain by
Butler and Tanner Ltd, Frome, Somerset

British Library Catologuing in Publication Data

Tinniswood, Peter
  Hayballs
  I. Title
  823'.914 [F]

ISBN 0–09–173859–8

1

In a snug ditch at the edge of a juicy meadow two old men lay side by side dozing peacefully.

A shire horse whinnied.

A roe deer coughed. Rooks squabbled.

It was a plump day.

The sun was plump. The downs were plump. The old cock pheasant was plump with summer.

Yet in the evening breeze there was a faint hint of the chills and damp of autumn.

The first of the winter black-headed gulls wheeled above the meadow, and their eyes were cold and resentful.

In the distance there was the sound of the crack of bat against ball. There were muted cheers, and high overhead a jet plane slivered its white trails across the brittle sky.

It was the last cricket match of the season.

The two old men did not stir.

Their clothing was almost identical.

They wore faded cord trousers, scuffed boots, white flannel vests and moleskin waistcoats.

One of the old men, however, wore a large and expensive gold watch on his right wrist, and as he twitched in his slumbers it glinted.

Their sleep was plump, and the tips of their noses were flushed.

The old cock pheasant whirred its wings and lumbered into weary flight as a man vaulted over the stile.

His gait was soft, his belly was large, his black hair, flecked with grey, curled over his shoulders, and he had a blue-chipped gap between his two front teeth. His chin was stubbled, his shirt was open to the waist and above his left nipple was tattooed the word 'Mild', and above the right nipple was tattooed the word 'Bitter'.

He was forty-three, and his name was Winston Hayballs.

He looked down on the two old men. A warm smile cracked across his strong-weathered face.

He chuckled.

And then very deliberately with the tip of his left wellington boot he kicked each of the old men firmly in the ribs.

'Now then, you old buggers,' he said. 'Time for tea.'

The old men awoke without rancour and proceeded to scratch the dark recesses of their armpits and crutches with deep languid contentment.

'Come on then. Time for tea. Can't delay it no longer,' said Winston Hayballs. 'The match is over. We lost. We was defeated look. Kept up our proud record right to the bitter end we done.'

He helped the old men to their feet. He dusted them down. He removed the slugs and snails from their moleskin waistcoats.

'You old buggers,' he said warmly. 'You leads the life of Riley, doesn't you, and that's without a doubt.'

The erstwhile comrades in slumber nodded solemnly to each other and set off in their different ways to their different homes.

The old man with the expensive gold wristwatch loped off with Winston Hayballs. His name was Grampy. He lived in a council house at the back of the village pub.

The other man directed his tracks towards the misting beech woods.

He lived in a palace.

He was the seventeenth Duke of Wiltshire.

2

The village of Winterleaf Gunner lies deep in a snuck and a snuggle of the smooth-cropped downlands of the West Country of England.

It has a church.

It has a pub.

It has a shop.

There is a slow chalk stream with deep pools. The water meadows are cluttered with buttercups. Barn owls hunt in the night. Woodcocks ride in the musty woods. There is a Cuckoo Tree, and in the spring the cuckoos gather there and call:

'Cuckoo. Cuckoo. Cuckoo.'

The whole village sings with them.

Winterleaf Gunner is the seat of the Dukes of Wiltshire but everyone in the district knows that its principal family is the Hayballs.

They live in four council houses in a tangled, rumpled lane just to the rear of the village pub.

The houses are painted white. They have green roofs.

The road is called Idle Lane, and in the winter the ruts and runnels are skated with ice, and in the summer whitethroats flutter softly in the banks of nettles and dock.

At Number Two lives Winston Hayballs. He has a wife called Doreen, three sons called respectively Roderick, Tarleton and Wood-cock, and a daughter called Baksi. They are of various ages.

Grampy lives there, too. He has his own bedroom, and from its window he can see, poking above the beech woods, the towers and turrets of Florey Palace, the home of his best friend, the Duke of Wiltshire.

Florey Palace is damp and cold. Grampy's bedroom is warm.

Next door to Winston Hayballs at Number Four lives his eldest brother, Asquith. He has a thin-shanked wife called Nola. She is Irish. They are childless, and Asquith is in prison.

Across the road at Number Three is the home of Winston's unmarried sister, Clementine. No one has ever dreamed of shortening her name, although in a moment of passion at the village fete a squaddie from Halifax once tried. She has six children. One works in the abattoir.

Finally at Number Five lives Venetia, widow of Winston's brother, Baldwin, who died of sadness during a stormy winter. Venetia has an eighteen-year-old daughter called Barbara, who is studying at a university somewhere in the Midlands. She has long blonde hair and cool thighs.

'What did you say she was studying for?' says Winston every time he meets Venetia.

'She's studying to be clever,' says Venetia primly and passes on her way with her umbrella.

As tea came to its natural end at Number Two Idle Lane purple-veined clouds reared up above the rim of the sparse downlands which overlooked Winterleaf Gunner.

'That's it then,' said Grampy. 'That's the end of summer.'

'Too bloody true,' said Winston Hayballs. 'And I can't stand sardines neither.'

He banged on the table with his fist, and his wife, Doreen, came scurrying in from the kitchen, where she was eating with her children.

'Yes?' she said. 'Was you calling by any chance?'

'Too bloody true I was,' said Winston Hayballs. 'I was calling loud and long and clear.'

His wife shuffled nervously and wiped her hands hurriedly on the hem of her pinny.

'What was you calling for?' she said.

'I was calling to say I doesn't like sardines,' said Winston Hayballs. 'I abhors sardines, I does.'

His wife nodded sadly and repaired silently from the room.

Grampy picked at his teeth with the spike from his gardener's clasp knife.

Then he said:

'Your wife is the ugliest woman I ever seen in the whole of my life.'

'Without a doubt,' said Winston Hayballs, nodding gravely. 'Without a shadow of a doubt she is ugliness personified.'

Grampy took off his trousers, hung them neatly over the radiogram and fell asleep in the knock-kneed rocking chair.

Winston Hayballs opened a bottle of home-brewed sloe and elder-berry wine, settled himself in the aged humpbacked armchair and commenced to read for the seventh time a history of the Spanish Armada.

He read intently, sucking sharply through the blue-veined gap between his two front teeth and grunting savagely.

After a while he looked up from his book at the sleeping Grampy and said:

'I been thinking.'

There was no response from the old man. His mouth sagged open. His top dentures rested on the tip of his lower lip. The hairs in his nostrils vibrated.

Winston Hayballs stood up and shook him fiercely by the shoulders.

'I been thinking,' he bellowed.

Grampy yawned, rubbed his eyes and eased a ruck out of his long woollen underpants.

'Oh aye?' he said. 'And what you been thinking about?'

'Sir Francis Drake,' said Winston Hayballs. 'I reckons through my researches of a reading nature that on the quiet he was an out and out shit look.'

Grampy yawned again.

'Well, I shouldn't bother about it,' he said. 'We won, didn't we?'

3

Next day the wind was mean.

It came from the east, and its throat was harsh.

Grampy rose early.

He dusted the bed fluff from his long woollen underpants. He slicked back his hair with Brylcream. He went downstairs to the kitchen, where his granddaughter, Baksi, was sitting at the Formica-topped table writing squintily into her homework book.

'Morning, Grampy,' she said with a smile.

Grampy scowled.

'I got a pain in my belly,' he said.

'That's because you needs your breakfast, you daft old bugger,' said Baksi, and she jumped from her chair and cut a thick hunk off the loaf of bread her mother had baked late the previous night before sawing wood for the stove and affixing a new plug to the video machine.

She spread the bread with swirling layers of tangy beef dripping, and she sang to the rhythms of the swish of the knife.

She was plump. She was young and saucy. She was happy.

She took a large tumbler from the dresser, went into the darkest depths of the cold pantry, and, singing softly to herself in time to the flow and flood of the dark red liquid gulping out from the neck of the stone pitcher, filled the glass to the brim with stiff draughts of her father's home-brewed port wine.

Grampy stuffed the dripping bread into the hip pocket of his cord trousers, and, clutching the tumbler of port wine tightly to his chest, grunted to Baksi and stepped out into the garden.

It was a true countryman's garden.

The weeds were rampant. The roses were lank with blight. Aged ice-cream wrappers mingled in profusion with flattened beer cans and rotting crisp packets. A rusting scythe with a splintered shaft lay crooked and weary against the side of a roofless kennel, which had once been the home of a lurcher called Aneurin.

Grampy walked carefully down the garden path, bracing himself so

10

that he would not slip on the black-slimed flags and ducking so that he would not gouge out his eyes on the thorns from the roses.

He beat his way through an angry hedge of berberis and hawthorn, and, kicking open a warped, one-hinged wicket gate, he stepped out into the wood.

It was a small wood.

In its heart was a glade.

In the glade was a beech tree.

And there, resting his back against its broad trunk, staring contentedly upwards into its mop-headed canopy, his knees scrunched up to his chest, was Winston Hayballs.

He was drinking from a pint pot of home-brewed port wine.

Grampy nodded cursorily.

'What do you reckon then?' he said.

'Not a lot,' said Winston Hayballs.

His chest was littered with the crumbs from his swift-bolted dripping bread. There were specks of fat in the stubble of his unshaven chin. There was a hole in the right knee of his grease-stained trousers, and he was wearing odd bicycle clips.

'I see you're all dressed up then,' said Grampy. 'You going out with one of your bits of fluff then?'

'Oh yes. Without a doubt,' said Winston Hayballs. 'I thought I'd hop into my motor, my car look, and drive over to Compton Blissett and meet that bit of fluff with the squat legs.'

Grampy settled himself on the spring-soft earth beside him, downed his tumbler of port wine in a single gulp, wiped his mouth on the tail of his shirt and said:

'Ah. Got squat legs then, has she, this bit of fluff of yours?'

'Oh yes. Without a doubt,' said Winston Hayballs. 'You knows the great virtue of squat legs in a woman, don't you?'

'What?' said Grampy.

'They don't get in the way,' said Winston Hayballs.

Grampy scratched his chin thoughtfully. He clucked his tongue solemnly and sighed. And then he said:

'That's philosophy, is that.'

Winston Hayballs smiled.

'I knows,' he said. 'It can come in quite handy at times, can a dollop of the old philosophy.'

An army helicopter roared low over the wood. Its clatter thudded

11

deep into their breastbones. The rasp of its blades twitched at the muscles of their necks.

Winston Hayballs spat and said very softly:

'Bastard.'

Grampy nodded, and he spat, too.

'Bastard,' he said.

Shortly afterwards they parted.

Grampy made his way to the far side of the wood. It was on an eminence and from this vantage point he could look out over the village of Winterleaf Gunner.

Jackdaws chacked in the drifts of wind around the slim and leggy steeple of the church.

Fan-tailed pigeons fluffed and preened on the lichened Dower House roof. Smoke wheezed from the chimneys of the cottages that lined the weary dogleg of the main street.

Swallows flocked above the still waters of the ancient trout hatchery tucked into a tight and narrow bend of the River Florey.

The army helicopter swooped low over the village again. Its exhaust roared and rattled, and the old half-blind Border collie chained up in the yard of the village shop threw back its head and howled.

Grampy shook his head sadly.

He climbed nimbly over the wooden fence that separated the wood from Cuckoo Tree Meadow, and, nodding amiably to the shire horse and the damp-nosed bullocks, headed off towards the village.

He hunched his head into the ice-lipped east wind that had begun to bend back the elms which rimmed the village green and its cricket pitch.

Grampy paused.

He looked around slowly.

It was his favourite spot in the whole of the world.

During his time away at the wars as he crouched in flinty foxholes, toiled in the blizzards of bleak mountain passes or shivered under rat-fouled blankets he had kept its picture firmly in his mind.

The pub. The church. The thatched scorer's box. The splintered benches ringing the old oak. The sullen pond with its moorhen and muscovy duck.

And in the distance high above the banks of beeches the towers and turrets of Florey Palace, seat of the Dukes of Wiltshire.

They owned every nook and cranny of Winterleaf Gunner.

12

For centuries they had guided and blighted its fortunes. For generations they had bullied and cajoled, threatened, imprisoned, tortured, transported and evicted its inhabitants.

They had seduced its maidens, killed off its young men in ill-led battles in foreign climes and overseen with haughty indifference the sickness and penury of its old people.

They were English aristocrats to the very core.

Grampy grinned and set off in his long, slow countryman's lope down the twisting, pot-holed drive that skirted the village green and led direct to the main gates of the palace.

As he passed by they opened and a navy-blue chauffeur-driven limousine edged out.

Hunched in the back seat was a small, balding man with fat cheeks, crisp black moustache, stiff white collar and pinstriped suit.

He glared at Grampy and flicked his shoulders.

His deep violet eyes flecked with gold flashed.

He was the Duke of Wiltshire's son, the Marquess of Sturminster.

He was the local Member of Parliament.

Grampy spat long and hard.

'Bastard,' he said.

He continued his walk, following the line of the high stone wall that enclosed the palace grounds. After a quarter of a mile he stopped. In a dark recess was a small green wooden door the height of a tall man's hips.

Grampy looked furtively over his shoulder from right to left.

Then he took out a large brass key from the pocket of his moleskin waistcoat, inserted it into the creaking-lock door, pushed sharply with his knee and stooped his way through the opening.

He slammed the door behind him.

He smiled.

The start of another day.

The start of a day that was like every other day he could remember during the course of his life.

With a spring in his step he set off to meet his best friend, the seventeenth Duke of Wiltshire – Baron Nadder, Earl Idle, Viscount Quidstock of the Chase and life president of the Winterleaf Gunner Allotment Holders' Association.

13

4

Grampy and the Duke of Wiltshire were born at the identical hour on the identical day of the identical year in those far-off years when ankles were slim and the century was young.

Every morning since they could remember they had met in the fruit store house set deep in the shrubbery at the bottom of the palace's stintless kitchen gardens.

There they had sucked through peaches, they had crunched through apples of every hue and shape, plunged their teeth deep into the hearts of juice-oozed melons, griped their stomachs on bullet-sharp redcurrants, sugared their tongues on fat, purple gooseberries and gorged themselves sick on nectarines and quince.

They had fought there, savagely and bitterly and without restraint.

They had wept there.

They had grieved silently.

They had laughed. They had grumbled and groused. They had caroused.

They had talked endlessly.

Always they had been content and staunch in each other's company.

Now, however, the fruit store house had long since been abandoned by the gardeners.

Ivy and honeysuckle festooned and spidered its walls and roof, but it was still sound and secure against the weather.

It was cool in the summer and warm in the winter, and the slatted windows let in the dusty sun and kept out the frost and scouring winds.

Inside little had changed.

There was no fruit, of course.

But the great trays on which it had been stored remained, stained and scrubbed and reeling with the rich aromas of distant bounties.

The ceiling was deeply smirched and reeked with the smoke from countless, cherished, sweet-cored pipes. The floorboards creaked and crooned. The wicker baskets piled high in all four corners were mellow and mature and sly with secret smells.

There were dormice in the eaves.

Grampy knew every inch of the grounds and gardens of Florey Palace. He knew every inch of the hothouses and conservatories. He had pruned and grafted. He had hoed and raked. He had worked there since he was a spindle-shanked boy and the one-eyed mare, Milly, had pulled the muck cart each morning from the stables, and grayling had browsed and darted in the shadow of the thatched wooden bridge that arched the River Florey.

When he started there had been thirty-six gardeners.

Now there were but three, and two of them had tired, old hearts.

The Duke of Wiltshire was waiting for him when he entered the fruit store.

'You're late, you bastard,' he said.

'No, I ain't,' said Grampy. 'It's you what's early.'

'How dare you contradict me, you scum,' said the Duke of Wiltshire.

'I ain't contradicting you,' said Grampy. 'I'm just saying you're wrong look.'

He took out the half-eaten slice of dripping bread from the hip pocket of his cord trousers and threw it onto a tray.

Instantly the Duke of Wiltshire snatched it up, rammed it into his mouth and gobbled it back greedily, smacking his lips and licking his fingers.

'Well then?' said Grampy when he had finished. 'What you got for me, you greedy old gannet?'

The Duke emptied the pockets of his moleskin waistcoat and spread the contents on the tray.

'Oh hell,' said Grampy. 'Not that bloody awful caviare stuff again? I seen hamster shit what looks more appetizing than that.'

He took out his gardener's clasp knife and prodded suspiciously at the produce laid out before him.

'No smoked salmon then?' he said.

The Duke shook his head.

'None of them canape things?' said Grampy.

The Duke shook his head again.

'You ain't been bloody trying, has you, you miserable old sod?' said Grampy grumpily, and he filled his mouth with a hunk of ripe Stilton cheese and a wedge of pineapple soaked in curaçao.

A drowsy, summer-sated wasp bumbled into the store house through a sagging slat in the windows. It landed with a fat-bellied thump on the tray and waddled towards a sliver of glazed passion fruit.

15

The Duke raised his fist.

'No,' said Grampy. 'Leave him be.'

The Duke nodded.

'Nice chaps, wasps,' he said. 'Buzz, buzz, buzz. Nanny Smithson was stung by a wasp once. She came from Skipton in the West Riding of the county of Yorkshire. Buzz, buzz, buzz. I was in the Western Desert once. With the chaps, you know. We were fighting Gerry. And he sent over this reconnaissance plane to spot us out. Buzz, buzz, buzz, it went. You should have heard it.'

'I did,' said Grampy. 'I was there.'

'So you were, old chap,' said the Duke of Wiltshire. 'So you were.'

Grampy finished off the remains of his crêpe hongroise, staring intently at his aged companion, who was chuckling to himself, rolling his eyes and twitching his thumbs.

'You know what's wrong with you?' he said.

'What?' said the Duke.

'You're failing,' said Grampy. 'You're going doodle alley pip.'

'You scum, you bastard,' shouted the Duke, and his deep violet eyes flecked with gold flashed. 'I am not failing. I've never felt so fit in the whole of my life. You're the one who's failing. You're growing old. You're growing senile. Good God, sir, it's obvious to anyone you're a damn sight more senile than I am. And I'm not the slightest bit senile. Not yet anyway.'

The wasp crawled to the side of the tray, teetered on the brink for a moment and then dropped to the floor. It landed on its back. It waved its legs.

'Buzz, buzz, buzz,' said the Duke, and with a smile he raised his boot and squashed the wasp to pulp.

Grampy stared at him silently again.

Then he said:

'You had a good night, did you, last night?'

'No I bloody well did not, sir. It was rotten,' said the Duke. 'Frozen to the gunwales I was. My God, the cold. Eskimo time. Blue noses. Blue toesies. I'm too old to be cold in my own bed at my time of life. Cold as a stepmother's breath I was. And you?'

'Snug as a bug in a rug,' said Grampy. 'That old central heating – he were rumbling away like a good 'un all night long he was. He's been a good friend to me, have that old central heating.'

The Duke of Wiltshire thumped his fist hard onto the tray.

'It's not bloody well fair,' he said. 'Why can't I have central heating?'

Speckles of ire appeared in his deep violet eyes flecked with gold. His old warrior shoulders were thrust back. The chin jutted.

And then his body softened.

His voice softened, too.

'The happiest day of my whole life was when I spent the night at your home when we were thirteen,' he said. 'I was so warm. We had dripping bread and home-brewed port wine for breakfast. Your sister showed me her naked titties. There was a dead fieldmouse in the trap in the kitchen. I'd never seen bare breasts before. Never seen them that often since, come to that. The seventeenth Duchess wasn't keen on that sort of thing, you know. Do you remember the Duchess? I do. Great big horse of a woman, she was. She used to neigh at the butler. On the night of our honeymoon I discovered she'd got pubic hair like us. Damned odd, I thought. Still do now, if you twist my arm.'

He sighed.

He smiled.

Then he continued:

'I was so warm when I stayed at your home. We had cow heel stew for supper. And in the morning your sister came into our bedroom and she said to me: "Have you ever seen things like this before?" And with that she flopped them out. Great whoppers they were. If she'd shown them to Adolf Hitler, he'd never have dared go to war against us. I've never been so warm in the whole of my life. I did enjoy spending the night at your home when we were thirteen.'

'Yes, I knows you did,' said Grampy. 'And when you got home to your palace, your old dad gived you the thrashing of your life look. He thought you'd run away to sea, didn't he?'

'He most certainly did,' said the Duke. 'Fearful whacking he gave me. Almost as beastly as the ones they used to give me at Eton.'

'Harrow,' said Grampy. 'You went to Harrow, you barmy old bugger.'

'So I did, sir,' said the seventeenth Duke of Wiltshire. 'So I did.'

The east wind snuffled its icy snout in the tangles of honeysuckle and ivy, but inside the store house it was warm and cosy.

The two old men lit their pipes.

They dozed fitfully.

Sometimes they spoke.

Sometimes they smiled and chuckled.

Memories coiled and swirled in their minds.

The screech of a Stuka dive bomber. Screams in the hull of a burning tank. Goldcrests' eggs in a nest of down. Azure and chestnut flash of kingfisher. Bounding white rump of roe deer. Crunch of sand and rattle of bayonet.

'I saw your ghastly son with the tattoos this morning,' said the Duke. 'He was in his motor, his car.'

'He would be,' said Grampy. 'He was off to see one of his bits of fluff.'

'Which one?' said the Duke.

'The one with the long legs from the foot clinic.'

'Oh her,' said the Duke.

They dozed again.

Fat sheen-black grapes from the hot house. Fat black stream of smoke from the tailplane of the dying Heinkel. The acrid wallow of Red Sea troopship. Scream of fox cub. Tumble of otter.

'I seen your vile son this morning,' said Grampy.

'Sturminster!' said the Duke. 'Bloody bastard!'

'That he is,' said Grampy. 'That he is without a doubt.'

The Duke suddenly leaned forward and said urgently:

'He's up to no good, you know.'

'How do you reckon that?' said Grampy.

'I can feel it in my bones,' said the Duke. 'First he opens up the palace to all those beastly tourist chaps with their smokers' coughs and their obese, slack-jawed offsprings. And now he's hatching something else up.'

'What?' said Grampy.

'I don't know,' said the Duke. 'But it's bound to be something horrid. It always is. Why doesn't he get himself a wife? Any old thing would do. I'm not fussy. She could be flat-chested with a bad temper for all I care. Nanny Smithson went to Oldham in the county of Lancashire to die. She had no love in her life, you know. There was no love in her bones. No love in her soul. She used to neigh at the butler. My God, how I hate Sturminster. If only he'd find someone like Nanny Smithson and take it all out on her.'

They dozed again.

Memories.

Buzz, buzz, buzz of spotter plane. Crack of rifle. Stray shot. Ripple of flames along cowl of engine. Steep bank. Slow glide to flinty desert. Shriek of metal. Fire.

Grampy woke up, prodded the Duke in the ribs and said:

'I remembers that spotter plane in the desert. We shot it down look. And when we got to the wreckage, all we found was bottles of scent. Bottles and bottles of scent. Bottle after bottle there was.'

'So there was,' said the Duke. 'So there was.'

'I tell you something else I remembers,' said Grampy.

'What?' said the Duke eagerly.

'I remembers the day of the village fete when we had dirt-track racing on Cuckoo Tree Meadow.'

'Do you?'

'Yes.'

'Good for you, old chap. Good for you, sir.'

A jay cackled. A woodpecker yaffled. The autumn swallows chittered.

At length Grampy stood up and said:

'I'd best be going look. It's time for dinner.'

'Yes,' said the Duke of Wiltshire. 'It's time for luncheon, too.'

5

The swallows left Winterleaf Gunner for Africa.

The fieldfare and redwing arrived from the Northlands.

They gorged themselves on the autumn berries. They sang sad remnants of the songs of summer.

One morning Winston Hayballs met his sister, Venetia, in the village shop. She was buying a zip.

'What did you say that daughter of yours was studying?' he said.

'She's studying to be clever,' said Venetia, and she rattled her umbrella primly.

Autumn lingered.

It was reluctant to go.

Old Granny Shergold reached her hundredth birthday with a cough and a tremble. A week later she died, and at her wake in the village pub Nansen Ticehurst set his turn-ups alight.

'Ghastly old woman she was,' said the Duke of Wiltshire next day in the fruit store house.

'Without a doubt,' said Grampy. 'Haven't you got no more of that French patty stuff?'

'No,' said the Duke.

'Bastard,' said Grampy.

For three days Winterleaf Gunner was lashed by gales.

The village cowered beneath them. They howled. They brought down two holm oaks and a horse chestnut and clattered the old bones of the thatched wooden bridge that spanned the River Florey.

Wilson Rappaport, owner of the Dower House, shot himself in the shed at the bottom of his garden.

They half-drained the swimming pool in his garden as a mark of respect.

'Ghastly fellow,' said the Duke of Wiltshire.

'Without a doubt,' said Grampy. 'Pass us another of them quail's eggs, will you?'

The gales blew themselves out and slank wearily and hangdog to the flat, crumbling coasts of the east and ruffled the surface of muddy creeks.

Clear, crackling nights. Misty mornings. Twin-engined army helicopters thumping the downs. A stray and lonely little auk bobbing on the village pond.

Thomas Fitchup won £131.27 on the football pools and went to live with his married sister in Margate.

In the House of Commons the Marquess of Sturminster made a speech on the subject of sexual morality in marriage. It was well received by those in the know.

A coping stone fell from the village church and killed a starling.

And then a respite from the cold.

Honey-gold sunsets. Deep leaf piles purring smoke. Bats hunting the dusk. Lazy afternoons mild with fat marrows.

Mrs Fokine's African grey parrot escaped from its cage and was never seen again, although Tarleton Hayballs swore he heard it talking at midnight in the wood at the back of his house.

The Marquess of Sturminster made a speech in the House of Commons on the folly of unmarried motherhood and extramarital sex. Winston Hayballs shot a fallow deer in the grounds of Florey Palace.

'What's this?' said the Duke of Wiltshire in the fruit store house.

'Venison sandwich,' said Grampy.

'Yum, yum,' said the Duke. 'Why the devil can't we ever have venison at home?'

Then winter struck.

Blizzards raked the flanks of the downlands. Snow drifted. Buses slid into ditches. The trout hatchery choked itself on ice. Blackbirds cowered and died in stilted hedgerows. Winterleaf Gunner was cut off from the outside world for eleven days. The pub ran out of beer and Cecil Woodyates, the undertaker's assistant, swore he could see goose pimples on the buttocks of the girl in the calendar. He touched it to make sure.

In the first week of November Winston Hayballs' eldest son, Roderick, joined the Royal Navy. In the second week his brother, Asquith, returned from his stint in prison.

'What do you reckon then?' said Winston Hayballs. 'Had a nice time, did you?'

'Piss off,' said Asquith Hayballs, and the following week he was committed to prison once more for assaulting a confectioner.

In the last week of November Clementine Hayballs gave birth to her seventh child.

Baksi cuddled it close to her plump breasts and said:

'Now I knows what I got bosoms for. To hold them tight to a rare little beauty like you.'

It rained solidly during the first half of December.

There was turmoil in the village wife-swappers' circle in the smart-young-executive estate in the lee of the Dower House. Mrs Godwin was discovered in bed with Edward Yardley, the twice-weekly commuting stockbroker. According to schedule she should have been in bed with the consultant obstetrician.

'What did you say that daughter of yours was studying?' said Winston Hayballs to his sister, Venetia, in the village shop. She was buying a magnifying glass.

'She's studying to be clever,' said Venetia, and she clipped her brother round the ankles with her prim umbrella.

On Boxing Day the Hunt gathered outside the village pub, and Grocott, the landlord, served stirrup cups to the gentry.

The Marquess of Sturminster fretted beadily on his coal-black stallion from Ireland, and cast his deep violet eyes flecked with gold on the drab gaggle of villagers waiting for the pub to open.

'Grocott!' he barked.

'Sir?' said the landlord.

'Will you stop these frightful people from gawping at me at once.'

'Certainly, sir,' said Grocott, and he turned and shouted at the top of his voice: 'Stop gawping.'

'Piss off,' said Winston Hayballs and he winked extravagantly at a girl with damp mushroom eyes seated astride a chestnut gelding.

Frost in January.

Harsh. Unyielding. Unlagging pipes. Chapping toes and hardening the tips of unmufflered noses.

The dormice slept snugly in the rafters of the fruit store house. Grampy slept snugly, too, in his oiled socks and his long woollen underpants.

The Duke of Wiltshire roamed the midnight corridors of Florey Palace shouting at the top of his voice:

'Sturminster, I'm cold. Damnit, you wet-toothed bastard, I'm freezing to death.'

Next day three men in Barbour coats and bright yellow wellington boots appeared on the village green with the Marquess of Sturminster. One had a camera. One took copious notes and whispered furtively into a pocket recording machine. The other prowled round the pond with a measure.

'He's hatching something up,' said the Duke of Wiltshire.

'Without a doubt,' said Grampy.

And then he yawned and said:

'Do you remember the day of the village fete when we saw the one-legged acrobat from Peru?'

'Of course I do,' said the Duke. 'He came from Brazil, didn't he?'

Rain in February.

Brimming vats of rain.

Hysterical, clawing fingers of rain scratching and screeching on window panes.

Sodden meadows. Slucking gum boots. Streaming, drumming gutters. The River Florey swollen and bruised with flood. Bloated carcasses of sheep wedged in forks of trees.

In the first week of March planning permission was granted to the village shop to build a lean-to extension to the outhouse in the yard.

'What about the extension to my bleeding garage?' said Grocott, landlord of the village pub.

'Don't you worry about that, my old wingsy bash,' said Winston Hayballs. 'You got another two years to go yet.'

'Two years?' said Grocott.

'Without a doubt,' said Winston Hayballs. 'That's the usual time it takes for the council to accept your bribe.'

He took a long gulp at his scrumpy, sucked through the blue-veined gap in his two front teeth, winked, grinned and said:

'Do you want to buy a swan I just shot by the hatchery? It didn't fall off the back of a lorry look.'

Then quite suddenly spring appeared.

It came in with a flush of wheatears. Chiffchaffs swayed exhausted on whispers of willow. Sandmartins flicked their white bellies, and rooks bowed and cawed high in the gossiping skulls of the gaunt elms.

Baksi lay awake at night.

The milky scents of her infant niece clung closely to her plump young body.

'The juices are flowing,' she whispered to herself in the darkness. 'The sap is rising. Oh yes, he's rising without a shadow of a doubt.'

The following morning came the news that rocked the whole of the village of Winterleaf Gunner.

'There's new folk from London moving into the old Dower House,' said Grampy.

'Oh really?' said the Duke of Wiltshire. 'By the way, what's this you're giving me today?'

'Swan sandwich,' said Grampy.

6

'They call themselves the Empsons,' said Winston Hayballs.

'Who does?' said Grampy.

'Them folks what is moving into the old Dower House.'

Grampy chuckled heartily.

'They don't know what they're letting themselves in for, poor buggers,' he said.

'That they don't without a doubt,' said Winston Hayballs, and he chuckled, too.

They were lying side by side against the trunk of the old beech tree in the glade at the heart of the wood at the back of their house.

The lesser spotted woodpecker looped, red-rumped and chequered, across the glade. Celandine glowed. Soft voles rustled. Badgers deep in their setts grunted in their sleep.

Grampy yawned.

'I seen that Baksi of yours in the grounds of the palace yesterday morning,' he said.

'Oh yes?' said Winston Hayballs, and he picked at a sodden clod of bread that had affixed itself to the roof of his mouth.

'What was she doing there then, that Baksi of yours?' said Grampy.

'Ah, she'll be out looking for a bit of nookie no doubt,' said Winston Hayballs.

'Oh,' said Grampy. 'That's all right then.'

An army helicopter clattered overhead. A soldier in a light-blue forage cap peered out through its open doors. He held a pair of field binoculars to his eyes.

'What's he doing?' said Winston Hayballs. 'It's too early in the year to catch bints with no clothes on sunbathing nude in their back gardens.'

'Bastard,' said Grampy, and he finished off the last of his home-brewed port wine with a gulp and a contented belch.

He looked over to his son, who was poking with intense concentration into the deepest recesses of his right ear with a spent match. His wellington boots were turned down to the ankles and covered with slime. There were grease stains on his belly and dry slivers of dandruff on his shoulders.

'You going off to meet one of your bits of fluff then?' said Grampy.

'No,' said Winston Hayballs.

'Why not?'

'Owing to the grounds that I ain't got none no more.'

Grampy raised his spiked and bushy eyebrows.

'Oh,' he said. 'Lost your knack, has you?'

'No,' said Winston Hayballs. 'What I done is I booted them all into touch look.'

'Why?'

'Cos they ain't got no powers of conversation.'

'What's conversation got to do with having your bit of nookie?'

'Plenty,' said Winston Hayballs. 'The whole of a man's life don't revolve round the state of his old Donger, you know.'

'No?'

'No,' said Winston Hayballs. 'A man needs to talk about other things of a permanent nature when he's had his bit of congress of a sexual nature on the sly. You take that bit of fluff with the squat legs from Compton Blissett.'

'What about her?'

'Well, I was over there last week look. And after we'd hit the old jackpot more or less mutually and I'd stored away my old Donger for safekeeping and she'd put back her teeth, I says to her: "Has you ever read *Cousin Pons* by that Honoré de Balzac, the French blokey from France?" "No," she says. "Is it a book?" Well, I just give her this look, I did, and I says: "Course it's a bleeding book. I read it, didn't I, from the public library?" '

'Well, that seems conclusive enough for me,' said Grampy. 'Many's the good fart I've had on the quiet in the public library.'

And then very slowly his eyes closed and his chin dropped to his chest.

He began to dream.

He crept shiftily into his memories.

He saw two young men standing stiff and wicked in the fruit store house. One had spindle shanks. The other had deep violet eyes flecked with gold.

The young girl with the ruddy cheeks smiled at them.

She stretched herself out on a tray of blushing peaches. They shed their juices beneath her. Her thighs glistened. Her breasts ran sticky. She scooped up the flesh of the peaches and ran it slowly over her body.

Slow squelch beneath her buttocks.

Coarse, chapped-red fingers, stubby and oozing with juice.

– Go on then. Say something, said the young man with the deep violet eyes flecked with gold.

– I don't know how to, said the young man with the spindle shanks.

The girl laughed.

She rocked with laughter, stuffing her fists into her mouth and thrashing her legs.

The two young men fled.

Grampy awoke with a start.

'What's that you was saying?' he said.

'I was talking about my bit of fluff in Nether Fenton,' said Winston Hayballs.

'What about her?' said Grampy.

'Well, I went to visit her the day after I'd had my literary contretemps with my bit of fluff in Compton Blissett look.'

'I see,' said Grampy, and with difficulty he stifled a yawn.

'Well, this bint in Nether Fenton, she's one of the best bits of fluff I ever had in the whole of my life look. Inventive. Got a deep navel full of secret promises. Makes a lot of noise when she's on the job. Know what I mean?'

'Mm,' said Grampy.

'Well, I thinks to myself, I'll try a new tack here look. What I'll do is I'll see what she's like when it comes to the old conversation stakes. So we clambers into the back of my motor, my car look, and she pulls down her kecks and hoiks up her skirt as per usual, and as per usual she's making these moaning noises in between taking puffs at her Park Drive. But what I'm doing is nothing, bugger all. I'm just propped up on my elbows looking at her and trying to get my toe out of the ash tray.

'Anyhow, when she's finished her fag, she smiles at me like a burst bag of cement and she says all archly like: "What's the matter, Winston? Having trouble hoisting the old mainmast, are we?"

'I shakes my head look. "No," I says. "Nothing like that. I'm just wondering what you thinks of General Mola's part in the capture of Valladolid." And what does she say? Nothing. Not a dicky bird. And, do you know, looking at her lying there with her knees bunged up close behind her earholes and the nicotine stains on the end of her nose, you'd have thought that the origins of the Spanish Civil War had never even took place. And that's when I realized I couldn't go on no more with my bits of fluff.'

'Mm,' said Grampy, awash and boistering in the dreams of his youth.

Winston Hayballs nodded gravely to himself and said:

'So I kicks her out of my motor, my car look, and I decides there and then quite dispassionate that in future and from henceforth and now on I shall only consort with bits of fluff what are intelligent and knows their onions as regards matters pertaining to the old grey matter.'

Grampy chuckled.

'In that case, my old beauty, you got your work cut out round here, hasn't you?' he said.

'Oh, I don't know,' said Winston Hayballs. 'Something'll turn up sooner or later. It always does in matters pertaining to bits of fluff.'

They talked on in the timid sunlight, and as they did so a large beige and apricot removal van edged its way slowly down the village street.

It was followed by a bottle-green Volvo estate car. The driver was Nancy Empson. Beside her sat her brother, William. And hunched up in a tartan travelling rug in the back seat was her father.

They were about to move into the Dower House.

Grocott, landlord of the village pub, watched them pass by.

'Bugger it,' he said. 'They don't look like beer drinkers to me.'

From the bedroom window of the veterinary surgeon Mrs Godwin observed the convoy with deep and naked interest.

She turned to her bed-bound and surfeited companion and said:

'Mm. Most interesting. They could be likely recruits methinks.'

The removal van and the bottle-green estate car turned off the main street and drove a short way down a stunted, rippled lane and pulled up outside the Dower House.

Nancy Empson stepped out of the car.

She was a bold, handsome woman in her late forties.

William Empson stepped out, too.

He was a thin, straw-haired man in his early forties. He was tall. He wore a compass round his neck.

He gazed around him gloomily.

'I'm going to hate it here,' he said.

'Nonsense, William,' said Nancy sharply. 'You're going to love it.'

28

'No, I'm not. I'm going to hate, loathe and detest it,' said William. 'Why did we have to move out to the country? Why couldn't we have stayed in London? I loved it in London. All those railway terminals. All those tunnels. All those deserted wharves. Why did we have to move to the country?'

Nancy Empson tapped her foot impatiently on the balding gravel path.

'You know perfectly well why we've moved here, William,' she said. 'It's why we've always moved – because of Father. Bloody Father, William. That's why we've moved.'

She turned to the car and bellowed:

'Well, come on out, Father. We're here.'

The rear door of the car opened stiffly and out stepped an elderly man. He wore a bright red shirt with a navy-blue tie. His trousers were fawn. His golf shoes were white and chocolate brown.

He looked up as the army helicopter roared overhead.

He smiled broadly.

'Whacko – helicopters,' he said. 'Do you know, chaps, I'm really going to like it here.'

7

The first person to visit the Empsons after their arrival in Winterleaf Gunner was Mrs Godwin.

Just before she called the Dower House was in turmoil.

The Empsons sat in the drawing room amid a wasteland of packing cases and black plastic sacks.

Nancy Empson wore a paint-stained fisherman's smock. Her black hair was unkempt. She wore no make-up and her fingernails were rimmed with black.

William Empson sat hunch-shouldered in the middle of the room muttering:

'I hate it here. I loathe it.'

Father sat on a packing case puffing at his pipe. He wore a bright green shirt and a canary-yellow tie. His trousers were black and white houndstooth.

'Chaos,' he said. 'Lovely, lovely chaos.'

'Father!' screamed Nancy.

And then the front doorbell rang.

Nancy clenched her fists, tautened the muscles of her neck and muttered softly but intently:

'Oh God. Oh, my God.'

When she opened the front door, she saw a tall, cool and elegant woman. Her hair was blonde.

Nancy fluffed at her hair, but then hastily put her hands behind her back to hide her black fingernails.

'Yes?' she said. 'What do you want?'

Mrs Godwin smiled briefly at her discomfort and cast a swift and mocking eye over her rumpled appearance.

'Welcome to Winterleaf Gunner,' she said. 'My name is Mrs Godwin.'

'What?' said Nancy. 'What's that you said?'

'Perhaps I might come in?' said Mrs Godwin.

'What?' said Nancy, the panic rising in her voice. 'Come in? Now?'

'That's right,' said Mrs Godwin, and she stepped inside.

Her perfume lingered in the hall as she made her way towards the drawing room.

Nancy hurried after her, ruffling at her hair and tugging at her fisherman's smock.

She called out plaintively:

'I'm afraid we're . . .'

Before she could finish Mrs Godwin had stepped into the drawing room.

She flickered a smile at the scene and then stared hard at William.

'Well, well,' she said. 'And who might you be?'

'That is my brother William,' said Nancy, scurrying into the room and raising her arms helplessly at the packing cases, the tea chests, the cardboard wardrobes and the mounds of black plastic sacks. 'That person sitting in front of you is my father and my name is Nancy Empson and I . . . and I . . .'

She shrugged her shoulders and sank back on a bulging cardboard box.

'Careful,' screamed William. 'There's all my notes on the Cambrian Railway in there.'

Mrs Godwin smiled once more.

'And how are you settling in here, William?' she said.

'Settling in? Settling in, did you say?' wailed William. 'I hate it here. I bloody well loathe it.'

And he fled from the room.

Father chuckled.

'Fearfully fraught sort of cove. Has been ever since he was in short trousers,' he said, and he raised his pipe in greeting to Mrs Godwin, gazing appreciatively at her ankles as he did so.

'Yes, well, I'm afraid we can't offer you sherry or anything,' said Nancy. 'The thing is we've been condemned.'

'Condemned?' said Mrs Godwin.

'Well, not us,' said Nancy. 'Our boiler.'

Mrs Godwin raised her eyebrows.

'You see, when we moved in yesterday, I smelled gas and William rang the emergency services, and they came and told us we'd got a gas leak – twenty-two per cent and rising. And so they cut off our gas, and when they saw the central heating boiler, they said it was dangerous and illegal, and so they hung this little card round its neck saying it was condemned, poor thing. So we've no gas and no hot water and

31

William's broken two panes of glass in the kitchen door and half the ceiling in the dining room has fallen down and most of the sockets in the house are live and make this awful bang when you put plugs in and . . . well, I'm afraid we're in a bit of a mess.'

Mrs Godwin nodded.

'In that case you need Winston,' she said.

'Winston?'

'Winston Hayballs. He's the village odd-job man and poacher. If you want any plumbing done, you call for Winston. If you want a tree chopped down, you call for Winston. If you want a salmon or a brace of pheasant or a side of venison or a hare or a woodcock, you call for Winston. Winston is a treasure, absolutely invaluable and divine. Without Winston we couldn't possibly survive in the village.'

'Then I'd better send for Winston,' said Nancy.

'Oh, there's no need to do that. Winston will be round very soon.'

'What?'

'You mark my words. Winston is certain to be here within the hour. He has a nose for these things,' said Mrs Godwin. 'What did you say your name was by the way?'

'Nancy,' said Nancy. 'Nancy Empson.'

'Well then, Nancy, if you or your father should need a bath, please don't hesitate to call on me.'

'I say,' said Father. 'A good old slog in piping hot water – whacko.'

He nodded cheerfully at Mrs Godwin, lingering his eyes with pleasure on the smoothness of her long, slim neck.

Mrs Godwin bade her farewells, and as she stood at the front door, she said:

'Remember my invitation, Nancy. And do pass it on to your brother, won't you? He'd be most welcome. Very welcome indeed, in fact.'

Within half an hour Winston Hayballs arrived at the front door of the Dower House.

He twisted the tips of his drooping Zapata moustache, spat on his wellington boots and rang vigorously at the front doorbell, knocking at the same time with his fists.

The door opened to reveal a tall, bold, handsome woman in her late forties.

Her dark hair was freshly brushed and combed, and it glowed. She wore a white cotton blouse, severely cut. Her pantaloons were black and silk. She wore gold lamé slippers. Her make-up was immaculate. Her fingernails sparkled.

Nancy Empson was in her pomp and in her prime.

She gazed haughtily at the ruffianly figure standing before her, picking his nose and grinning.

'Yes?' she said. 'What do you want?'

Winston Hayballs clicked his tongue appreciatively and winked and spat on his wellington boots again.

'Winston Hayballs,' he said. 'At your disposal, my old ducks, and at your service, too.'

And he brushed his way past her and stepped inside the house.

'Now look here,' said Nancy. 'Why does everyone just barge in here without being invited?'

'Oh, we always does, missus,' said Winston Hayballs. 'Old Wilson Rappaport, he always kept open house when he was alive.'

'But he's not alive now,' said Nancy. 'That is the whole point. We live here now. This is our house. It's our property.'

Winston Hayballs nodded.

'We'll see,' he said. 'We'll see.'

He poked his head into the drawing room. Father was sitting in a half-empty packing case, snoring softly, and embers from his pipe smouldered in the lap of his black and white houndstooth trousers.

'Who's the old codger then?' said Winston Hayballs.

'I beg your pardon?' said Nancy. 'That old codger happens to be my father, and he's a Master of Arts at the University of London.'

'Ah,' said Winston Hayballs. 'Clever old sod, is he?'

He smiled at her. He winked and commenced to make his way towards the kitchen.

'Now look here,' said Nancy hurrying after him.

'Oh, it's all right, missus,' said Winston Hayballs. 'No need to show me the way. I knows this house well. Oh yes, old Winston does, without a doubt.'

He ran his fingers along the dado rail and said:

'Well, he'll have to come down for a start. He's rotten to the core, is this dado rail. And I don't like the look of your skirting boards neither. Get on well with old Wilson Rappaport, did you?'

'I never met the man,' said Nancy. 'He died several weeks before I came to view the house.'

'That was the worst thing what you ever done in your life look,' said Winston Hayballs, stepping into the kitchen.

'I beg your pardon?' said Nancy, tripping on his heels as she followed him.

'The worst thing what you ever done in your life, missus, was to come down here and take over this house from Wilson Rappaport. What a man he was to be sure. What a laugh. A rogue and a vagabond. And you wants all your doors dipping, too.'

'What?' said Nancy, and her proud shoulders began to droop, and two tiny beads of perspiration appeared on her upper lip.

Winston Hayballs looked through the broken panes of glass in the kitchen door out into the back garden.

'You going to keep the swimming pool in the garden?' he said.

'No, I don't think so,' said Nancy.

'You do right, missus,' said Winston Hayballs. 'That swimming pool, he'll be a positive deathtrap look. Full of germs from top to bottom and crawling with toads. Course old Wilson Rappaport looked after it proper. He maintained it.

'Oh yes, without a doubt that's what he done. He heated it. He filtrated it. He scaled it out regular, and, of course, he didn't pay for nothing.'

'No?' said Nancy, and despite herself she found cosy corners of her mind warming to the fat-bellied poacher with the slimy wellington boots and the tattoos above his nipples, 'Mild' and 'Bitter'.

Winston Hayballs smiled at her.

'Yes, we had some times in this swimming pool look. Old Wilson Rappaport, he used to hold parties here and everyone in the village came. They'd get tanked up after a sesh at the pub, and they'd stagger over here, and they'd be jumping fully clothed in the pool, and some of them was bollock-naked, too.'

'I beg your pardon?' said Nancy, and to her surprise she found a blush coming to her cheeks.

'Why don't you sit down?' said Winston Hayballs. 'Park your arse.'

'Thank you,' said Nancy. And she sat down.

Winston Hayballs smiled at her again and winked.

'Oh yes, the thing about old Wilson Rappaport was he never paid for nothing as regards the swimming pool. He just by-passed the gas meter look. That's why you got all them pipes littered over your back garden. No legality to them. He botched them up himself.'

34

Nancy stretched out her legs and scratched her chin thoughtfully.

'That probably explains why we had our gas leak,' she said. 'Twenty-two per cent and rising.'

'Course it do,' said Winston Hayballs. 'And your electrics'll be up the spout, too, as well.'

'Ah,' said Nancy. 'That's one of the things I want to talk to you about.'

'Course it is,' said Winston Hayballs. 'And your roof needs doing, too.'

'Not according to the surveyor.'

'Oh, you don't take no notice of surveyors, missus,' said Winston Hayballs. 'They don't know nothing round here look. You get a surveyor in the city, and he knows something. He do without a doubt. But you get a surveyor here in the country and he . . . Do you know your extension's illegal?'

'Oh,' said Nancy. 'Is it important?'

'Course it is, missus,' said Winston Hayballs. 'When you lives in the country look, you has to have planning permission for everything. You even has to have planning permission, if you wants to go for a shit.'

'Now that's quite enough of that language, if you don't mind,' said Nancy.

'No, I don't mind, missus,' said Winston Hayballs. 'Come on then. On your hind legs, and I'll show you round the house.'

He marched purposefully out of the kitchen. And Nancy to her great surprise found herself following him meekly.

He went confidently from room to room, pointing out the defects.

'See this meter here?'

'Yes,' said Nancy.

'He needs slinging straight away. He's dangerous. And he's illegal, too, as well.'

'Oh dear.'

'And see this rad on your landing.'

'Yes.'

'Well, he needs throwing out. All your rads needs throwing out. And as for your roof.'

'What about my roof?'

'He needs to be completely re-tiled. Tell you what, missus. This house, he needs completely re-gutting from top to bottom.'

Nancy stood at the top of the stairs and tapped her feet angrily. The gold lamé slippers glinted, and her dark brown eyes turned coal black.

'I have to tell you, Winston, that it wasn't my plan when we moved here to have the house completely re-gutted,' she said. 'The survey simply said it needed a certain amount of work doing.'

'Ah yes, missus, but what did they mean by "a certain amount of work"? The word "certain", he do cover a multitude of sins. Without a doubt he do.'

He descended the stairs, prodding at the banisters with his stumpy fingers, clicking his tongue, sucking through the blue-chipped gap between his two front teeth and shaking his head sadly.

When he reached the bottom, he turned to Nancy and said:

'Tell you what I'll do, missus. I'll do your roof, rewire the house from top to bottom, put in new central heating and generally make the house habitable and fit to live in.

'My price to you? One thousand and seventy-six pounds inclusive of VAT and Vee Ay Tee and cash in hand at regular intervals to coincide with times when I'm skint. Now I can't say more fairer than that, can I?'

Nancy stared at him open-mouthed and speechless.

He slapped her on the shoulders and said:

'Right then, missus. He'll be a messy job. Noisy. Mucky. Bleeding inconvenient all round to man and beast. I'm not hiding nothing from you. But if you wants to live all comfy and conducive here, you'll just have to put up with it.

'I'll start on Monday look. And if you wants a bath in the meantime, you're very welcome to use my facilities. But bring your own towel and hang it over the bathroom keyhole if my Tarleton should be at home, dirty little sod he is. Right then, missus, I bids you good day look. And I think you've got a kink in the strap of your bra.'

And with that he slapped Nancy on the shoulders once more and left the house.

Nancy sat on the bottom step of the stairs for some time.

Her bold, handsome face was pensive.

She felt her breasts tautening. She felt a quiver in her secret parts. In the cold corners of her mind someone smiled, someone chuckled. A tongue clucked.

She clasped her hands to the side of her head.

She shouted at the top of her voice:

'No. No, no, no. Please, no.'

An army helicopter flew overhead and Father, roused from his slumbers, smiled and said:

'Whacko. Jolly Dee.'

8

Grampy munched placidly at the thick slice of Doboz Torte.

The rich caramels wreathed lazily in the upper reaches of his nostrils. When he had finished, he turned to the Duke of Wiltshire and said: 'I thinks old Winston's got hisself a new bit of fluff look.'

'Really,' said the Duke of Wiltshire, wolfing down the last morsel of his dripping bread. 'Anyone in my circle of acquaintance?'

'No,' said Grampy.

'Ah,' said the Duke of Wiltshire. 'Anyone in your ghastly circle?'

'I don't know,' said Grampy. 'He haven't said nothing to me. He haven't told me her name or the shape of her legs. But I can see it in the way he behaves look. When he gets hisself a new bit of fluff, he's forever shaving hisself twice a week and swilling out his navel in the back kitchen.'

'Good man,' said the Duke of Wiltshire. 'Can't beat the old field hygiene, can you?'

The two old men were sitting as usual in the fruit store house. It was raining. The rain drummed on the roof. It was the first of the summer rain: plump, fat and fizzy, warm to the breath, caring and loving.

The great magnolias in the palace grounds were in full bloom.

The first of the passage sandpipers were scuttling through the sodden hummocks of the water meadows. Hobbies scythed the sweet skies above the downlands, tumbling, gliding, looping the loop, rapacious for the first of the summer swifts.

Clementine had her seventh child christened Natalie Annette, and Baksi cuddled it constantly and buried its head deep into her pumpkinned breasts.

The Duke of Wiltshire began to snore wheezily.

His gaunt cheeks sagged and then fluttered. The broken veins on the bridge of his nose glowed.

Grampy stared at him silently and intensely.

Then he said softly to himself:

'He's failing. The old bugger's failing without a shadow of a doubt.'

He stood up and walked across the creaking floorboards, wincing as his knee joints creaked.

He opened the store house door and looked out.

It had stopped raining. The air was clear.

Yellow billow of kerria. First flush of rosemary blue. Fading mauve of crocus.

Grampy's winter-long eyes sparkled.

How he remembered those far-off days of his childhood.

Wrestling in the mud of Cuckoo Tree Meadow, scratching, biting, snarling, cursing, bloodied and bruised. Bathing naked in the still waters of the hatchery. Plop of kingfisher. Stab of heron. Stalking the shrubberies on the nights of the summer-scented balls.

He turned and looked at his companion, slumbering twitchily in the gloom of the store house, his head resting crooked on a tray, his left arm hanging limply by his side.

'You're failing,' he said. And then he shouted at the top of his voice: 'You're failing. And I won't bloody well have it.'

He dashed inside the store house and in a frenzy commenced to pummel the Duke of Wiltshire and shake him.

The old aristocrat struggled feebly against the onslaught.

When it had finished, he fought for breath and wheezed:

'Just having a nap, that's all. No harm in having a nap.'

Grampy looked down on him and said:

'What's the matter with you?'

'Nothing,' said the Duke.

'Yes there is,' said Grampy. 'I've known you all my life look. I knows you better than what you knows yourself. And I tell you there's something wrong. What?'

The Duke tried to fight free of his fierce, flashing eyes. He could not. So he shrugged his shoulders and said quietly:

'It's Sturminster.'

'What about him?'

'He's hatching something up.'

'Bollocks.'

The Duke of Wiltshire smashed his fist hard onto the tray.

'He is,' he shouted. 'He is. He is. He's stuffed the house full of these surveyor chaps with their maps and their little black waterproof notebooks. He's locked away in his study all day with ghastly thin-jawed creatures from the county council. There's these scum coming

39

down from London with those briefcase things and pockets full of fountain pens. There are these women with long necks and diphthongs. He's hatching something up.'

'Well, unhatch it then,' said Grampy.

'What?'

'Stand up and fight the bastard.'

'What?'

Grampy ground his teeth and narrowed his eyes.

His voice broke into a deep growl.

'You makes me sick, you does,' he said. 'You've let him trample all over you, you has.'

'I haven't.'

'You has, you old bugger,' said Grampy. 'He's took you over lock, stock and barrel. He runs the whole caboodle, he does. And all you does is slink and cower and grouse and grumble. Do something. Get back your rights. Get yourself in charge again.'

'I don't want to be in charge.'

'You does.'

'I don't. I don't.'

Grampy sat down heavily on an old cobwebbed barrel. He shook his head sadly.

'You used to be a lion,' he said.

The Duke of Wiltshire hung his head.

'When we was abroad soldiering, you was a lion. A rampant lion with not an ounce of fear in your bones. We followed you everywhere look. Without question. We'd have followed you to the ends of the earth. I'd have laid down my life for you, that I would have without a doubt. And you'd have laid down your life for me.

'You was loved.

'I loved you.

'I loved you like buggery.

'And now?

'Now I thinks you're a shit.

'You ain't a lion no more now, my old wingsy bash, my old mate. You're a weak-kneed sickly lamb, and all you does is cower and bleat pathetic.'

The Duke of Wiltshire kept his head down.

The rain returned.

It hissed through the ivy and the honeysuckle.

40

Then suddenly the Duke sprang to his feet and launched himself at Grampy. They fell to the floor. They wrestled, biting, snarling, cursing. They rolled on the floor, thrashing their legs, clawing and scratching and ripping. They hit the base of a pile of wicker baskets, which fell about them with a crash.

Baksi, creeping through the grounds and attracted by the noise, timidly poked her head round the door of the fruit store house.

When she saw the two old men, panting and wheezing and sobbing as they fought, she giggled.

She was still giggling as she made her way swiftly through the kitchen gardens and furtively entered a narrow side door in the east wing of Florey Palace.

9

Crunch!

Smunch!

Bumph!

The sledgehammer slammed into the brickwork.

The house shook. Hunks of plaster flaked from the ceilings. Ornaments rattled.

Crunch! Smunch! Bumph! Humph!

William Empson staggered out of his study, his hands clamped firmly to his ears.

'I can't stand it,' he shouted. 'I can't stand it. It's driving me mad.'

'William, don't be such an old fusspot,' said Nancy. 'It's only Winston.'

'Only Winston,' shouted William. 'If I hear those two words again, I shall disembowel myself on the spot. I shall personally garrotte myself.'

'Oh dear,' said Nancy. 'Oh dear.'

She followed William into the drawing room.

Father was sitting by the french windows with a tray containing a glass of milk, digestive biscuits, celery, radishes, gentleman's relish, cream crackers, olives, sardines and hard-boiled eggs.

He looked up from his morning paper, waved to them with his pipe and said:

'What-ho, chaps. I really love it here. Absolute perfection. And don't worry about the noise. It's only Winston.'

At this William dashed out of the room, sobbing and whimpering softly:

'I can't stand it. It's driving me mad.'

Nancy found him in the kitchen. He was sitting at the table, hands on his head, rocking slowly backwards and forwards.

'I hate it here,' he said. 'I'm going back to London.'

'You can't,' said Nancy.

'Why not?'

'Because you can't look after yourself.'

William sighed and nodded his head sadly.

'Why did we have to move here?' he said. 'We were so happy in London.'

Nancy rested her hand on the nape of his neck. With her other hand she massaged his shoulders gently. He grunted.

'You know very well why we moved here, William,' she said.

'Father. Bloody Father. Ever since Mother died all we've ever done with our lives is move from house to house because of Father. Father's got to move because of his chest. Father's got to move because of his legs. Father's got to move because of his . . .'

Crunch! Smunch! Brumph!

'I hate Winston,' said William. 'I do, Nancy. It's a wicked thing to say about another human being, but I hate him with a real throbbing passion.'

'There, there, William,' said Nancy, and she led him back to his study.

Everything was in order.

His bookshelves were stacked neatly. His stationery cabinet was situated at the perfect angle next to his writing desk, which was immaculate and tidy. The filing cabinets were solemn.

William sat down at his desk.

'How's your book going, William?' said Nancy.

'Well, when we were in London, it was going wonderfully well. I'd just reached the dénouement.'

'Well, I'm sure you'll be able to reach another one here, William,' said Nancy, smiling warmly. 'What's the book about by the way?'

'The Somerset and Dorset Railways. It's the definitive history,' said William.

'Good,' said Nancy. 'I'm sure it will be fascinating for devotees of the subject.'

She patted him on the head.

Crunch! Smunch! Berrrrumph!

A thin volume on the early history of the Manchester, South Junction and Altrincham Railway fell off the top shelf of the bookcase.

William groaned weakly.

Nancy left the room.

She went into the kitchen, poured herself a glass of sherry and sat down at the table.

She felt weary. She had worked non stop since they had moved into the house. Apart from the gas boiler, the electrics, the radiators and the roof everything in the house was shipshape and sparkling clean.

Once more she had made a home for her family.

Once more they had done nothing to help.

She sipped her sherry.

She remembered the houses of the past.

The great lowering Edwardian mansion in Dorset, where Father had run his private school. She had loved that. The dripping, slate-shrouded cottage in North Wales where they had moved after his retirement and his wife's death. She had hated that.

The narrow town house on the windy north-east coast. Father had loved it, but then his teeth had intervened. The fat and leafy stone house in Yorkshire with the tram stop outside the front garden gate, the morbid, monkey-puzzled vicarage in East Anglia with coots attacking the swampy lawns, the cottage nuzzling at the lazy creek. Those she had loved.

And now the old Dower House. How would she react to that? She looked round the dark, sly kitchen, and a sudden shiver rilled down her spine, and whispers of fear tugged at her heart.

And then the door opened, and in stepped Winston Hayballs.

His shirt was open to the waist and the folds of his belly glistened with sweat. His greasy, lank hair was covered in brick dust. His hands were bloodied.

He smiled at Nancy and said:

'By God, missus, you don't half look tasty today.'

'That's enough, thank you very much, Winston,' said Nancy sharply. 'Kindly remember who you're talking to.'

Winston Hayballs chuckled and slumped himself into the chair opposite her.

He lifted up his arms and sniffed deeply into the pits.

'Cor, I don't half niff, don't I?' he said.

Then he leaned across to Nancy and said urgently:

'Does you by any chance know the works of Jean-Jacques Rousseau? He's a philosopher look.'

'I know he's a philosopher, Winston,' said Nancy. 'He wrote *The Social Contract*.'

'Course he bloody did,' said Winston Hayballs. 'That's why it's in the public library.'

44

Father shuffled into the kitchen from the hall. He was wearing a pink silk shirt and a black velvet bow tie.

'What-ho, Winston,' he said. 'Just toddling off for a spell in the shed at the bottom of the garden. Fearfully pleasant shed as sheds go.'

He raised his pipe to them and pottered off into the garden.

'What's he want to go to the shed for?' said Winston Hayballs.

'To drink his gin,' said Nancy.

'What?'

'We're not supposed to know. But Father is a secret tippler. Every house we leave always has its great cache of empty gin bottles, and Father always says: "Good God, I wonder how they got there?" He drinks in the lavvy, too.'

'Well, it's more hygienic than doing the other, isn't it, missus?'

'Winston!' said Nancy. 'I wish you wouldn't talk like that. It's disgusting.'

'Oh, we all talks like that in the country, missus,' said Winston Hayballs. 'Very basic we are as regards the basic facts of life. You better get used to that now you're living here.'

'Yes, well, I'd rather come to grips with it in my own way and my own time, if you don't mind.'

Winston Hayballs winked at her and studied her thoughtfully.

She felt a blush coming to her cheeks.

She was forty-eight, and she was blushing.

She was blushing because she was being stared at by a fat-bellied country slob with stained teeth and greasy hair and flapping wellington boots.

Once more the shiver rilled down her spine.

She felt that someone else was staring at her, too.

Winston Hayballs chuckled again.

'In the old days I used to sit here by the hour with old Wilson Rappaport,' he said.

'Did you?' said Nancy.

'Oh yes. We used to talk about bits of fluff.'

'What?'

'Well, he was very fond of the fair sex and members of the opposite gender, was Wilson Rappaport,' said Winston Hayballs. 'I reckons that's why ultimate he topped himself in the shed at the bottom of the garden. Yes, that's why he done it without a shadow of a doubt.'

He stood up, sniffed at his armpits again and said:

45

'Right then. I'll just go and have a word with that William about the state of the rads in his study.'

'No, you can't go in now. He's working,' said Nancy, panicking.

But she was too late.

Before she could stop him, Winston Hayballs had marched down the corridor and barged open the door of William's study.

William sprang back from his typewriter with alarm.

'Hullo, William,' said Winston Hayballs with a friendly grin. 'Not disturbing you, am I?'

William buried his head in his hands once more, stifled a sob and said wearily:

'No, Winston, you're not disturbing me. Far from it.'

'That's all right then,' said Winston Hayballs.

He took a wrench from his back pocket and began to clank at the radiators, hammer at the skirting boards and whistle loudly and tunelessly through the blue-veined gap between his two front teeth.

He looked up.

'Sure I'm not disturbing you, William?'

'Not at all,' said William. 'I'm only trying to write my book. It's not important. Not important at all really.'

Winston Hayballs nodded wisely.

'You know, William,' he said. 'I don't know how you writer blokeys manage to write with all this noise and disturbance going on. Can you write when people are talking to you as well?'

'With great difficulty, Winston. With immense difficulty.'

Winston Hayballs sucked deeply between his gapped teeth.

'Well, that's just like me look,' he said.

'Is it?'

'Oh yes. You see, when I'm knocking down a wall or knocking the living shits out of a defunct rad, I can work and talk at the same time. Dead easy. A doddle. But I'm damned if I can go down to the pub and play a game of darts and talk at the same time. Can't be done look. I expect that's just the same as what you are, William.'

'Sort of,' said William.

Winston Hayballs made a space for himself on the desk by brushing a pile of neatly stacked papers to the floor and sat down.

'What do you write books about then?' he said. 'Mucky things?'

'I beg your pardon?'

'You knows what I mean,' said Winston Hayballs with a wink and a leer. 'Do you write mucky things about Hollywood?'

'No,' said William. 'I write books about railways.'

Winston Hayballs tapped the side of his chin with a stubby forefinger.

'Well, William, you can get up to some rare old dirty things on the railways, can't you?' he said. 'I remember last time I went across to Yeovil the day after the village fete. I went with Betty Hayballs look. Cor! You knows Betty Hayballs, of course.'

'No, Winston. I can't say I do.'

'You not met Betty Hayballs yet?' said Winston Hayballs, thrusting his left thumb into his navel and wriggling it violently from side to side. 'Well, you got a nice surprise coming to you, William, and that's a fact, my old wingsy bash. She's what I call nice and juicy and ripe, if you follows my meaning as regards her endowments. She's my first cousin, too, and she don't wear no knickers, if it's hot. Well, to get back to basics, William, there we are together, me and Betty Hayballs, in this empty compartment look, going across to Yeovil look and . . .'

'That used to be on the Somerset and Dorset Line,' said William.

'What did?'

'Yeovil,' said William, his eyes beginning to glint with excitement. 'It used to be on the Somerset and Dorset Line. They called it officially the Somerset and Dorset Committee. I'm writing a book about it.'

'A serious book?'

'Yes.'

'You're writing a serious book about railways?'

'Yes. That's how I earn my living.'

'And they ain't smutty books?'

'Oh no.'

Winston Hayballs sniffed the thumb that had been exploring the depths of his navel and nodded his head slowly.

'Well, that explains a lot, William,' he said. 'That do explain a lot without a doubt.'

He jumped down from the table, dislodging a stapling machine, a jar of coloured pencils and a packet of cough lozenges.

Before leaving the room he turned and said to William:

'Right then, William, carry on with the good work. And if you wants any research done as regards Betty Hayballs and our mutual trip to Yeovil, I'm your man.'

He slammed the door violently behind him, and a fat volume entitled *The Steam Railways of Bulgaria* fell off the second shelf of the bookcase.

Winston Hayballs found Nancy in the garden. She had her back to him. She was motionless.

Her back was straight. Her buttocks were firm. Her ankles were slim. Her hair glowed.

'Missus,' he whispered. 'Missus.'

She spun round with alarm and clapped her hands to her breasts.

When she saw Winston Hayballs her lips curled back with anger.

'Winston Hayballs,' she said. 'Don't you ever dare do that again. I am mistress of this house, and you will show me the respect and deference that is due to me. Do you understand that? Do you understand the situation between us? I am the employer. You are the workman. Kindly behave in that fashion. Remember your status. Do you understand that? Have I made myself clear?'

'Course you has, missus,' said Winston Hayballs, and he delicately plucked a greenfly off the front of her blouse. 'You coming to the cricket dance on Saturday night?'

'What?'

'It's the opening dance of the season look. Everyone in the village goes to it. It's expected of them. It'll be expected of you, too, as well.'

'But I don't like cricket.'

'Neither do I, missus,' said Winston Hayballs.

'Then why do you go?'

'In the hopes of picking up a new bit of fluff look,' said Winston Hayballs with a grin. 'By the way have you ever read the works of Adam Bede what is wrote by George Eliot?'

10

It was a perfect spring evening.

Winterleaf Gunner preened itself.

The cricket dance was to be held in the village hall. It was festooned with bunting and fairy lights.

Inside Nansen Ticehurst, the honorary caretaker, was sprinkling the floor with french chalk, and Grocott, landlord of the village pub, was setting up the bar.

In the kitchen the volunteer refreshment ladies were making up the buffet.

The two long trestle tables groaned with hams, poacher's pies, cheeses, joints of spiced beef and racks of cold lamb and side of venison.

There were savoury dips and meat pastes, loaves freshly baked at the village shop, fruit dumplings, tarts and tartlets, lardy cakes and date cakes, and in the centre of each table a glazed peacock, traditional present from the Marquess of Sturminster, who as always was to be guest of honour.

Miss Roebuck, the village postmistress, wreathed in steam, was scalding the innards of two vast tea urns, and the recently widowed Mrs Fokine was putting the finishing touches to the decorations on the trifles, the jellies and the blancmanges. She was wearing a long black velvet dress and white lace gloves.

Clementine Hayballs sat contentedly in a corner feeding her seventh child at the breast and stirring the custard for the fig and honey pudding.

Dusk sauntered through the village arm in arm with the smell of new-mown grass.

The lights of lonely farmsteads twinkled in the hunched mass of the distant downlands. The River Florey creamed itself round the piers of the old packhorse bridge. Cattle lowed.

Winston Hayballs completed his toilet by dousing his chest with liberal quantities of his eldest son's foot powder.

Then he went downstairs and said to his assembled family:

49

'Right then, you lot of miserable buggers, all ready to go, are we?'

'Yes,' said his two sons, Tarleton and Woodcock.

'Yes,' said his only daughter, Baksi.

He looked at her as she stood by the kitchen door in her brand-new dress, eager and wicked-lipped.

'Aren't you showing too much of your tits in that dress?' he said.

'No, Dad,' said Baksi. 'You got to let them breathe, ain't you?'

'Well, make sure they does it private then,' said Winston Hayballs. 'And keep them out of my trifle, too, while you're about it.'

He ushered his brood to the front door and turned to his wife, Doreen, and said:

'And there's no need for you to be idle while we're out. You can make yourself useful putting a new lick of paint on the door of the outside bogs.'

'Why can't I come with you instead?' said Doreen.

'Cos you're too bloody ugly, that's why,' said Winston Hayballs. 'And besides it's a complete waste of money buying a ticket for you. No one ever asks you to dance. And all you does is sit there taking up space and casting a damper on everything with your face. Just be satisfied with your lot and make sure my supper's ready for eating when I comes home.'

He stepped out into the spring night and breathed in deeply.

'Perfection,' he said. 'I wonder if she's ever read the works of Thomas Love Peacock.'

In the old Dower House the Empsons were preparing to leave for the village dance.

William stood glumly in the hall, hunch-shouldered and sulky.

'I hate dances. I loathe dancing,' he said. 'Why can't I stay at home and write my book?'

'Because it's expected of you to go to the dance,' said Nancy. 'We're living in the country now. So we've just got to muck in.'

'I hate living in the country,' said William. 'I like cities and parking meters and warehouses and Greek workmen's cafés and advertisement hoardings. I'd give anything to be back in Belsize Park.'

'This is your home now, William,' said Nancy sternly. 'This is our home and we make the best of it, don't we? And stand up straight, throw your shoulders back and do up that button on your braces.'

She dismissed him with a brisk wave of her arm and made her final inspection of Father.

He was wearing a lime-green brocaded smoking jacket, primrose-yellow shirt and cerise bow tie, tight pinstriped trousers and shining black patent leather dancing pumps.

'Perfect, Father,' said Nancy. 'I've never seen you looking more handsome.'

Father smiled contentedly.

'Well, I always was a bit of a dandy in my younger days. A real masher, you know,' he said. 'Your mother and I used to cut quite a dash when we went to those dances in India. Did I ever tell you about the dances your mother and I went to when we lived in India?'

'Yes, Father,' said Nancy wearily. 'Many many times.'

'I remember the ball we went to one Whitsuntide in the Ganges Valley. Or was it the Chota Nagpur Plateau?'

'It was the Ganges Valley,' said William.

'Was it, by Jove?' said Father. 'Well, wherever it was, it was a most fearfully interesting evening. Can't remember a thing about it, but it must have been a tip-top do for it to have remained so vividly etched in my memory.'

'That's right, Father,' said Nancy gently, and she led her party out into the spring night and breathed in deeply.

'Perfection,' she said. 'Absolute perfection.'

'No, it isn't,' said William. 'It smells of horses.'

Mrs Godwin stood naked in front of the full-length mirror in her bedroom.

She gazed at her reflection.

She ran her hands slowly over her body.

She fondled her boyish breasts.

She smoothed her thighs.

She closed her eyes and rolled her head slowly from side to side, revelling in the slick and slide of her blonde hair about her shoulders.

'You are a very beautiful woman,' she said. 'And very sexy, too.'

Then she dressed quickly, made her toilet and stepped outside into the spring night and breathed in deeply.

'And it's a very sexy evening, too,' she said. 'Oh yes, it's a really really carnal evening.'

In the fruit store house in the grounds of Florey Palace Grampy and the Duke of Wiltshire dozed fitfully as bats flittered and night beetles battered at the slats of the windows.

They both wore faded black frock coats with stained lapels and frayed buttonholes.

The Duke of Wiltshire wore grey cord trousers, Grampy's cord trousers were navy blue.

Their mufflers were white, and their medals clinked to the irregular heaving of their chests.

The Duke of Wiltshire had a black eye and a bruise on the bridge of his nose. Grampy had a swollen upper lip and contusions on his chin.

They awoke simultaneously.

They yawned and stretched out their arms and their legs.

They rubbed their eyes and scratched long and hard at their crutches.

'Another village dance then,' said Grampy lazily.

'Yes,' said the Duke of Wiltshire.

He smiled, and he chuckled.

'Do you remember the first one we ever went to?' he said.

'Oh yes. Without a doubt,' said Grampy.

He remembered other village dances, too.

The first year of peace after the Old War when young widows sat in the shadows of the village hall and the feet of the dancers seemed to sluck in the mud of Flanders. Black Bottoms and Charlestons, sleek hair with centre partings, salty kisses and swooning sighs. The Duke's first night as guest of honour and his formal first dance with the maid from the Dower House; he tall, haughty and shy, she blushing, bountiful and willing.

Grampy stood up.

'Best be going then,' he said.

'Yes,' said the Duke of Wiltshire, and he stood up, too.

He looked at his old friend and said:

'I must say you're looking damned handsome tonight.'

'You're not behind the door yourself, when it comes to that, my old wingsy bash,' said Grampy.

They stepped outside into the spring night and breathed in deeply.

'Dear oh dear,' said the Duke of Wiltshire. 'Didn't we used to be a devilish pair in the days of our prime?'

'We still is,' said Grampy. 'Course we are. Without a doubt. If I doesn't have at least two dances with that Mrs Fokine with the wet mouth, may both my legs be turned into two rolls of bedroom lino.'

The two old men made their way to the village dance in single file, Grampy following behind the Duke of Wiltshire.

He didn't want to take in what he saw.

He could not help it, though.

And it grieved him to see the falter in his companion's step and the tremble to his hands.

But as soon as he entered the village hall he forgot all about it.

11

The village cricket dance opened with a prayer.

It was given by the vicar, the Rev. 'Charlie' Barnett, who took time off from his whisky decanter especially for the occasion.

He said:

'Dear Lord,

'Don't worry, I'll make it brief.

'Well, here we go again. Another village dance. The start of another cricket season. Boring old game, isn't it? Still, if You invented it, it must figure somewhere in Your grand design, I suppose.

'Anyway, to cut a long story short, we thank Thee for Thy muni . . . munifi . . . for providing all the food, and keep up the good work.

'Amen.'

The villagers muttered their Amens, some aggressively, some sulkily, some enthusiastically as they cast their furtive eyes towards the bar, where Grocott was licking his lips and flexing his fingers, preparing himself for the first onslaught of the evening.

Before that, however, the Master of Ceremonies, Peary Ticehurst, son of Nansen, had a duty to perform. He had to introduce the guest of honour, the Marquess of Sturminster.

He did so.

The Marquess of Sturminster acknowledged the sparse applause with a stiff-necked cough. He perspired. He expressed his delight and his honour at being invited 'to set the festivities in motion'.

His fat cheeks huffed.

He referred to his notes, frowning and flustering, and then expressed his undying dedication to the welfare of all who lived in Winterleaf Gunner and his appreciation for the loyalty and affection they and their ancestors had shown him and his ancestors during the unfolding pageant of 'our beloved island nation's garlanded history' with all its vicissitudes and all its triumphs and the ever-changing weft and warp of the social scene and national mores, during which the villagers of Winterleaf Gunner had never wavered in their commitment to the old-fashioned virtues of steadfastness, courage in the face of adversity, respect for property and profound contentment with their lot and that of their children.

'Bastard,' said Grampy.

The Marquess of Sturminster finished his speech. The applause was tepid. He turned to leave.

'Hold on, mate. You can't go yet,' shouted young Scott Ticehurst, who was home on leave from the submarines. 'You got to do the dance of honour first look.'

The villagers cheered.

The Marquess of Sturminster flushed. His arms stiffened. He gulped. He tugged at his stiff white collar.

The band struck up 'The Anniversary Waltz'.

No one moved.

The band played on.

The Marquess of Sturminster perspired.

Miss Roebuck, the village postmistress, giggled.

And then out of the crowd stepped Baksi.

She walked confidently across the dance floor, her head held high, her hips swaying, her arms swinging haughtily.

She curtsied archly to the Marquess of Sturminster and then without a moment's hesitation took him in her arms and commenced to waltz him round the hall.

The guests applauded. They stamped their feet. They shouted.

Baksi's cheeks glowed. She wrapped her arms round the Marquess of Sturminster's neck. She whispered into his ear. He blushed deeply.

Winston Hayballs, first recipient of Grocott's scrumpy 'by a distance' stood on tiptoes and watched his daughter rilling her limbs.

'Not got a bad pair of knockers on her, has she, mate?' he said to his neighbour.

'Well, really!' said Mrs Fokine. 'And me just recently widowed through a dead husband.'

The dance finished.

The women gossiped. The men milled around the bar. The Marquess of Sturminster pushed his way tetchily through the crowd and confronted his father, who was sitting next to Grampy in a cool-lit corner.

'Right then, Father,' he said. 'Time to go.'

'What's that?' said the Duke of Wiltshire.

55

'I said it's time for you to leave,' said his son. 'We've done our duty. There's no reason to stay a minute longer.'

'Very well,' said the Duke of Wiltshire, and slowly he started to rise to his feet.

Grampy grasped him firmly by the tails of his frock coat and yanked him down into his seat.

'Wait a minute. Hold on,' he said. 'Your old dad ain't going nowhere yet.'

'I beg your pardon, Hayballs?' said the Marquess of Sturminster. 'What's that you said?'

'I said your old dad's stopping here,' said Grampy, bristling his jaw and jangling his medals. 'The night, he ain't started yet. There's enjoyment afoot, and he's going to make the most of it, or he'll get the tip of my boot up his arse.'

'I don't intend to stand here arguing with you, Hayballs,' said the Marquess of Sturminster. 'Father! On your feet!'

The Duke of Wiltshire stood up.

Grampy hauled him down into his seat once more.

'Stay where you are. Don't move,' he said.

And then slowly he stood up, braced his shoulders and glared down on the Marquess of Sturminster.

'You've sucked the juices out of your old dad, you has,' he said. 'In his youth, in his prime look, he was a lion. He had the roar of a lion. He had the prowl and the glare of a lion. He had the teeth and the mane of a lion.

'Then you come along. You killed your mother in your birth. And you spent the rest of your life killing your father. Softly. Slowly. Bit by bit. Slyly. Well, no longer no more, my old wingsy bash. Tonight he stays here. Tonight he enjoys hisself. Tonight he roars like a lion, and he prowls like a lion. And like a lion he gathers round hisself his pride.'

He moved closer towards the Duke's son.

He thrust out his chest.

He said very softly through snarled lips:

'Go. You ain't wanted here. Skedaddle.'

The Marquess of Sturminster paused for a moment.

His fat cheeks glistened. His mouth opened, but no words came. He glanced swiftly across to his father, who was dozing peacefully in his chair.

Then without further ado he turned on his heel and left.

Grampy chuckled and sat next to the Duke. He prodded him sharply in the ribs and said:

'Well then, what do you reckon?'

The Duke of Wiltshire smiled.

'I showed him, didn't I?' he said. 'By jingo, didn't I just show him?'

'That you did. You was like a lion without a doubt,' said Grampy. 'Come on. Let's get pissed.'

The dance had been in progress for more than an hour before Nancy met Winston Hayballs.

She gasped when she saw him.

He was wearing a navy-blue velvet suit. It was very well cut. He was wearing a green and black striped shirt. That was very well cut, too. Round his neck was a canary-yellow cravat with a pattern of blood-red fox heads. His hair was combed back and neatly cut at the nape. The stubble on his chin had been shaved away, and he was not wearing wellington boots.

'Winston!' she said. 'Is it really you?'

'Oh yes it's me without a doubt,' said Winston Hayballs. 'I'm all dicky dolled up look and rarin' to go. Fancy a bit of a jive, does you?'

And before she could answer he had taken her firmly by the hand and led her onto the dance floor.

The band was playing a slow foxtrot, but Winston Hayballs took no notice. He pulled Nancy hither and thither, spinning her round under his arm, spinning her behind his back and twirling her by the hips.

'Winston,' gasped Nancy. 'You're pulling my arms out of their sockets.'

'Good,' said Winston Hayballs, and he put his hands on his head, opened out his knees and waddled his belly.

The music stopped, and Nancy breathed a sigh of relief and made to leave the dance floor.

Winston Hayballs held hold of her hand tightly.

'Oh no you doesn't,' he said. 'We got a real smoocher next one.'

The band played a jive.

Winston Hayballs paid it no heed.

He clasped Nancy closely to him and shuffled round the floor, breathing heavily into her ears and running his hands up and down her back.

'Winston!' hissed Nancy. 'Will you let me go. People are looking.'

57

'Course they is, missus,' said Winston Hayballs. 'You're a handsome woman. Real tasty. Mature and ripe.'

'Winston! That is quite enough,' said Nancy, and with a pummel to his chest and a sharp kick to his shins she broke free of his clutches and returned to the table she had been sharing with her father and William.

William was not there.

His place had been taken by Mrs Godwin.

She was slim and elegant.

'Good Lord,' said Nancy. 'You've got a perm just like the one I had done in Southwold only it didn't suit me.'

Mrs Godwin smiled.

She said in her deep, slow voice:

'I've been watching you dancing. You seem to have developed quite a rapport with Winston.'

'Winston?' said Nancy. 'That disgusting, nauseating little man? Never never ever in the whole of my life have I met such a revolting, obnoxious, conceited, ignorant, foul-breathed, filthy-tongued little runt. And that's almost swearing.'

Mrs Godwin laughed.

Nancy felt rage boiling in her veins.

She hadn't felt such anger since her early days at Domestic Science College. She hadn't felt such lack of control over her emotions since her younger sister, Rosie, had left the family home to live with a half-Polish fabric designer.

She turned furiously to Mrs Godwin, but before she could speak William returned from the bar with a tray of drinks.

He had a large gin and water for his father, a small dry sherry for Mrs Godwin and a grapefruit crush for himself.

'Oh,' he said, when he saw Nancy. 'Sorry. Can I get you a drink?'

'That won't be necessary, William,' said Mrs Godwin. 'I should like to dance, if you please.'

'But I don't know how to,' said William.

'In that case we'll take a turn outside in the fresh air,' said Mrs Godwin, and she took William by the elbow and directed him through the throng and out into the night.

The village green was slumbering.

The barn owl hunted.

58

There was a nip in the air. Stars crackled. Wild geese late for their scanty northern summer flew high overhead and called.

Mrs Godwin linked her arm into William's and said:

'I'm feeling all shivery, William. I like feeling all shivery, don't you?'

'Not much,' said William.

They walked twice very slowly round the village green.

They did not speak.

Mrs Godwin placed her arm round William's waist and held him close.

'They tell me you're a writer, William,' she said.

'Yes,' said William.

'How terribly exciting. We've never had a writer in the village before. You'll be quite an asset to our circle.'

'Your circle?'

'A very discerning circle, William. Very exclusive. Very persuasive. You're going to love it.'

'Mm,' said William, starting as a muscovy duck fluffed out its feathers and grunted in its sleep.

'We give parties, too, William,' said Mrs Godwin. 'Our parties are most distinctive. Most unusual. Do you like parties, William?'

'Not much,' said William. 'I don't like staying up late when I'm writing.'

Mrs Godwin laughed.

It fluttered and lingered in the tender patches behind his ears.

Faint music from village hall. Pound of double bass. Throb of bass drum. Thin whine of clarinet. Applause.

Memories stirred in William's mind.

Tennis club hop at rough and windy north-east seaside town. Wide, flared skirt. Black leather belt. Rasp of nylon stockings. Pink coral earrings, 4711 cologne.

– William. Oh, William, it's dead easy if you just concentrate. Open your mouth. Don't keep your lips so tight. Relax, William. Relax. Give me your hand, and I'll put it somewhere nice.

William coughed.

'Yes, well,' he stuttered. 'Yes, well, I think I'd better be getting back to Nancy and Father.'

'Of course you must, William,' said Mrs Godwin.

She led him back to the village hall and their footsteps snailed through the heavy dew on the snuck-sharp, new-mown grass.

59

Before they went inside Mrs Godwin said:

'Now I don't think we should rush things, William.'

'Rush things?' said William. 'What things?'

'The course of our relationship.'

'What relationship?'

'Our relationship, silly. The relationship between you and me, William.'

She gave him a gentle push in the back.

'There you are, William. That's the way into the hall. Through the front door. Go back to your father and your Nancy. There's no need to walk me home. That can come later, can't it?'

She blew him a kiss and with a languid backward wave disappeared into the smooth-cheeked darkness.

An hour later the buffet was served.

Then the raffle was drawn.

Mrs Fokine won the first prize of a weekend for two in Weymouth.

She burst into tears.

Ted Cholderton, fast bowler, tail-end slogger and relief milkman, won the second prize of a hamper of tinned country produce.

Woodcock Hayballs won the third prize of a bottle of whisky.

'I'll have that look,' said Winston Hayballs. 'Here's fifty pee. Go and buy yourself a glass of Coke.'

The band emerged tipsy from the ladies' cloakroom and resumed their musical entertainment.

Baksi Hayballs danced with Scott Ticehurst.

'You coming for a bit of a romp down Cuckoo Tree Meadow then?' he said.

'No,' said Baksi. 'I got a prior session indoors arranged.'

Grampy and Nansen Ticehurst swayed softly in a corner next to the bar.

'Then this Stuka dive bomber appeared right out of the blue,' said Nansen Ticehurst.

'Did it?' said Grampy.

'Yes. Without a doubt,' said Nansen Ticehurst. 'It was black.'

'I knows it was black. I was there, wasn't I?' said Grampy.

Nansen Ticehurst nodded glumly.

'You would have been, wouldn't you?' he said. 'You been bloody everywhere, you has.'

Father sat next to the gently dozing Duke of Wiltshire and said:

'I don't know if you are au fait with India, Your Grace.'

'What's that you say?' said the Duke of Wiltshire sleepily.

'I was talking about India, Your Grace,' said Father. 'Fearfully agreeable place India. Your mother and I spent a great deal of our time there. Well, not your mother. My wife, I suppose it would be more correct to call her. She was more in the way of being Nancy's and William's mother when it came to maternal attachments.'

'Who's William and Nancy?' said the Duke of Wiltshire.

'My children, Your Grace,' said Father.

'Children!' said the Duke of Wiltshire savagely. 'Bloody pigs.'

Suddenly Grampy saw the two old men talking.

He pushed his way through the revellers. He took hold of the Duke of Wiltshire by the scruff of his faded old frock coat and dragged him to his feet.

'If you don't mind, matey,' he said to Father. And then he spat out: 'If you don't mind – newcomer.'

'Not at all, old boy,' said Father cheerily. 'Be my guest.'

Baksi danced with Ted Cholderton.

'You fancy a serious sesh of how's-your-father down by the hatchery?' he said.

'No, ta,' said Baksi. 'I made other arrangements of a more comfier nature, I has.'

The laughter grew more raucous. The pitch of soft southern voices was raised. Cigarette smoke scoured at squinting eyeballs. Foot odours coiled round table legs. The Rev. 'Charlie' Barnett fell off his chair.

'I want to go home,' said William.

'Wait,' said Nancy. 'It's not polite yet.'

She fanned herself.

The room whirled.

Memories whirled. Memories swirled.

College dances. Dances at the university union. Sharp-quiffed young men in navy-blue blazers and grey flannel trousers. Buttressed bras. Petticoats. Sickly saxophone.

The snuffling, giggling panting darkness of the union common room. Beery breath. Twang of elastic. Fumbling fingers. Tense necks. Clenched fists.

– I'd rather you didn't do that, if you don't mind.

– Oh, not at all. Sorry.

Tears at night. Sobbing herself to sleep. The soft creak of the lavatory door. Muffled cough. Clink of gin bottle.

Then Winston Hayballs appeared out of the crowd.

He sat down, and, resting his elbows on the table, stared deep into her eyes.

'You enjoying yourself, missus?' he said.

'It's very pleasant, thank you,' said Nancy.

Winston Hayballs smiled.

He had stuffed his canary-yellow cravat into the pocket of his velvet jacket. His shirt was undone to the waist and the tattoos above his nipples convulsed and pumped as he drank his pint of scrumpy greedily.

'You wants to let yourself go, missus,' he said, when he had finished his drink. 'Enjoy yourself look.'

'I don't need any advice from you on how to enjoy myself, thank you very much, Winston,' said Nancy.

'Oh, but you does, missus. Without a doubt you does. There ain't a woman in the whole wide world what is so experienced in the arts of enjoyment as she don't need a word of advice from old Winston on how to enjoy herself,' said Winston Hayballs and he winked, tapped the side of his nose with his left forefinger and said: 'Want to give it a whirl then? Or would you like the pleasure of escorting me to the village pond where we shall engage ourself in throwing stones at the ducks?'

'No,' said Nancy. 'Go away.'

Winston Hayballs sucked deeply into the blue-chipped gap between his two front teeth, stood up and said:

'I shall do as you bid me, missus. I shall leave and retire forthwith and straightaway and present myself to Betty Hayballs.'

Before she could stop herself Nancy said:

'Who's Betty Hayballs?'

'Ah,' said Winston Hayballs. 'She's the bit of fluff what I always goes to when I gets back-heeled look. Oh yes, old Winston always ends up with his first cousin when he finds hisself in that rare predicament. Well, she's got big endowments, ain't she?'

He smiled.

Then he walked purposefully out of the village hall with scarcely a stumble or a stagger.

'Come on,' said Nancy sharply to her father and William. 'Time to go.'

'Thank God for that,' said William.

The three Empsons walked home slowly to the old Dower House, which greeted them with a scowl.

'Fearfully pleasant old buffer, His Grace,' said Father as he pondered and poked at the skin on top of his beaker of Horlicks in the drawing room. 'I like old people. They remind me of the halcyon days when I was young in India.'

Presently Nancy herded them upstairs to their beds.

Later in her own bed she lay cold and rigid and lonely.

More memories.

He was portly for his age. He must have been born portly. He always seemed so plaintively at odds with his uniform. With his face, too, if it came to that.

Sputters of rain on the windscreen. Flash of lighthouse. Moon shadows of stiff-winged fulmars. Rattle of cufflinks.

– I say, Nancy. Why don't we . . . well, why don't we sort of . . . well, you know, Nancy, why don't we sort of get married?

The pause. Forever the pause. The pause growing longer and longer as the years rolled by.

– Oh, I don't know about that, Geoffrey. And don't forget you've put the car in reverse.

Suddenly she sat bolt upright in bed, and she found herself saying:

'I wonder what it's like to have big endowments?'

She giggled.

Her eyes filled up with tears and she said:

'Well, I should know, I suppose. When all's said and done, mine aren't all that small, are they?'

12

And then the bombshell hit Winterleaf Gunner.

The Marquess of Sturminster announced that he intended to rip up the village green.

It was his intention to build an access road from the main highway directly to the gates of Florey Palace.

It would rip out the heart of the village green.

The pond would have to be drained and filled in.

The cricket square would be torn up.

The elms and the horse chestnuts would be felled.

The thatched scorer's hut would be chopped up and burnt.

It was the first week in April.

The cuckoos had just arrived at the Cuckoo Tree in the meadow.

'Cuckoo, cuckoo, cuckoo,' they called.

The Marquess of Sturminster listened to their song with glee.

13

Nancy Empson was outraged when she heard the news.

It was brought to her by Lionel Woodyates, the milkman with the permanent thread of spittle between his lips.

Immediately she dashed out into the cobbled courtyard.

'Winston,' she shouted. 'Winston!'

'Yes, missus,' said Winston Hayballs. 'What can I do for you?'

Nancy looked up with a start.

Winston Hayballs was sitting astride the ridge of the stable roof high above her. He was not wearing a shirt. Sweat glistened in the folds of his belly. A thicket of wiry black hair matted his chest and sent tentacles twining towards the tattoos above his nipples.

His broad grin sharply sickled the curve of his Zapata moustache.

'Want to come up with me here, missus, and admire the view?' he shouted down to her.

'No, thank you, Winston,' said Nancy tartly. 'As you can no doubt see I'm not exactly dressed for climbing roofs at the moment.'

'No, missus, that you ain't,' said Winston Hayballs, clucking his tongue appreciatively. 'What I'd say you was dressed for is playing a part in one of the collected works of Oscar Wilde or Sir Arthur Quiller Cooch.'

Nancy bit her lip, clenched her fists and then said sweetly:

'Winston, I wonder if you'd be kind enough to come down from the roof. I have something I wish to discuss with you.'

'Certainly, my old wingsy bash,' said Winston Hayballs. 'These ridge tiles are playing merry hell with the nick in my arse.'

He slid down the slates with panache and grace and shinned nimbly down the drainpipe.

The sun shone.

The first of the timid swallows zinked softly into the musky darkness of the stables.

The cuckoos in the tree in the meadow sang lustily.

'Cuckoo, cuckoo, cuckoo,' they went.

Winston presented himself in front of Nancy, zipped up the flies of his trousers, winked and said:

'Right then, missus, what can old Winston do for you?'

The thick, sinewed neck. The hard knot of muscles in his forearms. The sparkle to his eyes. The boldness and mischief in his grin.

Nancy felt a singular flutter come to her temples.

She composed herself in an instant and said:

'I was wondering if you'd heard the news, Winston.'

'Oh yes,' said Winston Hayballs. 'Well, I always thought he was a bit of a shit house, that Andrew Lloyd Webber.'

'I'm not talking about him,' snapped Nancy. 'I'm talking about the plans to rip up the village green.'

'Oh that,' said Winston Hayballs. 'Yes, I heard all about that last night when I was having a sesh in the pub.'

'So what do you think?'

'What does I think, missus? I think let them get on with it, if that's what they wants.'

'What?' said Nancy. 'What's that you say?'

'Let them get on with it,' said Winston Hayballs. 'There's nothing we can do about it. It's all in the bag look. He'll have paid out his bribes fair and square to the planners all by the book.'

'Bribes?' said Nancy. 'What on earth are you talking about?'

Winston chuckled softly.

'I'm talking about the ways of the country, missus,' he said. 'Graft. Corruption. Privilege. That's how they runs things round here. Back-handers dished out right left and centre look. Aristocratic blue blood. Rank. Wealth. When you got all that, you gets just what you want in the country. Without a doubt you does, missus.'

'But he's going to wreck the whole village, Winston,' said Nancy. 'Doesn't that concern you? Doesn't it make you want to rage and rant?'

Winston chuckled again.

'No, missus, no,' he said. 'I don't give a monkey's either way. They can do what they likes with the village green for all I cares.'

'I don't believe what I'm hearing,' said Nancy, and her eyes speckled with anger and her cheeks reddened. 'If they destroy that green, the whole village will be destroyed. Centuries of tradition will be wiped out, annihilated, lost for ever. A whole way of life will be massacred. Doesn't it bother you? Don't you care?'

Winston smiled slowly.

He took hold of Nancy's arm.

'Come with me, missus,' he said. 'We'll sit under that old rose arbour look, and I'll tell you some home truths.'

Nancy allowed herself to be led to the stone bench. She sat down meekly and the new-budding roses clambered above her and bees fussed.

Winston Hayballs sat next to her.

She could feel the heat from his body. She could smell his deep, mysterious odours. She could sense his strength.

He gazed straight into her eyes, and she felt her cheeks redden once more.

Then he spoke.

'What you just said, missus. Well, it's all a load of old bollocks look.'

'Winston!' snapped Nancy. 'I won't tell you again about using foul language in front of me.'

Winston laughed.

'That's the country way of life, missus,' he said. 'That it is without a doubt.'

He moved closer to her.

She shuddered inwardly. Once again she had the strange feeling that someone was watching her. She took a swift glance over her shoulder.

'There's no need to do that,' said Winston softly. 'There ain't no one around to see us.'

'I don't care if there is. Why should I care? There's nothing improper going on. It's not as if . . .'

She stopped suddenly, flustered, bewildered.

Winston Hayballs was staring into her eyes. His smile was soft. His bearing was gentle.

She composed herself quickly and said:

'Right then, Winston, tell me all about these home truths of yours. And be quick about it. I've Father's lunch to prepare, and he'll play merry stink if I don't get it to him on time.'

'Calm down, missus,' said Winston Hayballs. 'You're coming out all of a dither and a dander, that you are.'

Nancy breathed in deeply and said calmly:

'The home truths, if you please, Winston.'

Winston Hayballs took a battered tin out of his hip pocket, commenced to roll himself a baggy cigarette, and, when he had lit and spat out the loose straggles of tobacco clinging to his lips, said:

'The country way of life, missus? I hates it, I abhors it.'

'What?' said Nancy.

'You know what the country way of life is, missus?' he said. 'Well, I'll tell you. Forelock tugging, that's what it is. Gossip. Back-biting. Jealousy. Malice. Duplicity. People with minds as thick as two short planks. People with brains like billiard balls. Scoffers. Liars. Cheats.

'The country way of life, missus? It's all dampness and cold and draughts whistling under your doors. It's always being skint and running out of baccy because the pub's forgot to order it. It's a life of whinging and whining. It's ugly women with rasping scalps and mouths like cement mixers. It's the stink of cow shit and the lack of adequate reading material. You ever seen books in people's houses round here? You ever heard of anyone speak of the works of Marcel Proust or the paintings of Tintoretto? Course you ain't. The country way of life? He's poison to a man of refinement and discernment like what I am, missus.'

During this discourse Nancy's mouth had sagged open.

And when Winston Hayballs had finished, she found herself gawping at him helplessly and shaking her head in disbelief.

For a moment she could not speak.

Winston winked at her. The sodden stump of the roll-up cigarette quivered in his lips.

He smiled.

'Cor blimey, you don't half look handsome, when you're all of a flummox, missus,' he said. 'There's some folk would say you looked real tasty, real desirable. That they would without a doubt.'

Nancy snapped her mouth shut.

Her eyes hardened.

'Wait a minute, Winston,' she said threateningly. 'If you hate the country so much why have you never taken your chance and moved out to the city?'

Winston Hayballs put his hands behind his neck and stretched out his legs.

'Simple, missus,' he said. 'On account of what you doesn't find in the big city.'

'I don't understand.'

'Then I'll tell you look,' said Winston Hayballs. 'What you doesn't find in the big city is pheasants, ain't it? And you doesn't find salmon and grayling and fat brown trout. You doesn't find wild swans and domestic geese let loose in the meadows. You doesn't find woodcock and partridge and quail and leaping deer with great juicy bellies and haunches rarin' to be soaked in cranberry jelly. The raw materials of my trade, missus. They ain't in the city. And that's why there's no living there for a poacher and a philosopher like what I am.'

Nancy felt his breath on her cheeks.

A sparrowhawk swooped low over the lawn, and the starlings shrieked and scattered.

'And there's something else as well what you doesn't find in the city,' said Winston Hayballs.

'What's that?' said Nancy.

'Bits of fluff,' said Winston Hayballs, and he slapped her warmly on the back.

Nancy stood up and smoothed down her white linen smock top.

'I've never heard such a lot of nonsense in the whole of my life,' she said.

Winston Hayballs grinned again.

'And stop grinning like that,' said Nancy. 'I can't stand men who grin at me.'

She began to walk quickly towards the kitchen.

Suddenly she stopped and turned back to Winston Hayballs, who was still chuckling to himself.

'Well, let me tell you this, Winston bloody Hayballs,' she said. 'If you won't do anything about it, I most certainly will. I shall get something done.'

'In that case, missus, you wants old Wilson Rappaport to organize things.'

Nancy found herself screaming at the top of her voice:

'But Wilson Rappaport's dead. He's long since gone. If people don't stop going on about Wilson Rappaport, I swear I shall go stark staring mad.'

She dashed into the kitchen and slammed the door behind her. She slumped down into a hard-backed chair her mother had bought in Dunoon and rested her elbows on the table.

The old postman's clock ticked. It tocked.

And for an instant she could have sworn that someone was watching her, smiling at her, grinning at her with a long, slow leer.

That evening Mrs Godwin presented herself at the front door of the

69

old Dower House and was led by Nancy into the drawing room, where Father was studying the public notices in the local telephone directory.

'Ah, what-ho,' he said, when Mrs Godwin entered the room. 'I saw five army helicopters today. Fearfully pleasant, don't you think?'

Nancy fluttered her hands and directed Mrs Godwin to a chintz-covered armchair next to the fireplace.

– Such elegance. Such assurance. Skirt drawn up just right above long, shapely legs. Slim ankles. Not a hair out of place. Make-up perfect. The perfume subtle. The lips moist and mocking.

'Yes, well, Mrs Godwin,' she said. 'May I offer you a drink?'

'How kind,' said Mrs Godwin. 'A dry sherry would be most acceptable.'

'Oh dear. We've only got sweet.'

'In that case I'll have a small whisky.'

'Gin. That's what you want,' said Father. 'Of course I don't drink the stuff myself nowadays. But when I lived in India, we drank oodles and oodles of gin. Oodles and oodles of the stuff. Did I ever tell you about the time I . . .'

'I'm sure Mrs Godwin doesn't want to hear your stories about India, Father,' said Nancy, handing her visitor a small measure of whisky. 'I'm sure she's far more important matters to discuss than your experiences in the subcontinent.'

'As a matter of fact, I have,' said Mrs Godwin, taking a slim, gold cigarette case from her handbag. 'I've come to talk to you about the planned desecration of the village green.'

'Ah,' said Nancy, slapping her thigh. 'Good-oh.'

– Blast! Why must I slap my thigh like that? It's so gauche. So adolescent. So jolly hockey sticks. I'm not like that. I'm a mature woman. I'm sophisticated. I'm experienced in the ways of the world. I'm terrific at Scrabble.

She rearranged the knot in her silk scarf and adjusted the cuffs of her starched white shirt.

'A quite appalling business, Mrs Godwin,' she said in measured tones. 'And I'm sure you'll find all the members of this household totally united in their opposition to it.'

'Good,' said Mrs Godwin. 'In that case I'm sure you'll be delighted to play a full part in the campaign I am organizing to kill the scheme stone dead.'

'Oh quite,' said Nancy. 'Rar-ther.'

– Rar-ther! There I go again. Jolly hockey sticks. Rags in the dorm. The old Joyce Grenfell routine. But I'm not like that deep down. Honestly, I'm not. Really. Cross my heart.

At that moment William shuffled into the room.

He held an open book in his right hand, and in his left hand crooked against the inside of his elbow he held a sheaf of notes.

'I'm just looking for . . .'

He stopped dead in his tracks when he saw Mrs Godwin. He blushed.

'Good evening, William,' she said. 'How lovely to see you.'

'Yes,' said William, and he turned to leave the room.

Nancy called him back sharply.

'William,' she said. 'Don't be so rude.'

'Sorry,' said William.

Nancy continued:

'Mrs Godwin is here on important business. Vital business, William. She is here to enlist our support in her campaign to oppose the plans to destroy the village green.'

'Oh that,' said William. 'Who cares?'

'I beg your pardon?' said Nancy.

'I couldn't care less about the village green,' said William. 'As far as I'm concerned they can run bulldozers over every inch of it. They can run bulldozers over the whole of the village. They can raze it to the ground, and then there'd be no excuse for staying on here and we could go back and live in London.'

Nancy sank back onto the piano stool. She clasped her hand to her bosom and said weakly:

'William. William, how could you do this to me?'

Mrs Godwin smiled.

'William,' she said.

'Yes, Mrs Godwin,' said William.

'I think it is high time you paid a visit to my house. I think it's high time you were instructed into the facts of life.'

There was silence.

Nancy felt her heart pumping. William felt his toes sticking to the inside of his socks. Father dozed peacefully.

Mrs Godwin took a fat oval cigarette from the slim gold case, tapped it three times on the lid and lit it with a matching slim gold lighter.

She exhaled the smoke slowly through her nostrils.

'Another small whisky, perhaps?' she said.

71

14

Winston Hayballs finished the last draught from his pint pot of home-brewed port wine.

He was sitting with his back against the trunk of the old beech tree in the glade of the wood at the back of his house.

Chiffchaffs sang.

Willow warblers sang, too.

The shire horse whinnied.

The sky was content.

Winston Hayballs closed his eyes.

Dreams.

The big city. Early morning streets, the gutters streaming with water and the smell of fresh bread and roasting coffee. Chestnut trees and winter braziers and tots of rum and waiters with ankle-length white aprons and zinc-topped bars and schoolboys in blue smocks and barges nuzzling the currents of the river.

The villa high in the hills. Hoopoes calling. Bee-eaters and wall-creepers. The scents of cork oak and eucalyptus. Mimosa and hibiscus. Slim volumes of Cocteau and Gide. Hispano Suiza parked in the front drive. Twin tattoos above left and right nipples, 'Rouge' and 'Blanc'.

The bedroom. Shutters creaking. Storks clacking. Stark shadows gashing white walls. A glass of champagne and an Egyptian cigarette. A sapphire-shelled tortoise bumping at the wash stand.

And then into the room she walks, the bold, handsome woman with the springy black hair and the white linen smock and the silk pantaloons and the gold lamé slippers.

She blushes.

She stands stiff and rigid as he undresses her.

He leads her to the bed.

He lies back on it.

He does not wink. He does not chuckle. He opens out his arms to her. Firm breasts. Deep, cool navel. Choice thighs, tasty, succulent. She licks her lips. She smiles. She smoulders.

'What do you reckon then?'

'Not a lot.'

Winston Hayballs jumped up with a start.

Standing before him was Grampy.

'What's the matter?' Winston Hayballs said in a panic. 'What's happening?'

'Nothing,' said Grampy. 'I just said: "What do you reckon?" and you said: "Not a lot." And then you jumped up as though someone had planted a firecracker in the arse of your trousers.'

Winston Hayballs grinned.

'Same as usual then, isn't it?' he said.

He sat down again with his back to the old beech tree and Grampy joined him.

'What are you grinning about?' he said.

'I'm thinking about bits of fluff,' said Winston Hayballs.

'Oh them,' said Grampy.

'Many's the bit of fluff I've had under this old beech tree,' said Winston Hayballs. 'Not any old bit of fluff mind. Not the ones with squat legs and thick ankles and nicotine stains and double chins and floppy tits. No, I'm thinking of the classy ones what I've had.'

'You've never had no classy ones,' said Grampy.

'I knows that,' said Winston Hayballs with a grin. 'But there's always a first time look, ain't there?'

Grampy took a long swig at his tumbler of port wine.

Memories.

Bits of fluff in the days of his prime. The girl in Sicily with the dark moustache and the broken teeth. The blushing maid at the old Dower House. The heron-legged moaner at the back of the cinema in Aldershot. The refugee from Latvia in the sodden shawl. The Arab girl. The daughter of the shepherd at the home farm when the hay was sweet.

He finished off his home-brewed port wine, turned to Winston Hayballs and said:

'What do you reckon to the news about the village green then?'

'Not a lot,' said Winston Hayballs.

'Bastard,' said Grampy and he stood up and strode off out of the wood and into Cuckoo Tree Meadow.

He met Sid Lopcombe who was scything the young nettles to brew for beer.

'Morning, Sid,' he said. 'What do you reckon?'

'Not a lot,' said Sid Lopcombe.

Rooks cawed.

'Rum news about the village green, ain't it, Sid?' said Grampy.

'Oh that,' said Sid Lopcombe. 'Well, it's no concern of ours, is it?'

'Bastard,' said Grampy and he loped off towards the village green.

It was deserted except for Lionel Woodyates and Nansen Ticehurst who were mowing the cricket pitch and spiking it.

He sat on the old splintered bench beneath the oak and lit his cherrywood pipe.

What matches he'd seen on that village green. What matches he'd played in. The six he hit into the yard of the pub. The tumbling catch he'd taken in front of the scorer's hut to win the game against Broad Absley. His old dad, drunk and arthritic, taking all ten wickets against Compton Blissett. Himself and the Duke scoring 123 undefeated for the first wicket against eleven gentlemen from Sturminster.

The Duke of Wiltshire?

'Bastard,' he said softly to himself and then he shouted at the top of his voice: 'Bastard!'

Nansen Ticehurst looked up from his mower and shouted:

'Morning. What do you reckon then?'

'Not a lot,' growled Grampy and he puffed fiercely at his old bent-stem pipe and the spittle at the bottom of the bowl slucked and spat sourly.

The cockroached brothel in Algiers. The heaving sheep shed high in the Italian hills. The giggling store room at the back of the dress-maker's shop. The drizzling yard with a canary singing from the tene-ment window. And all the time his eyes had only seen the village green and the elms and the chestnuts and the moorhen and the clover and Milly, the one-eyed mare pulling the heavy roller and all simmering in the sun of an English summer full of youth and innocent girls with saucered eyes.

He stood up and hurried on his way.

He was late for his meeting.

He fumbled with his key as he let himself in through the stooped gate into the grounds of Florey Palace.

He had hardly walked five yards before he bumped into Baksi.

She was breathless. Her hair was rumpled. Her cheeks were red. There were scratches on her legs and her eyes were sparkling.

'What the bloody hell are you doing here not in your school uniform?' he said.

74

'What's it got to do with you?' said Baksi.

'You young bugger,' said Grampy. 'You should be at school.'

'I am,' said Baksi.

'No you're not,' said Grampy. 'How can you be at school if you're here in the palace grounds with the buttons on your blouse undone?'

'I been doing nature studies,' said Baksi, and she cocked her head at him and flounced off haughtily.

Grampy walked on slowly and thoughtfully to the fruit store house.

He opened the door and stepped inside.

No one was there.

He sniffed. He smelled the old familiar scents of tobacco smoke. He smelled damp cord trousers and dusty moleskin waistcoat.

There was a note on a tray.

He opened it and read:

'You didn't come.

'I ate all the pâté and the glacé chestnuts.

'And I'm still a lion, you bastard.'

15

That evening a protest meeting was held in the village hall.

Mrs Godwin took the chair.

Storms swept in from the Channel approaches.

The wind slashed the surface of the pond on the village green, and the moorhens cowered.

The rain flattened the cocky young lupins in Mrs Fokine's front garden. It snaked in smoking spirals across the water meadows. It trailed its sodden skirts across the flanks of the downlands.

The shire horse sheltered beneath the Cuckoo Tree.

In the hall the villagers sat silent and sullen as Mrs Godwin, slim and slink, announced her plans to fight the destruction of the village green.

When she had finished her speech, she asked if there were any questions.

After a while Grocott, landlord of the village pub, stood up and said:

'Well, I don't reckon much to what you've said, missus.'

'Hear hear,' grunted Branwell Tidyman, proprietor of the village shop.

Grocott scowled at him and continued:

'I ain't no public speaker look, but I mean to say, when they builds this road and all them tourists come, it won't be bad for trade, will it?'

'Hear hear,' said Branwell Tidyman.

Mrs Godwin flicked her shoulders angrily.

'But surely, Mr Grocott, that's taking a self-centred attitude, isn't it?' she said. 'We're talking here about the village as an entity. We're talking about the dangers of the irrevocable breakdown of a way of life that has existed here for countless centuries. Surely we can't sit back and allow that to happen just for the sake of an increase in your trade? Surely the rest of you good people in the hall can't sit back and allow that to happen?'

The villagers shuffled their feet and coughed.

When they realized there was to be no distribution of free beer and poacher's pie, they stood up and departed en masse.

And so an action committee was formed.

Its chairman was Mrs Godwin.

The committee consisted of the consultant obstetrician, the twice-weekly commuting stockbroker, the minor TV personage and the wife of the prominent auctioneer and valuer. She had large hips. She was a member of CND and she ran a children's fashion boutique in the lee of the cathedral close in Sturminster.

Nancy Empson was elected secretary.

– Trust me to land up with a job like that. The old dogsbody once more. Good old Nancy, she'll do all the donkey work. Good old Nancy, reliable to a fault. Good old Nancy, she'll never let you down. It's not fair. I'm dressed just as smartly as Mrs Godwin, and I haven't got those stupid long fingernails either. I bet she gets butter stuck under them.

She looked at the well-fed, studiously-bored, smug faces of her fellow committee members, and her heart sank.

– It's doomed right from the start. Nothing will come of this. They're just doing it for a giggle. It's another of their 'activities'. It's something for them to do. It's an excuse for more of their parties with all that ghastly jungle music blasting out over the village. I hate them, and Mrs Godwin's seams aren't straight either.

She declined an invitation for drinks at the home of the stockbroker and, securing her plastic hood securely over her head, set off for home in the rain and the wind and the bleak darkness.

– Winston's right about country people. That's all they are – a pathetic shower of forelock tuggers. They're frightened of standing up for themselves. God, those incurable, irredeemably gormless faces. Those slack mouths. Those humourless eyes. Those cheap clothes. Those disgusting clothes. Why have the women always got the sleeves of their jackets half an inch too long? Where on earth do they buy those clodhopping shoes from? And smoking in the street, it's so common. It's so . . .

– Winston's right. They *are* a lost cause. Hopeless. Utterly bloody hopeless – and that's swearing. Why fight for them? Why bother? They don't appreciate what they've got. Give them a video recorder and a good bit of gossip, and they're as happy as pigs in . . . yes, Winston's right.

– Winston! Why bring Winston into it? That disgusting, nauseating, obnoxious little man with his fat boozer's belly and his greasy hair and his dirty teeth and that moustache that's always got gravy stuck to it.

– And I object to being called tasty. I am not tasty. I am not like one of his bits of fluff. I am a handsome woman. I know that. I overheard the golf professional talking about me at . . .

The bungalow with the green shutters overlooking the links. The golden retriever she had taken walks every morning over the dunes. The distant bay with its dredgers and raking packet steamers bound for the Isle of Man. Calling in at the clubhouse for drinks at lunchtime. Father playing the fruit machine. The golf professional with the dark, crinkly hair and the angora sweaters and the tight-swinging bum. She had loved it there. Then Father developed an allergy to the dog, and they had to get it destroyed.

– Why do I carry on? This bloody family. I toil for them. I slave for them. And do they appreciate me? No. Do they even notice me? No, not really. They eat me alive. They drink all my sap and my juices. Okay, William, you want to go back to London? Well, bugger off then. Okay, Father, you like it here. You like the army helicopters. Well, stay here and stew.

– And me? What shall I do? Shall I run away and leave them? Yes. Yes, terrific. But where would I go? The world's my oyster. But I don't like oysters. I got poisoned by them that time we went on the day trip to Calais and William got the screaming squitters and Father got something or other and I had to . . .

Just outside the village shop someone stepped out of the shadows and barred her way.

'Oh, my God,' she shrieked. 'Oh God.'

'Don't be alarmed, Mrs Empson,' said the figure. 'It's only me.'

'Only you?' she said with a tremble and a tremor to her voice.

'Yes,' said the figure. 'It's me. Venetia. Venetia Hayballs. I'm Winston's sister-in-law.'

Nancy peered hard into the blackness.

Slowly there came into focus a tall, angular woman. She had large, narrow splayed feet. Her nose was large, too.

'What do you want?' said Nancy nervously.

'I just wants to tell you I'm on your side.'

'On my side?'

'Yes. Regarding the village green. I think it's a sin and a shame what they want to do with it. Well, I've got a daughter at university, you see. She's studying to be clever.'

'I see,' said Nancy.

'I'm not frightened of airing my opinions in public, you see. Only I've got to think of my status look. That's why I'm airing my opinions to you in private.'

Nancy nodded slowly.

'The rest of the villagers thinks the same way only they're not people of breeding like you and me. They needs a leader to get them going. Not one of the newcomers. One of their own. That's why you needs Winston to help you.'

'Winston?' said Nancy.

'You must know Winston,' said Venetia. 'I hates him I does. I had a proper education, see, before I married into the Hayballs. I could ballet dance on my toes. I could eat cake with a fork. That's why I hates Winston and his foul language and his goings on with loose women and his boozer's belly and his dirty teeth and his . . .'

'Oh I don't know,' said Nancy. 'He's not all that bad surely?'

Venetia Hayballs laughed bitterly.

'Oh I see,' she said. 'You, too, is it?'

And then she disappeared into the darkness.

Nancy did not linger over supper. She hardly spoke a word to her father and her brother.

Later she tossed and turned in her bed as the storm fumed and bellowed at the night and rattled the timbers of the old bridge in the grounds of Florey Palace.

– Me too? What does she mean – me too? How dare she? The cheek of it. These people are absolutely intolerable. What are we doing here? They're not Us. I'm not cut out for this life. I've managed everywhere Father has taken us to. I've set up good homes. I've looked after their tummies. I've dosed them up when they've had colds. I've taken their clothes to the dry cleaners. I've coped. I've always coped. But here? How can I cope here? I can't. I just can't cope.

Presently she fell asleep.

Her sleep was peaceful and undisturbed.

Next morning the storm had disappeared.

Winterleaf Gunner was fresh.

Grampy and the seventeenth Duke of Wiltshire walked slowly side by side round the village green.

They passed Nansen Ticehurst who tugged at his forelock and said:

'Morning, Your Grace. Beautiful morning without a doubt.'

'Morning, Lopcombe,' said the Duke. 'It is indeed the most exquisite morning.'

Grampy grasped him by the arm and stopped him dead in his tracks.

'That ain't Sid Lopcombe, you barmy old sod,' he said.

'No?' said the Duke of Wiltshire.

'No, it's Nansen Ticehurst,' said Grampy. 'He bloody near copped his lot with us when we was storming that pillbox.'

'Good. So he did,' said the Duke. 'Poor chap's aged quite a bit since then, hasn't he?'

The white-candled chestnuts were serene. The sullen pond made an effort to smile at the sunlight. Moorhens battled for territory. The muscovy ducks placidly preened themselves on the banks.

'Bloody things,' said Grampy. 'Reminds me of a road accident what's gone wrong, they does.'

They continued their slow stroll.

They passed Lionel Woodyates who doffed his cap.

They passed by Mrs Fokine, who dropped a whinnying curtsey.

They were stopped by Father, who was taking a morning constitutional with his pipe and William.

'Morning, Your Grace,' said Father. 'Fearfully pleasant day.'

'It is indeed,' said the Duke. 'Fearfully pleasant.'

'Reminds me of those superb mornings we used to spend in the hills, when I was living in India.'

'Ah, stationed in India, were you?' said the Duke.

'Rather,' said Father, slapping his thigh. 'I was with your mother at the time. Well, not your mother, you understand. Nancy's mother to be more accurate. Anyway, Your Grace, to cut a long story short, I'd just been to inspect the locos in the Chitteranjan works at Chitteranjan when . . .'

'Come on,' said Grampy, yanking the Duke of Wiltshire by the scruff of his collar. 'We ain't got all day to waste on idle gossip.'

Father raised his panama hat.

'Morning, Your Grace,' he said. 'Fearfully pleasant to have a chinwag about the old times, eh?'

The Duke of Wiltshire smiled and when at length Grampy seated him firmly on the splintered bench beneath the oak tree said:

'Agreeable old bastard, don't you think?'

'Him?' snarled Grampy. 'He's one of them bleeding newcomers.'

'Really?'

'I told you before, you daft old bugger,' said Grampy. 'I told you he just moved into the old Dower House.'

'Really? Well, I hope he'll be very happy. I must visit him and pay my respects.'

Grampy scowled at him.

'You don't understand nothing, do you?'

'What do you mean?' said the Duke.

'It's them bloody newcomers what's destroying this village,' he said. 'And you're the one what's to blame.'

'Me?' said the Duke.

'You,' said Grampy. 'You let them build all them swanky houses here with their gramophones playing all night long and their women showing off their tits in them bathing costume things. You let them rip up the grass verges so's they can drive their cars without looking where they're going. You let them build whacking great pylons all over the place so's they can have electricity to work their electric toasting machines. You just sat back and you let them wreck the whole village look.'

'It's not me that's done that,' said the Duke. 'It's Sturminster.'

'It ain't bleeding Sturminster,' said Grampy. 'It's you. You let him walk all over you and now you're letting him rip up the whole of the village green here just so he can bring bloody tourists and more new-comers into Winterleaf Gunner. It's not his fault. It's yours, cos you won't stand up for yourself. You're a coward, that's what you are. A yellow-backed coward with white feathers fluttering out of his arsehole.'

A V-shaped squadron of mute swans flew over the green, wheezing softly to themselves.

Larks sang. Lapwings called.

Then very slowly the Duke of Wiltshire raised himself from the bench.

He stretched out his arm.

He yawned.

And then he bellowed:

'How dare you talk to me like that, you bloody scum.'

Grampy's pipe dropped out of his mouth.

'And stand up while I'm talking to you. Stand up, blast you.'

Grampy stood up.

'Take your hands out of your pockets. Straighten your back. Throw out your chest.'

Grampy did as he was bid.

81

The Duke of Wiltshire glared at him.

'You scum,' he said. 'Remember your station in life, when you talk to me. I know Sturminster's a stinker. I know he's an arid fat little worm with dried-up juices who needs a woman to stir his loins and send the blood coursing and stiffen his mainmast. But that is between him and me. It is nothing to do with you. Do you understand that?'

Grampy, standing rigid to attention, nodded.

'You bloody upstart,' said the Duke of Wiltshire. 'You live in your ghastly hovel covered in mouse droppings and stinking of sardines, and you have the effrontery to talk to me who lives in a palace.

'I live in a palace, sir, even though the hot water pipes don't work in my bedroom and I don't know how to work the bloody immersion heater.

'I am an aristocrat. And you are scum. Remember that. Remember your station in life.'

His deep violet eyes flecked with gold glinted at Grampy, who stood rigid, not moving a muscle, staring straight ahead.

Rooks squabbled in the elms.

A drowsy fly buzzed round Grampy's nostrils and nuzzled at his eyelids.

He did not flinch.

Mrs Fokine's stooped old King Charles spaniel sniffed at his trousers and growled at his boots.

But he did not flinch.

And then he smiled.

And he stepped forward, and he thumped the Duke of Wiltshire hard in the chest.

The Duke staggered backwards, and Grampy had to grasp him by the lapels of his jacket to keep him upright.

'You old bugger,' Grampy said. 'That's more like, eh? You're standing up for yourself at long last. Good for you, my old wingsy bash.'

The Duke smiled happily.

'Yes, it was rather good, wasn't it?' he said, and then linking arms with Grampy, he made his way towards the fruit store house in the grounds of Florey Palace.

The two old men were too late to catch Baksi straddling her man on one of the ancient peach-sodden trays.

They were too late to see her look down on him, her head rolling from side to side, her hands slowly kneading her ribcage.

They were too late to hear her whisper:

'There, my love. There, there. That's nice, ain't it? That makes the old juices run, don't it? Oh, it do without a doubt.'

Just before they stepped inside the sated store house the Duke of Wiltshire paused and said:

'Pleasant old cove, that chap in the panama hat. I really must pay him a visit some time.'

16

The Duke of Wiltshire was as good as his word.

Three days later he presented himself at the front door of the Dower House.

He was wearing an I Zingari blazer, woollen tartan shirt, MCC cravat, pinstriped trousers and a panama hat.

House martins darted and whisked at flies.

The two bay trees which Nancy had brought from London glowered grumpily at the sun. They missed the soot.

The front door was opened by Father, who said:

'Yes?'

The Duke of Wiltshire doffed his panama hat and then with an expansive sweep of his arm passed it across his chest and rested it on his heart.

He smiled broadly at Father and said:

'Herbert Henry.'

'Beg pardon?' said Father.

'Herbert Henry, seventeenth Duke of Wiltshire, Baron Nadder, Earl Idle, Viscount Quidstock of the Chase and former life president of the Winterleaf Gunner Norwich Canary Society.'

'Ah, it's you, Your Grace,' said Father. 'Didn't recognize you in those white tennis pumps.'

He smiled at the Duke and after a while he said:

'What do you want?'

'I've come to visit you,' said the Duke. 'I've come to pay my respects and welcome you to the village.'

'Ah,' said Father. 'And do you want to come in as well?'

'What do you reckon?' said the Duke.

'Come in,' said Father. 'It's only me.'

So the Duke of Wiltshire stepped into the old Dower House and was led into the drawing room by Father.

'Sorry Nancy's not here to greet you,' said Father. 'She's on the lavvy at the moment. Biggies, I think.'

'Good,' said the Duke. 'Stout fellow.'

Father shuffled his way across the faded Indian carpet to the drinks cabinet and said:

'May I get you your fancy, Your Grace?'

'Call me Herbert,' said the Duke. 'I'll have an extremely large brandy followed almost immediately by another one.'

'Certainly, Herbert,' said Father.

He poured out the drink and handed it to the Duke, who took a long reflective sip at it, then downed the remains in a single gulp.

He smacked his lips and said:

'I'm ready for the next one now.'

And as Father replenished his glass he said:

'On the other hand, if you don't want to call me Herbert, you can always call me Dook.'

'Dook?' said Father.

'It's short for Duke,' said the Duke.

'Ah,' said Father. 'In that case I'll stick to Your Grace.'

He sat opposite the old aristocrat and sipped at his glass of tawny port.

He smiled at the Duke, held up his glass and said:

'Never touch the stuff, old boy.'

The Duke nodded and presented his glass to be refilled.

Father obliged.

They sat in silence.

Then the Duke of Wiltshire said:

'Shall we talk to each other?'

'Why not?' said Father. 'Did I ever tell you about the time your mother and I went to Cochin? Or was it Goa? Doesn't matter really. Both in India, aren't they?'

'So they tell me,' said the Duke of Wiltshire, settling himself happily in the deep armchair as he prepared for the delights of his companion's story.

Father moistened his lips, flexed his vocal chords and said:

'Well, we were playing bridge with this dentist chappie, when this little black bugger with the . . .'

And that moment Nancy entered the room.

The Duke of Wiltshire sprang to his feet and Father said:

'Ah, Nancy. May I introduce you to Herbert?'

'Herbert?' said Nancy.

'The Duke of Wiltshire,' said Father.

Nancy staggered backwards. She gasped. Her neck flushed scarlet. Her knees began to shake.

The Duke of Wiltshire stepped forward and offered his hand to her.

'Pleased to make your acquaintance, madam. Your father was just telling me about this little black bugger he met in Cochin. Or was it Goa?'

'Goa,' said Nancy.

And she blushed again and said:

'Father, why didn't you . . . excuse me, but I must . . . well, it's just that I . . .'

Before she could finish Winston Hayballs entered the room.

He looked at the Duke of Wiltshire and said:

'Oh hello, you old bugger. Now then, Nancy, I'm having trouble with your stench pipe look.'

'What?' said Nancy.

'Your stench pipe,' said Winston Hayballs. 'You ain't got one.'

'Winston!' said Nancy. 'How dare you come barging in here and . . . I'll come with you to inspect it.'

'No, don't go, my dear,' said the Duke. 'You're a damned handsome woman. I haven't been in the presence of such a handsome woman since I don't know when.'

'Oh,' said Nancy weakly. 'Oh.'

'Wonderful pair of shoulders you've got, my dear,' said the Duke. 'Absolutely capital. And the old pins are in pretty good shape, too.'

'Thank you,' said Nancy. 'I don't know what to say. I . . . I . . .'

The Duke continued happily:

'You remind me of a maid my mother used to employ here in the good old days. You're a much older version, of course, but . . . but . . . Carletta. That was her name. She'd deep brown eyes. And when you touched her skin, it was . . . yes, yes. Carletta. That's what they called her. Carletta.'

Winston Hayballs sniffed hard and wiped his nose on the back of his wrist.

'Well, missus, are you coming or ain't you?' he said.

'Yes,' said Nancy eagerly. 'Of course. Yes.'

She smiled nervously at the Duke. She made to curtsey, but Winston Hayballs took her by the hand and pulled her out of the room.

He led her firmly and purposefully along the hall, through the kitchen and into the courtyard, which was basking in the sunshine and the song of willow warblers.

He sat her on the bench in the rose arbour, looked down on her and began to chuckle.

'What are you laughing at?' said Nancy.

'You, missus,' said Winston Hayballs. 'What a lark, eh?'

'What lark are you talking about?' said Nancy.

'You and the old Dook,' said Winston Hayballs. 'You weren't half flummoxed there, eh?'

'I was not flummoxed,' said Nancy. 'It was simply the fact that I was taken unawares. I'll kill Father when I get him on his own. And stop laughing like that.'

Winston Hayballs stifled his mirth, and then he looked grave.

'You don't want to take no notice of that silly old sod,' he said. 'He's gaga look. Pots for rags. Has been this past twenty-four years or more.'

'That's not the point,' said Nancy. 'He's a Duke, a peer of the realm, and he should be shown proper respect. And I will not have you coming into my drawing room and calling a member of the House of Lords "you old bugger".'

Winston Hayballs sucked hard through the blue-chipped gap in his two front teeth and shook his head.

'You got a lot to learn about the ways of the country, hasn't you, missus?' he said.

Nancy sighed.

'Yes, Winston,' she said. 'That I have without a doubt.'

'Tell you what I'll do,' said Winston Hayballs. 'I'll take you out this evening in my motor, my car look, and I'll teach you everything about what you needs to know to lead a happy life here.'

'That won't be necessary, thank you very much, Winston,' said Nancy.

– Go out with him in his motor, his car? Me? I'm a mature, sophisticated woman. I've been to Switzerland.

Winston Hayballs coughed.

'Lost in your thoughts, are you, missus?' he said.

'What?'

Winston Hayballs chuckled.

'I said it before and I'll say it again,' he said. 'You looks real tasty when you're incommoded.'

'Will you stop using that word "tasty", Winston?' said Nancy sharply. 'I take great exception to it.'

Winston Hayballs nodded.

'I'll remember that for future reference,' he said. 'Right then, do you want to go and see where your stench pipe ain't?'

'No, I most certainly do not, Winston,' said Nancy. 'Just for once I should like to be left alone. Just for one brief second I should like to have a little time to myself instead of worrying about the welfare of other people. It's not a lot to ask, is it? I'm not asking for the world. I'm just asking for a little space in my life. I'm asking for a little time I can devote to me. To me, Winston. Nancy Empson. Good old Nancy. Do you understand that?'

Winston Hayballs stared at her for a moment, his head cocked to one side, his eyebrows raised, his lower lip protruding moistly. Then he said:

'Right then, missus, I'll see what I can do about your missing stench pipe.'

He turned on his heel and made his way to the back of the stables and suddenly Nancy felt lonely.

She shivered.

Once more she had the sensation that someone was watching her, someone was listening to her heartbeat, boring his eyes right through her clothes and devouring her body.

She tried to stand up, but she couldn't.

'Cuckoo, cuckoo, cuckoo.'

The shire horse whinnied.

An army helicopter roared.

– I can't cope with all this. It's savage. It's not refined. I've no control over it. I hate not being in control. It makes me frightened. I hate being frightened. I'm frightened of being frightened. I hate this house. I hate this village. I hate living in the country. I loathe it and I can't cope with it.

Then suddenly she remembered her father and the Duke of Wiltshire.

'My God,' she said out loud. 'How rude of me. I must get them something to eat.'

She stood up. She looked round in panic.

– What do Dukes eat? I suppose they must eat what we eat. It's probably nicer, but basically it'll be the same. After all their stomachs are just the same as ours and . . . Winston! Winston'll know what Dukes eat. Winston knows everything.

She turned to call to him.

But then she stopped.

She straightened her shoulders, jutted out her chin and said:

'Nancy Empson. Take a grip on yourself. For pete's sake, take a grip on yourself, woman.'

She gulped hard and then strode firmly into the house.

She went upstairs to her bedroom, drew the curtains and stripped off her clothes.

Before going to her wardrobe she looked at herself in the mirror.

– I am a handsome woman. I'm a tasty woman. I'm real tasty look. I got big endowments, that I has without a doubt.

She giggled.

She put her hands on her hips, stuck out her left hip and buttock, pouted her lips and looked at herself through the tops of her eyes.

And once again she felt the eyes boring into her.

She clasped her hands to her breasts and then to her secret parts. Goose pimples rippled over her whole body. She began to shake and shiver. Her nipples tautened till she thought they would explode. She opened her mouth and screamed, but no sound came.

Then quite without warning a great calmness came to her.

It caressed her. It crooned to her. It whispered to her.

She smiled.

Her eyes sparkled.

She sat in front of her dressing table and adjusted her make-up.

She dressed herself in her pencil-slim black skirt and her cream crocheted sleeveless jumper with the high neck. She put on her new black patent leather shoes with the tottering heels.

She looked at herself once more in the mirror of the dressing table, brushing her hair and smiling.

Then she put on her earrings and the slim gold bracelet her mother had bought in St Andrews and went downstairs to the kitchen where she prepared a tray of thinly cut cress sandwiches, brandy snaps and cream and a pot of china tea.

When she took these into the drawing room she found her father, the Duke of Wiltshire and Winston huddled over the coffee table.

They were eating huge, lop-sided hunks of cheese and onion sandwich and drinking bottles of stout by the neck.

89

'Father!' gasped Nancy. 'What on earth are you doing?'

'He's having some nosh, some tucker look. I made it with my own fair hands,' said Winston Hayballs, spraying breadcrumbs all over the carpet. 'Take a pew and have a swig of my stout. I'll wipe the neck with my hankie if you doesn't mind being hygienic.'

Nancy stared at him speechless as he took a grease-smeared, mucus-stained handkerchief from his pocket and wiped the neck of the stout bottle.

The Duke of Wiltshire stood up and came over to her.

He touched her bare arm. His hand lingered. His hand ran slowly down to her wrist.

'Yes, madam,' he said. 'You are without a doubt the most handsome young woman it has been my good fortune to meet in many a long year.'

'He says that to all his bits of fluff, don't you, you randy old bugger?' said Winston Hayballs.

The Duke of Wiltshire chuckled, and then he bowed courteously to Nancy.

'We're having the most spiffing time,' he said. 'I should take it as a great privilege if you would do me the honour of joining us at table.'

Nancy allowed herself to be led to the table. She sat down.

The Duke of Wiltshire took a long swig from his bottle of stout, belched softly into the back of his hand and said:

'Your father's been regaling us with the most fearfully interesting stories about his days in India.'

'That's right,' said Winston Hayballs. 'The old bugger's been rabbiting away for ages.'

'The old bugger?' said Nancy.

'That's me,' said Father with a happy smile. 'And the other old bugger's Herbert. I was just telling him about that curious cove we knew in Madras who made hat stands out of balsa wood. Or was it towel rails?'

'Towel rails,' said the Duke of Wiltshire.

And at that moment the door burst open and Grampy entered the drawing room.

His boots were caked in cow slime.

'Got you,' he bellowed at the Duke. 'I knew I'd catch you here, you bastard.'

90

And with that he marched across the room to the Duke, fists raised and teeth gnashing.

The Duke cowered back in his chair, raising his forearms in front of his face.

But it was to no avail.

Grampy dragged him to his feet, knocking over the table and scattering stout bottles and cheese and onion sandwiches onto the Indian carpet, and the two old men commenced to wrestle slowly, cursing and groaning.

'Winston,' screamed Nancy. 'Do something.'

Winston Hayballs sighed, shook his head, made his way to the two ancient combatants, took hold of them by the scruff of their necks and banged their heads together sharply.

They sank to the floor, rubbing their pates and whimpering softly.

Winston Hayballs returned to his chair and continued his drink.

'Did I ever tell you about the mud wrestlers your mother and I once saw in Darjeeling? Or was it Rawalpindi?'

'Trivandrum,' said William, as he entered the drawing room. 'It was in Trivandrum you saw the wrestlers.'

He held up a wad of typescript.

'I've just finished another chapter,' he said. 'It's about the points system at Yeovil Junction.'

'William,' screamed Nancy at the top of her voice. 'William.'

'Yes?' said William.

'Bugger off. For Christ's sake, bugger off.'

17

Three hours later the Empsons were reaching the end of their dinner.

They had had lamb chops, new potatoes, peas and mint sauce followed by apricot flan and cream.

Nancy glanced up at her two eating companions.

William was sulking, the cheese and biscuits uneaten on his plate.

Father was daubing a brown Ryvita biscuit with gentleman's relish and reading the advertisements for cattle auctions in the local newspaper.

He was humming softly to himself.

He caught Nancy's gaze and smiled at her.

'I made a chum this afternoon,' he said. 'Fearfully pleasant old stick, don't you think? He once garrotted a German bombardier, he was telling me.'

'Oh, my God,' said William, and he slammed down his cup, stood up and left the room.

– I shouldn't have sworn at him like that. I've never sworn at him before. Never ever. I've never sworn at anyone in public. Fancy swearing in front of a member of the House of Lords.

– What's coming over me? I'm losing control. I'm losing my grip of things. I forgot to put salt into the potatoes. I didn't put enough coffee in the percolator. I can't cope. I just can't cope.

There was a ring on the front doorbell.

'I'll go, Father,' said Nancy wearily.

'Whacko,' said Father, and he smiled at her and said: 'Do you know, Nancy, I wouldn't half mind buying a cow. We could train it to give us milk, couldn't we?'

When Nancy opened the door, she found Winston Hayballs standing there, grinning at her.

He was wearing the blue velvet suit and canary-yellow cravat he had worn at the village dance.

His hair was slicked back and there was no stubble on his chin.

He smelled of washing-up liquid.

'I come to take you out, missus,' he said. 'I come to take you for a spin in my motor, my car look.'

'What?' said Nancy.

'He's over there look,' said Winston Hayballs. 'The blue one with the dents and covered in horse shit. You'll like him, missus. Very comfy. Very agreeable. Good engine. Classy upholstery. Got him for seventy-two quid from old Jim Filbert with the cast in his right eye. Right then, put your coat on and we'll go.'

'Winston,' said Nancy. 'I am not going anywhere with you.'

'Why not?'

'Because ... well ... because I'm going to listen to a concert on the Third Programme.'

'Oh yes?' said Winston Hayballs. 'A bit of Brahms, is it? Or is it a bit of the old Poulencs?'

'It's Richard Strauss if you must know.'

'Well, you can listen to him in my motor, my car look,' said Winston Hayballs. 'I expect we can pick up old Richard Strauss on the radio.'

He smiled at her.

'Come on then, missus,' he said. 'We're losing the best part of the evening.'

And to her intense astonishment she found herself returning to the drawing room and saying to Father:

'I'm just going out for a while, Father.'

'On your tod?'

'No. No, Father. I'm going with ... well, as a matter of fact I'm going with Winston.'

'Ah, Winston,' said Father. 'Fearfully pleasant cove. His father paid us a visit this afternoon. Did you by any chance meet him?'

Still in a daze Nancy took her navy blue leather trenchcoat from the cloakroom and allowed herself to be led to the car by Winston Hayballs.

She sat next to him meekly in the front seat.

Meekly she allowed him to fasten her seat belt.

She said not a word as he tooted the horn three times and set off with a screech of tyres and a roar of exhaust.

The main street of the village was deserted. A pair of jackdaws squabbled on the wall of the village pub. One of Sid Lopcombe's bantams lay dead at the side of the road.

Winston switched on the radio.

93

It hissed and spat at him and then settled itself comfortably into emitting an irregular series of low-pitched grunts and belches.

'That don't sound like Richard Strauss to me,' said Winston Hayballs. 'I'd say it was more of your early Stockhausen, wouldn't you, missus?'

Nancy did not reply.

She sat still and tense, gazing straight ahead through the fly-squashed windscreen.

– What am I doing here? What am I doing with him in an old claptrap car like this? I've been in the front seat of an Alvis in my time. And a Lanchester. And a Lea Francis. Or was it a Humber? Stop it. Stop it, Nancy. Take a grip on yourself.

She turned to Winston and said stiffly:

'I wonder if you'd mind turning the wireless off. It doesn't seem to be getting us anywhere, does it?'

Winston Hayballs chuckled.

'That it ain't missus,' he said. 'I must go to the dry cleaners again with my trousers so's I can get another coat hanger for the aerial.'

He switched off the wireless, opened his side window, thrust out his elbow and commenced to sing softly.

He had a sweet voice, surprisingly high, but mellow and tuneful.

Nancy glanced at him out of the corners of her eyes.

He was tapping the steering wheel in time to the rhythm of his song. He was smiling. There was a small square of blood-sodden toilet paper on his neck.

– If they could see me now they'd have kittens at the golf club. They wouldn't believe it. Well, some of them would, I suppose. Good old Nancy, they'd say, getting stuck in and trying to make a go of things. Good old Nancy, making another new life for her family and keeping things sweet with the locals. She always was marvellous with tradesmen and the little man who came round to do the garden.

Winston Hayballs turned the car over the old packhorse bridge and commenced to follow the narrow road that wound its way up the valley of the River Florey.

The woodlands of Crannock Chase billowed with hanging oaks and beech.

Jersey cattle browsed, gentle-nosed and limp-eyed, in the water meadows. Buzzards spiralled and mewed. A goat, tethered at the side of the road, did not look up as they passed by.

– What's it doing here miles from nowhere? Who owns it? I expect there's a little farm hidden away in the tuck of the valley below. I wonder what they're like, those people who live in the farm. Are they an old couple desperately waiting for a letter from their daughter in New Zealand? Or are they young and in love and just setting up house for the first time and they can't afford a television or the reception's so bad it's not worth getting one and he's tall and slim with crinkly dark hair and she's plump with a cheery face and they're just waiting for it to go dark so they can go upstairs to bed and they won't draw the curtains because no one can see them and it's more exciting that way, anyhow, and he'll rip off her clothes and he'll whisk her up in his arms and he'll hurl her onto the bed and he'll smother her breasts in kisses and he'll . . . Nancy, stop. Stop it at once, Nancy. Pull yourself together.

The car crested the brow of the hill with a snort and whine and Winston Hayballs said:

'Well, here we are, missus. The village of Gridley Miskin at your disposal.'

It was a scant and scattered village. The houses were lank, with shifty windows. There was a corrugated-iron Methodist chapel. A gaggle of sullen youths were sitting astride their motorcycles staring silently at two giggling girls, propping up the side of the bus shelter.

And in the centre of the village was a huge yard. It was parked to the brim with container lorries and trailers. The vehicles were large and new and their radiator grills smirked in the last of the evening sun.

Suddenly Nancy found herself flooding into talk.

'It's amazing, isn't it?' she said. 'How many times do you come out into the country to a one-horse dump like this and find a whacking great haulage contractor's bristling with lorries? Why? I mean, what possible work can they find round here? What are they doing here, Winston?'

Winston Hayballs smiled slowly.

'Ah, that's another one of them great unfathomable mysteries about the countryside, missus.'

Just before they reached the far end of Gridley Miskin Winston Hayballs pulled the car into a pub yard hidden from the road by a clump of yew trees.

He helped Nancy out of the car with a bow and a wink, pointed expansively to the pub and said:

'Here we are. Feast your eyes on that, missus.'

95

The pub cowered forlornly.

Two of its upstairs windows were boarded up. There was a patch of stale sick on the front step.

Winston Hayballs smiled.

'Smashing place look,' he said. 'I brings all my bits of fluff here.'

'What?' said Nancy. 'What?'

Back at the old Dower House William was pacing up and down the drawing room.

Father looked up irritably from his Biggles book and said:

'I wish you'd stop doing that, William. Fearfully distracting, you know, old boy.'

'It's Nancy,' said William.

'What about her?'

'She swore at me.'

'I shouldn't worry about that,' said Father. 'Your mother always used to swear at me. "Jigger me," she used to say. "You've burned another hole in the front of your cardigan." Fearfully observant woman, your mother.'

He returned to his book and William resumed his pacing up and down.

Then he stopped and said:

'And now she's gone off with Winston. What on earth is she doing with Winston?'

Father put down his book with a resigned sigh.

'Fraternizing with the natives, old boy. Buttering them up,' he said.

'What?'

'The first thing your mother did when we were posted to a new station in India was to fraternize with the natives. Did I ever tell you about that ablutions wallah we had in Hyderabad? Your mother took quite a shine to the little black bugger. She taught him how to play the cello. Fearful noise he made. Morning, noon and night all we heard was the noise of his ghastly cello. Ruined the ablutions facilities for months.'

He smiled and stood up.

He waved his pipe at William and paused at the drawing room door.

'I think I'll just take a short constitutional to the shed at the bottom of the garden,' he said. 'Don't know why I'm going. Something to do, I suppose.'

He left the room.

William followed him and repaired to his study.

His typewriter needed a new ribbon. This was the third day running Nancy had forgotten to change it. What was going on with her? She'd forgotten to renew their subscription to the Woodland Trust and there was a distinct lack of salt in the potatoes she had prepared for dinner. And now she'd gone off with Winston. Winston! Winston, of all people. Winston? Wait a minute. Perhaps he knew how to change a typewriter ribbon.

The front doorbell rang.

He answered it.

Mrs Godwin stood there.

'Ah, William,' she said. 'Just the man I want to see.'

She stepped inside and made her way into the drawing room.

William spluttered in her wake.

She said:

'I'd like a small whisky, if you please, William.'

'Certainly,' he said. 'Have we got any?'

Mrs Godwin smiled slowly.

'I think you'll find it in the drinks cabinet,' she said.

'Ah,' he said. 'Good-oh.'

She was wearing dove-grey slacks.

He liked women in trousers.

Her loose blouse was blush pink.

Pink was his favourite colour, just pipping by a short head the distinctive vermilion livery of the old Midland Railway.

He handed her the glass of whisky.

'Thank you, William,' she said. 'Are you alone in the house?'

'Well, sort of,' he said. 'Father's in the shed at the bottom of the garden and Nancy's out with Winston.'

'Winston?' said Mrs Godwin, and she laughed.

It was a laugh full of deep, languid pools and lazy ripples.

'So it's started already?' she said.

'What's started already?' said William.

'Sit down, William,' said Mrs Godwin.

'Thank you.'

He sat down.

Gosh, she'd got long fingernails. The West Indian ticket collector at

Belsize Park tube station had got long fingernails, too. He'd always wondered if she'd been infringing company regulations.

Mrs Godwin lit a cigarette, let the smoke dribble slowly over her lower lip and said:

'I've come here, William, because I want to co-opt you.'

'Co-opt me?'

'Onto our committee.'

'Your committee?'

'Our action committee to save the village green.'

'Oh no,' said William. 'I don't want to get involved in that.'

'Nonsense,' said Mrs Godwin.

'Pardon?'

'Nonsense, William,' said Mrs Godwin. 'We need a man like you on the committee. We need a writer. Someone to write up reports for the local newspaper. A man "in the know". A man of the world.'

'But I'm not a man of the world,' said William. 'I don't know how to write for newspapers. I write books about railways. I couldn't care less about village greens. And this particular village green, I hate. I loathe it. I loathe everything about this village. I've never been so miserable in my life living here.'

'In that case, William, you'll have to come to one of our parties, when we start them up again.'

'Pardon?'

'You'll love our parties, William. They'll give you a chance to get to know us. And we're dying to get to know you. You're all the talk in the circle. A famous writer in our midst! We're absolutely avid to make the most of you. And as for me, William - well, I just can't wait.'

'Oh,' said William.

Mrs Godwin smiled and flicked a speck of ash off her dove-grey slacks.

'Good. That's settled then,' she said. 'Consider yourself well and truly co-opted.'

'Let me make it quite plain to you, Winston, once and for all and finally,' said Nancy. 'I am not – repeat not – one of your bits of fluff. Is that quite clear?'

Winston sucked in deeply through the gap in his two front teeth.

'Cor, missus,' he said. 'I've said it once and I'll say it again - you don't half look tasty when you got your dander up.'

'I have not got my dander up,' said Nancy. 'And I do not look tasty.'

Winston buried his mouth deep into the swirling, matted heart of his pint of scrumpy. He drank greedily. He withdrew his mouth, wiped the foam from his lips on his sleeve, smiled, winked and said:

'I tell you something about old Winston, missus,' he said. 'When old Winston declares that a woman what is in his company is tasty then tasty she be, whether she likes it or not. And that is true without a shadow of a doubt. Has you ever read the works of Mrs Gaskell, by the way?'

They were sitting in the snug bar of the pub.

It was cold. It was damp. The floor was stoneflagged and dirty. They were sitting on narrow benches cramped close to the peeling walls. The table wobbled. There was no ice for her gin and tonic.

– I like it here. It's nice. I feel safe here. I feel secure. I feel at home. Good gosh, Geoffrey would have done his nut if he could see me here. Geoffrey liked what he called 'roadhouses'. He liked to see Jaguars and Austin Healeys parked in the car park. He liked a good artificial log fire and bowls of crisps and silverskin onions on the bar counter and an aquarium on a wrought-iron stand. He didn't like olives on the bar counter, but he was very partial to rugby club fixture lists and collecting boxes for the Royal National Lifeboat Institution. He'd have hated it here.

When Winston Hayballs returned from the bar with another pint of scrumpy and a gin and tonic, she smiled at him and said:

'Thank you.'

'You're welcome, missus,' said Winston Hayballs. 'But I wouldn't drink too much more of that gin stuff or you'll be wanting to pee all night on the way home.'

She laughed.

– I laughed? Me, Nancy Empson, laughing at a vulgarity like that? What's come over me? I once slapped Geoffrey's face for talking about dog dirt in mixed company. Well, I almost slapped his face. I would have done, too, if he hadn't been in uniform. He's right. If I have any more, I really will need to have a pee and goodness knows what the toilets are like here.

Before she could stop herself she turned to Winston Hayballs and said:

'Winston. I'm throwing myself on your mercy.'

'Oh yes, missus?' said Winston Hayballs.

They were sitting close together on the bench. Their thighs were touching. She thought she could smell foot powder.

'I'm pleading with you, Winston,' she said. 'I'm pleading with you to help us. You're the only man in the whole village who can.'

'Can what?'

'Help us win the battle to save the village green,' said Nancy, and she was intense that she had taken hold of Winston Hayballs' wrist. 'You're the kingpin in the village without a doubt. You must be our leader. I want you to join our action committee.'

'Oh that,' said Winston Hayballs. 'All he is, is just an excuse for another round of wife-swapping.'

'What?' said Nancy.

'Wife-swapping, missus. It's endemic in the country among folks of your classes.'

'What?'

Winston Hayballs took another sip of scrumpy and smiled.

'Let me tell you something what you doesn't know, missus,' he said. 'That Mrs Godwin, she's cock of the rock in the village wife-swapping circle. It's not going on at the moment look. No, they finished the last round five months ago. Two divorces and an attempted suicide came out of that. But they'll be starting up again soon. Oh yes, they'll be starting up again directly. And this committee of yours is the excuse. New blood, see. New recruits. They don't give a monkeys about the village green. All they want is a valid reason for resuming their clandestine activities of having their bits of nookie on the side.'

'I've never heard anything so disgusting in the whole of my life, Winston,' said Nancy. 'You are talking about cultivated, civilized people. You are talking about stockbrokers and obstetricians. You are talking about people in good odour with their bank managers. And, I might say, Winston, it ill behoves you with your bits of fluff on the sly to cast aspersions on people whose horizons stretch a dashed sight farther than stench pipes and big endowments. I know for a fact that Mrs Godwin takes *Which* regularly each month. I hate you, Winston, and I want to go home.'

'Certainly, missus,' said Winston Hayballs. 'Just let me finish my pint and have a slash, and I'll oblige you directly.'

William walked Mrs Godwin home in the snuffling dusk.

She held his arm tightly.

'I think Nancy's a very singular lady, William,' she said as they passed by the village pub.

'Do you?' said William.

'Oh yes. She's very handsome. Very bold. A pity about her dress sense, but she's certainly got a certain something about her. Quite a few of our circle have remarked on it most favourably.'

'Mm,' said William.

They were almost knocked down by Baksi Hayballs who was dashing back home, redolent with guilt and tangy with the scents of loving and the old fruit store house.

Venetia Hayballs scurried past them on her way from the village stores where she had been late-night shopping for a length of elastic.

'I think you and Nancy will be quite an asset to our circle, William,' said Mrs Godwin as they began to walk up the front path of her house.

'In what way?' said William.

Mrs Godwin squeezed his arm.

'In every way, William,' she said. 'In every way you like. In every way you could possibly dream of.'

She paused at the front door.

She kissed him on the lips.

'I would invite you in, William, only I'm expecting a visitor,' she said. 'Never mind. One day very soon you'll be a visitor, too, won't you?'

The headlights of the car picked out darting deer and startled rabbits.

An ashtray rattled.

Winston Hayballs sang at the top of his voice.

– I should be angry with him. I should be livid. But I'm not. I should be angry with myself going out with him in his motor, his car. But I'm not. Why? I've always been an angry person deep down. I'm always taking things back to the shops. I'm always having rucks with American Express. That's why I won't have any truck with those ghastly mail order catalogues. That's why I won't buy a telephone answering machine. I think you can tell the character of a person by the message they leave on the answering machine when you call them up. I hate them. You never know what to say and . . .

'You got a regular bloke then, Nancy?' said Winston Hayballs.

'I beg your pardon?'

'You got a regular bloke what writes you letters on notepaper regular and is desirous of claiming you in the fullness of time for his own?'

101

'No, as a matter of fact, I haven't,' said Nancy. 'But I have had the odd bloke or two.'

'Oh yes?'

'Yes. I was once almost engaged to be married.'

'Who to?'

'Geoffrey Wilkinson. He was a navigator in the RAF.'

'And what happened to him.'

'He crashed and got killed.'

'Ah,' said Winston Hayballs. 'It happens to the best of them, missus. Them boys, they goes up in them planes and half the time they don't know what's what, do they?'

'That's right,' said Nancy. 'And the other half of the time they don't know what's what about anything else.'

– He looked so portly in his uniform. Portly? Nice word, portly. He crashed in Germany. I like Germany. All those castles on the Rhine and eating elvers. Poor Geoffrey. His sister was distraught when he died.

It began to rain.

The wipers swished on the windscreen in a resigned and elderly fashion.

Winston Hayballs took his left hand off the steering wheel and rested it on Nancy's hip.

'That Geoffrey of yours,' he said. 'No use crying over spilled milk, is it? You got me now. Well, you got me for the evening, ain't you?'

'Yes,' said Nancy. 'Won't your wife be alarmed?'

'No, missus,' said Winston Hayballs. 'She's used to it look. She don't mind me having my bits of fluff on the side.'

'I've told you before about calling me . . .'

'Well, bits of fluff make a marriage a damn sight more interesting than what it would be normal, don't it? I wouldn't mind if she had her own bit of spare on the side, mind. She wants to herself. Oh yes, without a doubt. Trouble is she's so bloody ugly no one'll look at her. More's the pity, eh?'

He chuckled and said after a while:

'I wish I'd married a beautiful woman like you, missus.'

'What?'

'Well, stands to reason and makes sense, don't it?' said Winston Hayballs. 'I could have gone my way. And you could have gone yours. Would have made all the difference in the world to our marriage.'

The car approached the outskirts of Winterleaf Gunner.

Winston Hayballs' hand was still resting on Nancy's hip.

He removed it to change gear as they edged their way past the skip outside the home of the minor TV personage.

– He's going to put it round my shoulders. I know he is. He'll put it round my shoulders and he'll start to stroke them and I've got nice shoulders. When I used to go horse riding my instructor was always saying I'd got nice shoulders though what he saw in them under my hacking jacket I'll never know. I like having bare shoulders and bare arms. I'll kill him, if he touches them. I'll bite him and I'll scratch his eyes out.

Winston Hayballs stopped the car outside the front of the old Dower House.

He did not touch her shoulders or her arms.

He just rolled himself a cigarette and said:

'Yes, if you don't believe me about that Mrs Godwin, just you ask Wilson Rappaport.'

'But he's dead.'

'Course he is, missus,' said Winston Hayballs. 'That's why he shot himself look. Because of Mrs Godwin. He shot himself in the shed at the bottom of your garden because she led him on and then back-heeled him without warning and without remorse.'

He leaned across her and opened her door.

'See you tomorrow then, missus,' he said. 'You'll be pleased to know I got you a new stench pipe free and gratis and without payment.'

She went inside.

The car scrunched on the gravel.

– I'd have killed him if he'd tried to kiss me.

18

A week later Baksi announced she was pregnant.

It was the day of the first meeting of the Village Green Action Committee, and Nancy Empson had decided to wear the severe black suit she had worn on the day of Geoffrey's funeral, although the earrings would be different.

It was Sunday morning.

The Hayballs' house smelled of foot powder and bicycle oil.

Baksi was sitting in the kitchen varnishing her toenails, when she made the announcement.

Her eyes were glinting and her plump, firm young breasts swung free in her loose pink cotton tee-shirt.

'Well, that's wonderful news, my darling, indeed it is,' said Clementine Hayballs, who was smoking a thin-drizzled cigarette, feeding her infant child at the breast and dicing up carrots for the Sunday lunch. 'Does you by any chance know who the father is?'

'Yes, but I'm not telling,' said Baksi. 'All I'll say is he's someone important.'

Winston Hayballs, who was washing his feet in a dented bucket, looked up from his *Sunday Times* supplement and said:

'I see that Margaret Drabble's gone and wrote another of her bloody awful books.'

Doreen Hayballs, who had been standing in a deep corner, nervously tapping the colander against her gaunt thigh, said:

'Is that all you can say? Is that all the comment you can make? What's she going to do about her GCSE exams when it comes to passing them?'

'Oh, I expect she'll already have a hatful most likely,' said Winston Hayballs. 'These lady novelists aren't behind the door when it comes to being too bleeding clever by half.'

'I'm not talking about her,' said Doreen. 'I'm talking about our Baksi.'

'Oh Baksi?' said Winston Hayballs. 'Well, I reckons she's already passed her practical biology with flying colours, don't you?'

He chuckled, stood up, put on his socks and wellington boots and began to make his way to the garden door.

He chucked Baksi beneath her chin and said:

'Now you take a tip from your Auntie Clementine and don't go marrying no one till you're sure you got no chance of getting hitched up with a blokey what's better than the one you had before.'

Then he turned to Doreen, who was standing at the sink ripping up a sad and listless cabbage.

'And I don't want to hear another word from you about it, do you understand?' he said. 'All you got to do to keep in my good books is make sure my dinner's fit for eating when I come back from my sesh at the pub.'

He stepped outside into the late April morning.

Spring was in full spate.

In the wood at the rear of his house the trees were newly frocked in timid green. Small birds thrust out their breasts and sang their sweet soaring songs of threat and lust.

Cuckoo Tree Meadow glowed with oxslip and buttercup, and the shire horse was whinnying, frisking its tail and kicking out its hind legs with the snow-white, rampant feathers fluttering on its fetlocks.

On the swollen, sparkling waters of the River Florey coots hissed and fought and dabchick trilled and presented each other with garlands of weeds.

Spring smirked at him.

It fluttered its eyelids, pouted its lips and shamelessly offered itself body and soul to him.

He sighed.

On the whole he preferred winter and a good hack and a spit into the heart of a roaring log fire.

He commenced his regular Sunday walk through the village.

Two lady joggers from the wife-swappers' circle, bosoms heaving in soft, velvety track suits, cast hungry, predatory eyes at him.

Nansen Ticehurst, clearing up the debris from the previous night's dance at the village hall, nodded his head at him and said:

'What do you reckon then?'

'Not a lot,' said Winston Hayballs.

He was stopped by Venetia Hayballs, hotfoot back from a fruitless mission to the village shop in search of gravy granules.

'I just heard the news about your Baksi,' she said.

105

'Oh yes?' said Winston Hayballs.

'I think it's disgusting I do. You wants to give her the strap and send her off incognito. And I tell you something else.'

'What's that?'

'I just heard about you taking out Miss Empson in your motor, your car. I think it's disgusting I do. You wants to pay heed to your station in life and leave her to folk what understands her refinement and proper breeding connections.'

'I'll bear that in mind,' said Winston Hayballs with a chuckle and then he looked grave and said: 'What did you say that daughter of yours was studying for?'

'She's studying to be clever,' said Venetia Hayballs. 'And she's going to Barcelona this summer to learn how to speak real Spanish at the university what they've got there.'

'Well, as long as she don't get up the spout, it'll be all right, won't it?' he said.

He dodged the jab of her umbrella and continued his stroll.

He turned into the rumpled lane which led to the old Dower House. Nancy was working at the front door, carefully bathing the leaves of the two bay trees she had brought from London.

She was wearing her fisherman's smock and she had a green silk scarf turbaned round her dark, springy hair.

'Morning, missus,' he said. 'What do you reckon?'

'Not a lot,' said Nancy.

And then she slapped her thigh and said:

'I must stop saying that. It's so common. It's so vulgar. It isn't me at all.'

Winston Hayballs chuckled and sucked at the gap between his two front teeth.

'I'm just going for a sesh at the pub,' he said. 'I was wondering if you'd care to join me. We could have a couple of hands of crib, if you wants.'

'No, thank you, Winston,' said Nancy. 'I don't think it would be quite apropos, do you?'

'Why not?' said Winston Hayballs. 'You enjoyed our night out at Gridley Miskin, didn't you?'

'As a one-off, Winston, it was quite interesting,' said Nancy. 'But I have no wish to repeat it in the future, if you don't mind.'

'Please yourself, missus,' said Winston Hayballs. 'One day we might repeat it in the past, mightn't we?'

He doffed his woollen hat at her and turned away down the lane.

She called him back.

'Yes?' he said. 'Changed your mind about coming for a sesh, have you?'

She rubbed her hands agitatedly on the front of her smock, and then it all came flooding out.

'It's the first meeting of our Action Group tonight and I know in my bones it'll be awful and nothing will come of it and I know it'll be all dry sherry and expensive leisure wear and I'll feel out of place and my pen will run out while I'm taking the minutes and I'm sure to be wearing the wrong shoes and that frightful Mrs Godwin will be smirking and showing off her ankles and . . . Winston, you've got to help.'

'Me, missus?' said Winston Hayballs. 'Why me?'

'Because you're the only one in this ghastly village who's got the guts to stand up and fight. You've got integrity, Winston. You've got a sense of honour, a sense of decency. You know what's right and you know what's wrong. It's your duty to help us.'

Winston Hayballs scratched slowly at the recesses of his left armpit and nodded slowly.

'Duty, missus?' he said. 'I ain't got no duty to no one but myself. Number one, that's the only duty old Winston got in life. That's why I'll be round shortly to take you out for another trip in my motor, my car look.'

As he walked away down the lane he heard her shouting:

'I hate you, Winston Hayballs. I loathe you. You're despicable and you smell of chain guards.'

He chuckled to himself.

He passed by Horace Fisherton who said:

'What do you reckon then?'

'Not a lot,' he said.

'I just been informed of the news regarding your Baksi's condition,' said Horace Fisherton.

'Oh yes?'

'Yes,' said Horace Fisherton. 'I reckons she's got the correct sort of hips for it, don't you?'

'Oh yes. Without a doubt,' said Winston Hayballs.

He came to the village green and sat down on the splintered bench beneath the oak tree.

Lionel Woodyates and Ted Cholderton were dragging the heavy roller across the pitch in preparation for the afternoon's match against Bowerhampton.

Chestnuts. Elms. Rooks. Moorhen. Muscovy duck. Low-skimming swallows. Distant thump of shire horse hooves. Lazy hunch of heron neck.

– I could have been a maker of lutes look. Oh yes, without a doubt I could have made lutes in an old stable in a back yard in one of them cities with underground railways. I likes timber I does. I got an affinity with it. Them logs I chops in autumn, they're wasted on fires for winter. I could build a ship out of them I could. I'd build an ark and we'd read *Cousin Pons* and the works of Thomas Love Peacock, and we'd listen to the music of Richard Strauss and I'd make a crib out of maple for my first grandchild and I'd rock it back and forth and tell it not to grow up into a silly bugger like what they all are round here. Oh yes, without a doubt I got an affinity with timber and women with dark springy hair.

He stood up, tossed a greeting to the two rollermen and made his way to the village pub.

Grocott, the landlord, poured him his pint of scrumpy and said:

'I heard about your Baksi.'

'Oh yes?'

'Yes,' said Grocott. 'I'm opening a book on who the father's going to be. Evens Ted Cholderton and ten to one Bar.'

'I'll have a fiver each way on Bar,' said Winston Hayballs.

Three hours, ten pints of scrumpy and three whiskys later Winston Hayballs was eating his Sunday lunch with Grampy in the dining room.

Doreen, Baksi, Tarleton, Woodcock, Clementine and her seven children were eating their meal in the kitchen.

Grampy stuffed a wadge of gravy-sodden Yorkshire pudding into his mouth and said:

'They just told me about Baksi.'

'Well, they would, wouldn't they?' said Winston Hayballs.

Grampy sighed.

'My old mother,' he said. 'My old mother was fourteen years of age, when she give birth to her first illegitimate birth.'

'Is that so?'

'Yes. It was me. And I've never looked back since.'

They finished their roast beef. Winston Hayballs banged on the floor with the flat of his wellington boot and Baksi brought in the bread and butter pudding.

They ate in silence and then Grampy said:

'You got to help.'

'Help in what?' said Winston Hayballs.

'Saving the village green,' said Grampy. 'I'm too old now. I done my whack look. It's your turn now. Us Hayballs, we got a reputation to live up to. We're the only ones in the whole history of Winterleaf Gunner what's had the guts to stand up against them buggers in the palace. Well, you're chief cook and bottlewasher in the family now. Do your duty.'

'I ain't doing nothing,' said Winston Hayballs, and he wrinkled his nose and said: 'That Doreen, she's put nutmeg in the pudding again. She knows I hates nutmeg.'

Grampy stood up silently.

He looked down on his son, scooping up chunks of bread and butter pudding with the blade of his knife and snuffling at the thick custard.

He said quietly:

'You was a clever little sod when you was a boy. You was forever reading books, you was. I used to thrash the daylights out of you with my razor strop to bring you to your senses. You passed your examination for the Eleven Plus and you cried something bitter when I wouldn't let you go to the grammar school in Sturminster. I wanted you to be one of us look. So I kicked the living arse out of you, and I belted you round the ear and I burned all your books and I smashed all your records for the gramophone. And then bit by bit, day by day, week by week, I began to notice the difference. You stopped locking the lavatory door behind you. You began to smoke and chase the girls. You got yourself tattooed and let your hair grow long and greasy and I thought to myself: I done it. At long last he's one of us.'

He continued to stare at his son.

Winston Hayballs picked up the plate, pressed it to his lips and sucked back the remains of the custard.

And then Grampy roared at the top of his voice:

'But I was wrong, wasn't I? You ain't one of us. You never will be and I wish to God I'd still got my old razor strop hanging from the back of the kitchen door. That I do without a doubt.'

He slammed the door violently behind him and marched out of the house.

It was cold in the ditch at the side of the meadow.

The wind had backed to the east, and it was mean to the bones.

Grampy and the Duke of Wiltshire lay side by side, smoking their pipes.

'You wasn't at the fruit shed this morning,' said Grampy.

'I know,' said the Duke of Wiltshire. 'I just couldn't get up. I was so tired. I'm always tired these days.'

'Bollocks,' said Grampy. 'You're just bleeding lazy, that's all you are.'

'I'm not lazy,' said the Duke of Wiltshire. 'I'm tired. I'm old. I'm cold and I want to go home.'

He began to shiver and he clung to Grampy for warmth.

Thump of ball against bat. Faint applause.

Scatter of rooks.

Grampy pushed his aged companion away from his chest and said:

'It's just an excuse, that's what it is.'

'An excuse?' said the Duke of Wiltshire, blowing on his fists and huddling his elbows tightly into his ribs. 'What do you mean – an excuse?'

'An excuse for you to sit back and do nothing about the village green.'

The Duke of Wiltshire let out a low, plaintive moan.

'I'm sick of the village green,' he said. 'Let them do what they like with it. Who cares? I don't. I shan't be here to see it when they've finished. All I want is peace and quiet and warmth. I want a peaceful death. I want a long, slow, warm death.'

He smiled, cuddled himself up into a ball and fell asleep.

Grampy propped himself on a stiff elbow and stared at him.

The lion of his youth. The lion of the days of his prime. Storming the pillbox with the bullets whipping up the gravel round their ankles. Stalking the maid from the old Dower House with the dew seeping up to the backs of their knees. Shriek of Stuka. Bleat of troop-ship siren. The giggling. The heaving. The wild cries.

After a while Grampy stood up.

He woke the Duke of Wiltshire by prodding him in the ribs with the toe of his boot.

He put his arm round his neck and dragged him to the thatched scorer's shed.

He placed him in Nansen Ticehurst's wheelbarrow, covered him with a sheet of tarpaulin used to protect the pitch from rain and marauding dogs, and wheeled him to the front doors of Florey Palace.

He rang the bell.

A footman answered the door.

He was tall. He was young. He had deep, brown, smouldering eyes with here and there and now and then a fleck of gold.

He said:

'Yes.'

'I brought you a present look,' said Grampy.

The footman licked his lips. He looked over his shoulders. Then he descended the flight of stone steps and picked up the handles of the wheelbarrow.

'Not that,' said Grampy. 'It's old buggerlugs I brought you. I wants the barrow and the tarpaulin back. They're worth a damn sight more to the village than what your master is.'

He walked slowly to the fruit store house.

He sat down.

From the hip pocket of his cord trousers he took out a half-eaten dripping sandwich.

He placed it carefully on the bench in front of him.

And small salty tears welled up in his eyes.

19

The first meeting of the Action Committee was not a success.

When Nancy presented herself at Mrs Godwin's front door, her hostess said:

'Where's William?'

'William?'

'Yes. He's been co-opted to the committee.'

'When?'

'When I came to visit him at your home a few days ago.'

'You visited William at my home?'

'That's right, Nancy,' said Mrs Godwin with an icy smile. 'I believe you were out with Winston at the time.'

– I'd like to plunge a skewer straight through her rib-cage. I've never taken such an instant dislike to a person since I heard Andy Williams being interviewed on Radio 2. She's so smug. So superior. So cool. So beautiful. Yes, she really is a beautiful and sophisticated woman, and I'm wearing totally the wrong sort of shoes.

'Come along in, Nancy, and I'll introduce you to the gang,' said Mrs Godwin, and she smiled again. 'I like your shoes. You must tell me where you got them from some time.'

– Bitch. And it's not like me to use that word either. When we saw a bitch on the lead in the park, Mother always insisted we call it a 'lady dog'. Where was that park? There was always this mad old lady riding a sit-up-and-beg bicycle round the paddling pool and throwing scraps of bread to the children from a carrier bag. Will I end up as a mad old lady, writing poison pen letters to snooker players on the television, sitting on a bench outside the public library and howling like a monkey, wearing a fur coat in summer and . . . Poole in Dorset! That was where the park was. Poole in Dorset.

The introductions were made.

Nancy remembered not a single name.

Clinking glasses. Laughter. Perspiration. Banter. Rapacious eyes. Dull eyes. Wet lips. Mean lips. Aftershave and mascara. Double chins and slack bosoms. Wrinkles. Blotches. Braying voices. Sly, shifty voices.

Thin wrists jangling with bracelets. Hairless chests rasping with medallions.

– My God, they're so ugly. Ugly faces. Ugly bodies. Ugly manners. How can they be wife-swappers? I wouldn't want to swap with any of them. No, that's being very ungracious, Nancy. It's being very silly. Most unlike you.

– Mrs Godwin's beautiful. She's no chicken, I grant you, but she's beautifully preserved, and she's a pretty little thing in the corner there in the lilac boiler suit and that one with no bra and the frizzy perm could be quite attractive if only her thumbs weren't quite so blunt. It's the men. They're the ugly ones. So arrogant. So pleased with themselves. Such ugly manners. Have you noticed? They're all sitting down and the women are standing. Typical.

They made no effort to start the meeting.

They drank.

They touched each other.

A man with gold-rimmed half-moon spectacles and a bottle green leather thong round his neck touched Nancy's arm and said:

'When we start our parties again, Nancy, you really must come along.'

'Thank you very much,' said Nancy and she pulled her arm away from him.

– Me go to one of their parties? What do they think I am? I don't wear lilac boiler suits. I don't wear a chain round my ankle. I don't wear tight trousers that show the nick in my bottom. I wear severe black suits and a sensible vest that's driving me insane with all this heat. If only I could have a damn good scratch.

Suddenly Nancy was aware that Mrs Godwin was crouching on her haunches in front of her and resting her hands on her knees.

The touch was confident, familiar, mischievous.

'We've made a decision, Nancy?'

'Oh yes,' said Nancy.

'Yes, we've decided to send a delegation to the Marquess to put our case.'

'Ah,' said Nancy. 'Well, I'm afraid I didn't hear the formal motion and the names of proposer and seconder.'

Mrs Godwin snorted.

'Well, you wouldn't, Nancy. There's never any formality among our circle here.'

'I see.'

113

Mrs Godwin raised herself slowly to her feet, pressing her hands hard on Nancy's knees as she did so.

'May I get you another drink?'

'No thank you,' said Nancy hastily. 'I think it's time I should be wending my way.'

'Good for you,' said Mrs Godwin.

Then she clapped her hands sharply and the congregation fell silent. She paused for a moment, smiled and then said:

'This is just to announce, ladies and gentlemen, that our secretary is about "to wend her way".'

A flush came to Nancy's cheeks.

Her neck stiffened and locked. She felt she would faint, if she turned it to the left.

She gritted her teeth and said:

'Well then, cheerio, everyone. I'll write up the minutes just as soon as I get home.'

She thought she heard a titter.

Before she had left the room they had resumed their drinking and cracking the jokes she could not understand.

Mrs Godwin escorted her to the front door and said:

'Now remember. Next time you must bring William. I insist. Tell him that, won't you?'

How nice to get outside into the cool fresh spring night. How lovely. It had been sickly inside. So sneery. So shallow. So worthless.

– They don't care a fig about the village green. It's just a game to them. It's an excuse to meet up in their lilac boiler suits and their embroidered denim shirts. I've never met such an awful shower in the whole of my life. Wife-swappers? Rubbish. They're just the same as those dreadful people who used to bray and bicker at Geoffrey's open mess nights. I know what they're about. They're about being different from me.

The sky was clear.

The moon was full.

– I wonder what people are doing in Portugal now? Are peasants baking bread? Do they have lynx in Portugal? I know they've got them in Spain. I wonder what people are doing in Funchal? I wonder what Geoffrey's doing.

Winston Hayballs stepped out of the shadows, but she was not alarmed.

Very calmly she said:

'Oh, it's you. What do you want?'

'I been waiting for you,' said Winston Hayballs. 'I come to walk you home.'

'Thank you,' said Nancy.

They walked silently side by side for a while. Winston Hayballs had his hands plunged deeply into his trouser pockets and from time to time he slouched his feet.

At length he spoke.

'I don't want to talk,' he said.

'No?'

'No. I wants to be silent.'

They walked on past the village pub and the village shop and Mrs Fokine's cottage and the sub power station in the alley at the side of Miss Roebuck's bungalow.

And then Nancy said:

'Why do you want to be silent, Winston?'

'Cos I been thinking, I has.'

'What about?'

'About what certain people has been saying to me today. It's made me feel lonely.'

'You, Winston? Lonely?'

Winston Hayballs stopped.

'Do you want to sit on the wall here, park your arse like?'

'Winston!' snapped Nancy. 'How many more times must I tell you about your language?'

But she sat next to him on the low stone wall in front of the village shop.

He hunched his shoulders and scuffled his feet in the dirt.

'I'm going to be a granddad,' he said.

'You, Winston? A granddad?'

'Yes,' said Winston Hayballs. 'That Baksi of mine told me, informed me like, that she's up the spout.'

'How awful, Winston,' said Nancy. 'What are you going to do about it?'

'Me?' said Winston Hayballs. 'I ain't going to do nothing, missus. It's a fact of life round here, ain't it? You can't get no more basic than the facts of life in the countryside. There ain't no way you can fight against it look.'

She felt outraged.

She felt sick at heart.

The wantonness of it. The indifference. The cruelty. The disgusting vulgarity.

Then she found herself giggling and she said:

'You a grandfather, Winston? You'll have to wear woolly slippers. You'll have to wear a long nightshirt and carry lumps of barley sugar in your pockets. You won't find bits of fluff wanting to go out with a grandfather, will you?'

She could not stop herself. She burst out laughing.

'Come on,' said Winston Hayballs. 'I'll see you home.'

He helped her off the wall and they set off for the old Dower House.

– How awful to laugh at him. I know he's a disgusting, nauseating little man with a boozer's belly and dirty teeth, but he's got his feelings, hasn't he? They might not be like ours. I mean dogs don't have feelings like us, but you can always tell when they're happy and when they're sad, can't you?

They came to the front door.

Nancy fumbled for the key in her handbag.

Winston Hayballs said:

'I don't mind you laughing at me, Nancy. Old Winston, he don't mind having the piss taken out of him.'

'No?' said Nancy softly.

'No,' said Winston Hayballs. 'I got my consolations, see.'

'What consolations?'

'That old wood at the back of my house look,' said Winston Hayballs, and he sighed deeply and contentedly. 'Listen. Every morning I gets up at five in the morning. And in the summer and the spring I goes down to the bottom of my garden and there's a wood there. He's a little wood look. And I goes deep inside him, and I hears the birds singing. Chiffchaffs, warblers, nightjars churring away. And I sits down with my back against this old beech tree, and I listens to them. Oh yes, old Winston listens to them real intent like, and he thinks to hisself: You're dead lucky, you little buggers. If you was any bigger, I'd shoot you with my shotgun and have you in my stockpot as quick as look at you.'

Nancy laughed.

'Winston. You're incorrigible,' she said.

Winston Hayballs nodded his head rapidly and sucked through the gap between his two front teeth.

116

'That I am,' he said. 'That I am without a doubt. Well then, Nancy, good night.'

'Good night, Winston.'

When she entered the drawing room, Father raised his pipe to her and said:

'What ho, old girl. Been out for a spin with Winston, have you?'

'No, I have not been out with Winston,' snapped Nancy. 'If you must know, I've been out to a committee meeting.'

'Ah, a committee meeting,' said Father. 'I used to love committee meetings when your mother and I were out in India. They wouldn't have been the same without her, you know. She was the most intimidating quorum I ever met in the whole of my life, your mother.'

At this William walked into the room and said:

'I've finished another chapter. Well almost. I ran out of typing paper just as I came to Evercreech Junction.'

Nancy turned to him and said:

'I've got a bone to pick with you, William.'

'Oh yes?'

'I've just been to a meeting of the Village Green Action Group.'

'Crikey,' said William. 'I forgot all about it.'

'You're telling me,' said Nancy. 'And you also forgot about informing me that Mrs Godwin had visited you at this house. You forgot to tell me that Mrs Godwin had co-opted you.'

William shuffled his feet.

Then he said quietly:

'No, I didn't.'

'What?'

William glared at her defiantly and said:

'I didn't tell you, because there was no reason for you to know. You don't have to know everything about us, Father and me, Nancy. We do happen to have lives of our own. We're not just minor planets revolving around you. We're not just worthless tokens you can manipulate, just so you can justify your own self-imposed martyrdom.'

'William!' said Nancy weakly.

'And I'll tell you another thing,' said William. 'She kissed me on the front doorstep when I took her home.'

He left the room, and Father said:

'Ah, kissing. Fearfully fond of kissing I was in my young days. Your mother wasn't very good at it, though, you know. No. When your

117

mother kissed me, it was an operation rather like removing the washer off a cold water tap.'

'Father,' screamed Nancy. 'Father!'

The bedroom was hot.

She stuck out her right leg from beneath the duvet cover.

Then after half an hour she felt cold, and she began to shiver.

– I'm not a martyr. I don't manipulate them. I don't look on them as worthless tokens. I slave away for them because I love them. I bully them and badger them because it's my duty. I've sacrificed my life to them because I care. I care about everything. Why must I be the only person in the whole wide world who cares?

– I care about the whales. I care about acid rain. I care about the Amazon rain forest and the North Sea and preserving the BBC. I care about Father. I care about William. I care about the village green. I care about . . .

– He called me Nancy.

– Good Lord, for the first time Winston called me Nancy.

20

Next morning Father was cock-a-hoop.

He came into the small sewing room Nancy had converted with Winston Hayballs' help from the maid's room at the rear of the house, brandishing a letter.

'I've got a letter,' he said.

'So I can see,' said Nancy, who was embroidering a new cushion for the green Volvo Estate.

'It was hand-delivered,' said Father.

'Who's it from?' said Nancy.

'Herbert.'

'Who's Herbert?'

'Dook.'

'Dook?' said Nancy. 'Who's Dook when he's at home?'

'The Duke of Wiltshire,' said Father. 'He's invited you, me and William round for tea this afternoon.'

'This afternoon?'

'Yes. Do you think he'll give us chocolate digestives?'

'I'm not worried about chocolate digestives, Father,' said Nancy, jumping from her chair in a panic. 'What am I going to wear?'

'Togs.'

'What?'

'Togs,' said Father. 'Your mother always used to wear togs on these occasions. They never suited her, of course. They always used to look as though they wished they were on someone else. Curious things, togs.'

'Father,' said Nancy. 'Would you please stop talking such nonsense. If we're going out to tea, I've got a million and one things to do. I bet William's still got staples in his best blazer from the dry cleaners. I bet all his decent shirts are covered in typewriter ink. And what about you, Father? What are you going to wear?'

'Chukka boots.'

'What?'

'I shall wear chukka boots. Always wear chukka boots, my dear, when

119

you don't want your feet to get in the way,' said Father, and he waved to her with his pipe and pottered about cheerfully.

Nancy dashed to her bedroom and flung open the doors of her wardrobe.

– What on earth am I going to wear? I mean, what does one wear when one goes to afternoon tea with a Duke of the Realm? Do I need a tiara? I haven't got a tiara. I've got that long gown I bought when we thought Father was going to be made a freeman of Stockport. I wore it at . . . No, I didn't. I wore it at . . . Don't panic, Nancy. Don't panic, woman. A cocktail dress. That's what you wear when you go for afternoon tea at a palace. I haven't got a cocktail dress. I've loads of dresses, but I've never been to cocktails in them. Well, not specifically. Don't panic. Compose yourself.

She composed herself.

She went downstairs very calmly.

She walked into the back garden very calmly, and there, as she expected, she found Winston Hayballs, hammering at the sides of the drained and disconsolate swimming pool with a sledgehammer.

'Winston,' she said very calmly. 'I wonder if I could have a word with you.'

'Certainly, missus,' said Winston Hayballs, and he threw down the sledgehammer, spat on his hands, and climbed out of the pool.

He smiled at her.

'Right then, missus,' he said. 'What can old Winston do for you?'

'I want your advice, Winston.'

'Certainly, missus. At your disposal. Fire away.'

'This afternoon I am to take tea with the Duke of Wiltshire and I was wondering if you could advise me on the appropriate clothing that would be appropriate for the occasion.'

– What am I asking him for? He's a poacher. He's got scratches all over his belly. He lives in a council house. His daughter's going to have an unmarried baby. He's an uncouth lout and I must be mad demeaning myself in front of him. What's got into me? What's going on with you, Nancy? You're not coping again.

Winston Hayballs put his hand on her shoulder.

He let it lie there softly.

He said gently:

'You don't want to bother yourself about that, missus. Just you wear what you wants. Whatever frock you puts on, Nancy, you'll look the most beautiful, the most tastiest and handsomest woman what have ever set foot in that palace in its whole history. Oh yes, Nancy, without a doubt you will.'

She lay in her bath an hour later.

The water lapped at her chin.

It suckled her breasts.

– He called me Nancy again. He called me Nancy and he was wearing wellington boots. Bloody cheek. I bet he's never used bath salts in the whole of his life. The works of Jean-Jacques Rousseau – I bet he's never read a single one. I bet he's never read anything. All he's good for is sticking in stench pipes and crawling through the undergrowth shooting and maiming deer and boozing in the pub and leering at his bits of fluff on the village green and . . .

– The village green!

It came to her in a flash.

The village green! She had the perfect chance. She was taking tea with the Duke of Wiltshire. She'd put the case to him. She'd go straight to the horse's mouth. Never mind deputations. Never mind petitions and letters to the local newspaper. She'd have it out with the Duke there and then. She knew he liked her. He'd called her handsome. She'd heard him. She'd beguile him. She'd bewitch him. She'd use all her female charms on him. How could he resist her? This was her moment.

For the first time in her life she'd behave like a real woman and get her man.

'Good old Nancy,' she sang to herself as she stepped out of the bath. 'Good old Nancy. What do you reckon then?'

Over on the other side of the village Grampy and the Duke of Wiltshire sat in the fruit store house in the grounds of Florey Palace.

'You wants to get them railings fixed on that old wooden bridge, you does,' said Grampy, finishing the last of his plover's breast pâté.

'What's that?' said the Duke.

'Them railings. They're rotten,' said Grampy. 'I almost fell arse over tit in the river this morning when I leaned on them, I did.'

'Mm,' said the Duke.

He had a large red woollen muffler wound tightly round his neck. He wore an ulster overcoat. He coughed violently. His whole body wracked and contorted. His eyes watered and his face turned the colour of puce.

When he had finished, he groaned and clasped at his ribs.

'What's to do with you?' said Grampy.

'I'm not well, I'm very ill,' said the Duke. 'I must have caught a chill at the cricket match on Sunday.'

'You ain't caught no chill, matey,' said Grampy. 'What you caught is a chronic dose of guilt.'

'Guilt?'

'Guilt about the village green.'

'Oh God,' said the Duke of Wiltshire. 'Not that again?'

'Yes, my old wingsy bash – that again,' said Grampy. 'And it always will be again and again look till you shifts yourself and does something about it. You're a Duke. Well, bloody well put your foot down and behave like one.'

The Duke of Wiltshire sighed and said:

'I never wanted to be a Duke.'

'What did you want to be then?' said Grampy.

'I wanted to be scum like you,' said the Duke, and his eyes clouded over and a gentle smile came to his lips. 'Yes, I always wanted to be like you – menial, shifty, foul-tempered, dishonest, narrow-minded, totally beastly in every way and finally buried in a damp, narrow plot in the village churchyard. Damned pleasant way of living out your days, don't you think?'

He remained dreaming and dozing for quite a while.

Then he opened his eyes and said with a smile:

'Still, there's one bright spot on the horizon.'

'What's that?' said Grampy.

'I've invited the Empsons round to tea this afternoon,' said the Duke. 'Fearfully agreeable cove, the old feller, don't you think?'

Grampy stood up and advanced towards him.

'Don't hit me,' said the Duke, shielding his face with his forearms. 'Please don't hit me. I'm wearing three vests.'

The Empsons presented themselves at Florey Palace, as requested, at precisely half past three in the afternoon.

The footman with the dark brown eyes flecked here and there with gold led them to a sitting room off the main hall, threw open the doors and announced with a stiff bow:

122

'Mr Guy Empson, Mr William Empson and Miss Nancy Empson, Your Grace.'

'Ah, capital, capital,' said the Duke of Wiltshire, and he let out a volley of sneezes. 'Show them in, if you please, Filbert.'

The footman directed them into the room and shut the door softly behind them.

The Duke rose to his feet, shook them warmly by the hand, and directed them to seats in the deep bay window which overlooked the fountain and the lake and the massed banks of beeches.

He pointed to an ornate, inlaid table on which was a tray loaded with the impedimenta of afternoon tea.

'Would you like to be mother, my dear?' he said to Nancy. 'I'm afraid all the maids have got gum boils or something.'

'Certainly, Your Grace,' said Nancy, and she smiled at him and fluttered her eyelids.

'Damn fine daughter you've got there, Empson,' said the Duke. 'Splendid set of teeth on her. Congratters, old boy.'

'Thank you, Herbert,' said Father. 'Your mother and I tried to do our best.'

'How do you take your tea, Your Grace?' said Nancy.

'Out of the cup,' said the Duke. 'Never got the hang of drinking it out of a saucer.'

'I once knew a chap in Cawnpore who always drank his gin out of a saucer,' said Father.

'Did you, by Jove?' said the Duke. 'Do tell. I'm all ears.'

Father settled himself happily in his chair, tapped together the tips of his fingers and said:

'Well, apparently, according to your mother, he'd got in some scrape over the procurement of regimental tiepins. Or was it collar studs? Anyway, to cut a long story short, Herbert, this chappie had got a Staffordshire bull terrier and . . .'

'Sandwiches, Your Grace?' said Nancy.

'Ah, stout fellow,' said the Duke.

He gazed long and hard at the plate she held in front of him, and then he nodded gravely and said:

'Yes, you're right, my dear. They're sandwiches right enough.'

Nancy smiled sweetly and bent low towards him, her breath ruffling the silky white hair of his lustrous sideboards.

'I was wondering if you'd care for one,' she said.

123

'Certainly. Anything to oblige,' said the Duke. 'I think I'll have six.'

Nancy turned to her father and offered him the plate of sandwiches.

'I say,' said the Duke. 'Splendid backside she's got on her. Well done, Empson.'

'Thank you, Herbert,' said Father.

– This is awful. They're talking about me as though I were a horse. Have I overdone the lipstick? Am I showing too much bosom? I bet that label's sticking out at the back of my jumper.

The Duke of Wiltshire turned to William, who was glumly sipping at his tea and staring listlessly out of the window at an elderly gardener trudging across the lawn with a rusty bicycle wheel over his shoulder.

'Well then, young Empson,' he said. 'And what do you do with yourself all day long? Play footer?'

'No,' said William. 'As a matter of fact I write railway books.'

'Well, I suppose somebody's got to do it,' said the Duke of Wiltshire and he patted the sofa, indicating that he would like Nancy to sit by his side.

She did so.

The old man chuckled.

'By jove, it's ages and ages since I sat next to a ravishing young creature like you, Nancy,' he said. 'Congratulations.'

'Thank you,' said Nancy.

'Anyway, to get back to the Staffordshire bull terrier,' said Father.

'Ah yes, the old pooch,' said the Duke. 'Was he a brute, Empson?'

'I don't know, Herbert,' said Father. 'I never actually met it.'

The Duke of Wiltshire was about to speak, but then a look of fear spread across his face.

He clutched at his chest and cried out.

Then he began to cough. His whole body heaved. He bent himself double, clasping at his knees. The veins stood out on his temples. His shoulders pumped.

At length he finished.

He gasped for breath.

He panted.

He mopped his brow.

He smiled weakly.

There was silence for a moment and then Father said:

'I did meet his mother, though. Now she was a real brute.'

The door opened and the Marquess of Sturminster stepped into the room.

'Ah,' he said. 'I wasn't aware that you were receiving visitors.'

And he turned to go.

'No, don't go,' said the Duke. 'I'd like to introduce you to my new chums.'

The Marquess of Sturminster hesitated and then reluctantly he stepped forward.

He nodded curtly to Father, when he was introduced. He shook hands with Nancy. His grip was flaccid and damp. He blushed and turned his deep violet eyes flecked with gold away from her.

'And this young fellow here is William,' said the Duke. 'He writes books about railways.'

'Is that the case?' said the Marquess of Sturminster.

'Yes,' said William. 'I'm writing a book about the Somerset and Dorset.'

'Is that the case?' said the Marquess of Sturminster. 'I wonder if perhaps you are aware that it was once the company's intention to build a branch line that would have passed through Winterleaf Gunner?'

William's eyes lit up.

'Really?' he said. 'I didn't know that.'

'Not many people do,' said the Marquess coldly.

He turned to leave the room.

William jumped to his feet and said:

'I don't want to be a nuisance, but I wonder if you have any documents relating to the subject? No one's ever mentioned it before. And if I could . . . well, it would cause a sensation in the railway world if I could . . . well, if only I could get my hands on them, it would be the jewel in the crown of my book so to speak.'

The Marquess stared at him coldly again.

Then he said:

'My dear Mr Empson, documents we have. Where they are I do not know specifically. The last time I saw them they were buried under masses of cardboard boxes in the archives in the library.'

William stretched out his hand as though to clutch the Marquess's sleeve, but then he thought better of it and said:

'I wonder if I could . . .'

'Follow me,' said the Marquess.

'I say,' said William to Father and Nancy. 'I say.'

And with a hop and a skip he scampered after the Marquess of Sturminster who strode out of the room without a backward glance.

'Sturminster,' snorted the Duke of Wiltshire. 'Fearful shit house.'

He stopped himself and took hold of Nancy's wrist.

'My dear young woman. A thousand apologies. Unforgivable to use such ghastly language in front of you like that.'

He began to stroke the back of her hand.

He patted her knee.

'Am I forgiven?' he said.

'Of course you are,' said Nancy.

Father smiled and began to fill his pipe.

'This chap who drank gin out of his saucer was a shit house, too.'

'Was he, by Jove, Empson?' said the Duke. 'Do tell.'

Nancy disentangled herself from the Duke's hands and walked to the window.

She heard them gossiping happily. She heard the Duke break into a bout of coughing and sneezing. She heard her father slucking at his pipe.

– Well, go on then, Nancy. You've dolled yourself up. You've smiled at him. You've fluttered your eyes at him. He's been stroking your hand. He's been patting your knees, dirty old devil. No, he's not a dirty old devil. He's very sweet and he's got the most dreadful cough and I love his sideboards and you've set it up so now you've got to strike while the iron's hot. Show you care, Nancy. Show you care.

She stepped back from the window.

'I wonder if I could have a word with you, Your Grace?'

'Certainly, my dear,' said the Duke. 'Park your bum next to me on the sofa and fire away.'

Nancy sat down on the sofa.

The Duke took hold of her hand.

'And then after we'd had the monsoon drains fixed, we turned our attentions to the joists in the lavatory,' said Father. 'Well, as you can imagine . . .'

'Father,' screamed Nancy. 'Shut up.'

She turned to the Duke of Wiltshire and she began to gabble.

'Well, the thing is, Your Grace, I know it might be rude to bring it up now, I mean, we are having afternoon tea, but I think it's too important to remain silent about. It's the village green, you see, and . . .'

The Duke snatched his hand away from her and groaned wildly.

'Oh, my God, not that again?' he said. 'Why won't people realize that it is nothing to do with me? It's Sturminster. He's the one who's responsible. Leave me alone. I'm tired. I'm ill. I'm sick and tired of the bloody village green. All I want is to be left in peace. How dare you come barging in here all lathered up in lipstick and rouge and . . .'

He broke into another violent attack of coughing and retching.

Nancy did not move. She could not.

The door opened and in stepped William followed by the Marquess of Sturminster.

'It's terrific in there,' he said. 'It's fantastic. There's oodles and oodles of stuff and the Marquess has given me the free run of it. I can come to the library any time I like. He's put everything at my disposal, haven't you, Lionel?'

'That is indeed correct, William,' said the Marquess of Sturminster.

He tapped William diffidently on the shoulder. William grasped his hand and shook it vigorously.

And before she could stop herself Nancy marched up to the Marquess, looked him straight in the eyes and said:

'I think you're an absolute shit.'

'I beg your pardon, madam?' said the Marquess.

She was almost sobbing as she blurted it out.

'You're wrecking the whole village. You're destroying it. You're poisoning it and polluting it. And why? Just for your own selfish ends. You don't give a fig about anyone here. All you're concerned about is you. It's disgusting. It's obscene. And I hate you. I loathe you. You're an out and out shit house.'

Silence.

The Marquess of Sturminster began to retreat towards the door.

William stared at his sister with panic and misery in his eyes.

Father puffed placidly at his pipe.

The Duke of Wiltshire fell to the floor with a thump.

They all turned to him.

His face was turning blue.

His legs were twitching and his lips were bared and quivering.

'Oh, my God,' said Nancy. 'Oh, my God, what have I done?'

21

The Duke of Wiltshire lingered between life and death.

He had double pneumonia and complications.

He refused to enter hospital.

He lay white, feeble and silent in the great bedroom, in which his wife had died while giving birth to their only son.

A vast coal fire brooded solemnly in the grate.

Sometimes it mumbled and grumbled.

Filbert sat silently on a stool at the foot of his master's bed, and his dark brown eyes flecked here and there with gold were moist.

May came in with squalls that echoed the distant gales which had sunk fishing boats in the Bay of Biscay and grounded a dredger in the mouth of the Tagus.

The first of the summer swifts came to Winterleaf Gunner.

They scythed the blustering skies and they screeched.

Mrs Fokine's King Charles spaniel died of kidney failure and she bought a Border terrier pup.

Nansen Ticehurst fell off his bicycle on his way home from the village pub and Freddie Knoyle, the mobile fishmonger, overturned his three-wheel van at the foot of the hill outside Market Bruton.

'Oh, my God, what have I done?' said Nancy as she watched Winston Hayballs filling in the grave of the stricken swimming pool.

Winston Hayballs leaned on his spade.

'You ain't done nothing, missus,' he said.

'Yes, I have,' she said. 'I've killed him.'

'No, you ain't, Nancy. He ain't dead yet look. And even if he does snuff it, there's no blame attached to you. He's an old man. And old men die. It's a fact of life in the country. I expect it's the same in the city, too.'

He smiled at her and winked.

'Tell you what, missus,' he said. 'Why don't you and me go out this evening for a spin in my motor, my car look, and we'll have a sesh in the pub up Gridley Miskin?'

'I do not want a sesh in a pub, Winston,' said Nancy. 'That is the last thing I want in the whole wide world. Never again will I have a sesh in a pub with you. And that is final.'

The Marquess of Sturminster made a speech in Bolton praising the virtues of thrift and family unity.

Thomas Fitchup returned from his sojourn with his married sister in Margate. He did not like starched sheets, he said.

One morning the Duke of Wiltshire awoke from a disturbed sleep and said:

'Filbert.'

'Yes, Your Grace,' said the footman, moving anxiously to the side of his bed.

'Stroke my brow, Filbert, there's a good chap.'

Filbert stroked his master's brow.

The Duke closed his eyes and sighed.

'Ah, what a lovely, soothing hand, Filbert,' he said. 'There was a hand just like that used to stroke my brow in days gone by years and years ago when I was young.'

'Yes, sir,' said Filbert, and tears spouted in his eyes.

'Filbert,' said the Duke.

'Yes, Your Grace.'

'I don't mind if you want to fart.'

'Thank you, Your Grace.'

In the fruit store house in the grounds of the palace Grampy sat alone.

On the tray in front of him was a score of uneaten dripping sandwiches. Some were covered with mould. Others were warped and dry.

He looked at them and said softly:

'Why did I have to go and do it? Why did I have to go and hit the old bugger? Why won't they let me go in and see him?'

He swept the sandwiches to the floor with his fist.

'If they don't let me in I'll burn the whole bloody place down,' he roared. 'And may Him up in the Heavens strike me dead if I don't throw myself on the flames and perish hand in hand with my old mate.'

Then he sighed and said quietly:

'I don't half fancy some of that stuff what looks like hamster's snots.'

That evening William, just back from his researches in the library at Florey Palace, said casually to Nancy:

'Are you going to the meeting tonight?'

'What meeting?'

'The Village Green Action Group,' said William. 'It's an emergency meeting. Mrs Godwin phoned me about it this morning.'

Nancy scowled at him.

'No, I am not going to the meeting, William,' said Nancy. 'Never again will I go to a meeting. I do not care about the village green, William. I do not care about anything. I do not care about you. I do not care about Father. I do not care about dolphins and the preservation of the green belt. I do not even care about myself. Do you understand that, William?'

She repaired to her sewing room, sobbing softly.

On his way to Mrs Godwin's William was stopped outside the village shop by Venetia Hayballs, who had just purchased a blancmange mould.

'I hasn't seen your sister recent, Mr Empson,' she said. 'Not been took badly, has she, by any chance?'

'No,' said William. 'She's in prime condition.'

Venetia Hayballs prodded him slightly with the tip of her umbrella and said:

'You wants to take care of your sister, Mr Empson. She's a rare woman. She's a woman of refinement and breeding. Just like what I am. My daughter's at university in Spain, you know.'

'Oh yes?' said William. 'What's she studying?'

'She's studying to be clever,' said Venetia Hayballs.

Mrs Godwin met him at the front door.

She was wearing a silk satin kimono and dark pink velvet slippers.

She showed him into her back room.

There was no one there.

'Oh, I'm early, am I?' said William.

'Early, William?' said Mrs Godwin. 'What for?'

'The meeting.'

'What meeting?'

'The emergency meeting. You phoned me up about it this morning.'

'Did I indeed, William?' said Mrs Godwin. 'Well, I must have made a mistake. Silly old me.'

She sat him down on the fur-covered divan.

She poured him a whisky.

She smiled at him very slowly.

And very slowly she kicked off her slipper.

Three hours later William raced through the hall of the old Dower House shouting at the top of his voice:

'I like it here. I love it here. Do you understand? I'm happy here. I'm happy. I'm happy.'

Father, returning from the shed at the bottom of the garden glowing and redolent, said:

'All right, old boy. All right. No need to set it to music.'

Then he linked arms with William and said:

'Did I ever tell you about that curious blighter I knew in Assam, who used to drink rum out of a titty bottle?'

The days grew longer.

Roderick Hayballs sent his mother a postcard from Le Havre. Grocott, landlord of the village pub, took his annual holiday to Gorleston. The flowering currant in Sid Lopcombe's side garden was struck by blight.

Every evening after she had finished her homework Baksi would slip through a side door into Florey Palace and in the secret room she would look deep into the gold-flecked eyes of her lover, and she would say:

'There, there, my lovely. You ain't frightened of women at all, are you really?'

The sun shone.

Winston Hayballs shot a mink in the hatchery on the River Florey. He skinned it and presented the fur to Nancy.

'How awful, Winston. How dreadful,' she said. 'Take it away. It's so disgusting. It's so barbaric.'

She sobbed herself to sleep that night and did not hear William, hair rumpled, tie askew, staggering in through the front door and bellowing:

'I like it here. I'm happy. I'm happy.'

Then one morning quite suddenly as the month was drawing to its close the Duke of Wiltshire sat bolt upright in his bed and said:

'Filbert.'

'Yes, Your Grace?' said the footman, springing to his bedside.

'I wish to speak to Empson Senior.'

'Certainly, Your Grace.'

'Send for him immediately.'

'Certainly, Your Grace.'

As Filbert loped on his way to the old Dower House to deliver the summons he was stopped by Grampy, who said:

'How's the old bugger going on then?'

'The old bugger?'

131

'You know who I mean, you poncy little nancy boy. When I asks you a question, you bloody answers me, or you gets a thick lip. You understand that?'

Filbert nodded.

'Right then,' said Grampy. 'How is he?'

'He's taken a turn for the better,' said Filbert. 'He's asked to see Mr Empson Senior.'

Grampy's pipe fell from his mouth.

22

The following morning Father reported to Florey Palace.

He was wearing a navy-blue shirt, mauve bow tie and grey flannel trousers.

Filbert showed him upstairs to the bedroom.

'My dear Herbert,' he said as he approached the bed. 'How are you keeping, old boy?'

'His Grace is extremely ill,' said the doctor, who was packing his case. 'I have to tell you that I do not approve of this visit. His Grace needs peace and rest. Any untoward excitement could prove to be most serious for his condition.'

'Bugger off, you old charlatan,' roared the Duke.

The doctor bowed stiffly and left the room.

The Duke of Wiltshire smiled and patted the side of his bed.

'Do sit down, Guy,' he said.

'Thank you,' said Father, and he obliged.

'You don't mind me calling you Guy, do you?'

'No,' said Father. 'It's my name.'

'Thought it was. Good for you,' said the Duke. 'Well then, tell me all the news about India.'

Father lit his pipe, stowed the spent match carefully in its box and said:

'Well, we had the most fearful monsoon once.'

'Did you, by Jove?' said the Duke. 'Do tell.'

Father talked on happily. He told of camp fires in the cold nights of Bengal. He told of the shortage of envelopes during his days in Madras. He told of firework parties in Bangalore and ballroom dancing in Mandalay. He told of half-chat railway booking clerks and dyspeptic jewellers and myopic chartered surveyors.

Filbert brought them tea and biscuits.

And from the grounds down below Grampy bellowed:

'Come out, you old bastard. Come out and let me see you.'

As the days passed by Father talked on, and the colour returned to the Duke of Wiltshire's cheeks and the doctor expressed himself astounded at the swiftness of his patient's recovery.

'Let me in,' roared Grampy. 'Let me in, you old bastard.'

Father tapped out his pipe in the palm of his hand and inserted the dottle into the breast pocket of his blazer.

'And then your mother and I decided to make a bicycle tour of the Naga hill country,' he said.

'Did you, by Jove?' said the Duke. 'Do tell.'

'Well, it's quite simple really, Herbert,' said Father. 'We went by charabanc instead.'

Nancy sat in her sewing room.

She was not sewing anything.

She had not sewn for days.

She just sat there staring at the wall.

Sometimes she stood up and dusted the passepartout-framed photograph of Geoffrey in his uniform.

She did not hear Father returning from his morning meeting with the Duke of Wiltshire and shouting at William:

'I'm happy, William. I like it here. I'm fearfully happy.'

She just stared at the wall.

– I dressed myself up like a tart. I called him a shit house. What's happening to me? I could have been married to Geoffrey, if only I'd said. I could have had a house in Bedfordshire. Well, not exactly Bedfordshire. It's too flat and too near his mother.

– We'd have had a house in Herefordshire. I like Herefordshire. I like black and white timbered houses. We'd have had a black and white timbered house in Ledbury with two children. We'd have had their portraits painted, if we could afford it. We'd have tobogganed in the winter. And in the summer we'd have gone to Worcester and looked round the cathedral. And what of Father? What of William? Oh yes, they'd have been there, too. How could they have possibly looked after themselves? Leave it all to Nancy. She'll cope. She'll buy them their singlets and clean their razor blades and make sure they change their underpants. Good old Nancy.

– Good old stricken, love-lost, useless, worthless Nancy.

There was a tap on the door.

She did not respond.

'It's me. Winston. Are you in there, missus?'

She did not answer.

The door opened and Winston Hayballs poked his head in.

'Hullo, missus,' he said. 'I wonder if I could have a word with you.'

She did not move.

He came into the room and sat down on the Lloyd Loom chair by the window.

He had buttoned his shirt to the neck. He had doused his wellington boots in water. His flies were done up.

'I wants to ask you something, missus,' he said.

She stared straight ahead at the wall.

'Why have you been avoiding me, Nancy?' he said. 'Why have you been keeping out of old Winston's way?'

She said nothing.

'You ain't said a word to me for days. When you've seen me, you've dashed back into the house. You've locked yourself away in this room. Why, Nancy? Why are you doing this?'

She said softly:

'I can't cope.'

'What can't you cope with, Nancy? You tell old Winston all about it.'

He came across to her and knelt at her feet.

'They're happy,' she said. 'Father and William, they're happy. I can't cope with it. They don't need me any more. They don't need me to boss them and bully them. They laugh all the time. Why are they laughing? We've never had laughter in any of our houses before. Never ever. Our houses have always been noted for their lack of laughter. What's going on? What on earth is going wrong with our family? What's going wrong with me?'

'There's nothing wrong with you, Nancy.'

She looked across to the photograph of Geoffrey in his uniform. The knot in his tie was too slack.

'There ain't nothing the matter with you, missus, that won't be cured by one thing,' said Winston Hayballs. 'Do you want to know what that is?'

She nodded.

'What you needs is a man,' said Winston Hayballs. 'You needs a man to love you and protect you and take you for seshes at the pub in his motor, his car look.'

She beat at his head with her fists.

She hit him so violently that he fell backwards onto the floor.

She kicked at his belly. She kicked at his legs. She kicked at his face.

'Get out,' she screamed. 'Get out, you nauseating, disgusting little man with your foul breath and your dirty teeth and your . . . Get out. Get out.'

Mrs Godwin lay in her bath.

A cabbage white butterfly beat aimlessly and damp at the window panes. The curtain billowed.

'Are you happy, William?' she said.

'Oh yes,' said William. 'Fantastically so.'

'And you like your life in Winterleaf Gunner?'

'I should say so,' said William. 'That library is tremendous. There's so much material there. I've not come to the branch line stuff yet, but . . .'

'Pass the towel, William.'

She stepped out of the bath, shaking the moisture delicately off her toes. William handed her the towel.

'Would you like to dry me, William?'

'Yes,' said William. 'I came across some fascinating stuff this morning about quarry rights. Apparently in the eighteenth century they were . . .'

'Gently, William. Gently.'

'Sorry. Anyway, there was this house-building boom in Bath and . . .'

'Shall we go to my bedroom, William?'

'Yes. And it engendered this tremendous demand for high-quality stone and . . .'

'William.'

'Yes.'

'Shut up.'

It was still damp and cold in the snug bar of the pub at Gridley Miskin even though the evening sun was in full flood.

The landlord had placed his Amazon parrot on the bar counter among the jars of pickled eggs and sticks of liquorice root. It sulked beadily.

Winston Hayballs took hold of Nancy's hand and squeezed it.

She sighed.

They did not speak on the way home.

136

She waved to him as he drove off in the car.
As she climbed the stairs slowly she whispered to herself:
'Do something, Nancy. Do something positive.'

23

Two days later Grampy knocked on the front door of the old Dower House.

'I come to see your father, missus,' he said, when Nancy appeared.

'I'm afraid he's not in, Mr Hayballs,' said Nancy. 'I think he's up at the palace.'

'In that case, I'll come in and wait for him,' said Grampy, and he pushed his way past her and established himself in the kitchen.

Nancy ruffled her hair and clenched her fists behind her back.

'Is there any way I can be of assistance, Mr Hayballs?' she said.

'Call me, Grampy, missus. Everyone else do in the village.'

'Right, Grampy,' said Nancy. 'I was asking if I could be of assistance.'

'Have you got a bottle of beer?'

'I think so,' said Nancy. 'Winston usually keeps a few in the pantry.'

She fetched him a bottle of beer. He opened it with the blade of his clasp knife and drank from the neck.

'We had an old dog once,' he said. 'It was a lurcher. Yes, he was a lurcher and he grew old and arthritic in his limbs. He kept bumping into things look and he was forever sitting in the corner, staring at you and panting. So we got another one. A pup. We thought he'd liven the old dog up look. Give him a new lease of life. He didn't. He was so bloody lively. He was so bloody new. He was so bloody bossy and full of himself that he killed the old dog stone dead. Within a week it was. The old dog just keeled over one evening and died. Yes. He keeled over and died that old dog of mine.'

He rested his elbows on the table and stroked his chin thoughtfully.

Nancy coughed nervously.

'Yes,' she said. 'What a sad story. Would you care for a sandwich?'

Grampy ignored her.

He finished his beer slowly.

He wiped his mouth on a newly-ironed tea towel, stood up and said:

'Right then, missus, I'll be off. I'll not detain and keep you from your work no longer. There's no need to show me out. I knows a short cut through your back garden.'

He left her.

He strode purposefully through the village.

Venetia Hayballs tried to detain him outside the village shop, but he brushed her aside roughly.

He nodded curtly at Lionel Woodyates and ignored the greeting of Raymond Longmarsh, the retired schoolmaster.

He came to the village green.

Parked by the pond was a Land-Rover. Resting against it were surveyors' red and white poles and the base for a theodolite.

He looked round carefully.

No one was in sight.

With a grim smile he picked up the base for the theodolite and tossed it into the pond. Then one by one he hurled the surveyor's red and white poles into the water. The muscovy ducks scattered.

He twitched his shoulders, set his jaw squarely in the direction of the palace and marched off, his back rigid, his arms swinging stiffly by his sides.

In the palace Father and the Duke of Wiltshire were talking earnestly in the nursery.

It was the Duke's favourite room. Here he took his breakfast each morning. Here he read the books of Talbot Baines Reed and Percy F. Westerman and Douglas V. Duff. Here he tucked into aniseed balls and liquorice bootlaces bought for him from the village shop by Filbert.

He was dressed in maroon-and-white-striped flannel pyjamas and purple silk dressing gown. He wore a white muffler round his neck and a cloth cap on his head. He was sitting on the rocking horse his father had brought home from the war against the Boers.

'I feel absolutely top hole today, Guy,' he said.

'Good,' said Father, who was sitting on the roof of a doll's house made of sumac and zebrawood.

'The old quack's delighted with my progress,' said the Duke, popping another humbug into his mouth. 'He says he's convinced it's you and your yarns that's doing me the power of good.'

'Whacko,' said Father. 'And you're doing me the power of good, too, Herbert.'

'Really, Guy?' said the Duke. 'How spiffing.'

'You're my chum, you see,' said Father.

'I say, Guy.'

'I've never had a chum before.'

139

'No?'

'No. Your mother didn't like them, you see.'

'I say, Guy. Why ever not?'

Father poked into the recesses of the bowl of his pipe with a pearl-inlaid smoker's companion.

He sighed.

'Well, she maintained that chums always tramped in dirt on the living room carpets,' he said. 'She maintained that chums brought in dog hairs on their trousers and smelled of sprout tops.'

'And did they?'

'I don't know. I never had any, you see, Herbert,' said Father. 'I almost had a chum once when we lived in Poole in Dorset. He was a Monsignor of the Roman Catholic persuasion. He used to ride a Rudge bicycle.'

'I say, Guy. How interesting. Did it have a three speed?'

'Oh yes. Well, he was a Monsignor, you see. It was expected of him.'

'Bloody left-footers,' snarled the Duke and he began to rock up and down testily on the rocking horse.

Father rammed the bowl of his pipe with tobacco from his pouch and lit it noisily. Burning embers settled lazily on the front of his cardigan and added to the archipelago of small holes.

'Did I ever tell you about the problems we had buying packets of Bisto in India?' he said.

'Yes,' said the Duke. 'It must have been fearful for you.'

'Oh it was,' said Father. 'You see the spanner in the works was . . .'

He was interrupted by the sounds of heavy footsteps and raised voices.

The door of the nursery was flung open and in stepped Grampy followed by a flustered and dishevelled Filbert.

The Duke cowered on his rocking horse.

'Don't hit me,' he cried.

'I ain't come for you,' said Grampy. 'I come for him.'

He pointed at Father, who raised his pipe and said:

'What-ho. Been fearfully pleasant this a.m., don't you think?'

Filbert approached the Duke of Wiltshire timidly.

'I'm sorry, Your Grace,' he said. 'I tried to stop him, but . . .'

Grampy turned to him and yelled:

'You. Vamoose.'

Filbert scuttled out of the room with a whimper.

Father lit his pipe and said:

'I was just telling Herbert here about . . .'

'I don't care what you was telling him,' said Grampy. 'What I cares about is what you're doing to him.'

'Sorry, old chap. Not quite on your wavelength there.'

'Look at him,' said Grampy. 'Sat on a bleeding rocking horse in the middle of a nursery. You've turned him back into his second childhood. You've turned him into a babe in arms.'

'No he hasn't,' said the Duke. 'I've always liked the nursery, and the rocking horse is the most comfortable chair in the whole of the palace.'

'Shut up, you old sod,' said Grampy.

He turned once more to Father and ground his teeth.

'I blames you for everything. You newcomers, you've destroyed the whole village.'

'Oh, I say, that's a bit steep, isn't it, old boy?' said Father, carefully tamping down the top of the bowl of his pipe.

'You and your bloody biscuit tin houses. You and your loud voices and your women with hair like sheepdogs. You and your brats with smart-arsed Christian names and too many teeth. It's because of you and your lot they're ripping up the village green.'

'Oh, I don't know about that,' said Father.

Grampy could scarcely contain his rage. His lips foamed with spittle. His face was scarlet. He pounded his fists on the lid of the ebony Jack-in-the-box.

'But it's you what I blames most of all,' he said to Father. 'I blames you specific for what you've done to him. It's you what's turned him into a feeble-minded gibbering simpleton. It's you what's turned him into a lily-livered coward what won't stick up for hisself and do his duties to the village. It's you what's destroyed him. It's you what's killing him. Clear off. Leave him alone.'

'No,' said Father.

'What?' said Grampy.

'I will not clear off and leave him alone,' said Father. 'He's my chum.'

'What?'

'He's my chum.'

'He ain't your chum and he don't need you. I'm his chum and he needs me.'

141

'If you don't mind my saying so, old chap, but I think that's a matter for Herbert here to decide, don't you?'

'Herbert?' shouted Grampy. 'Herbert?'

Very slowly, with infinite menace, he picked up a child's croquet mallet and began to advance slowly towards Father.

'Run, Guy,' shouted the Duke. 'For God's sake, man, run for your life.'

Grampy raised the mallet above his head, and Father fled.

He fled down winding staircases chased by Grampy.

He fled into the drawing room and raced through the french windows with Grampy in hot pursuit, cursing and waving his mallet.

'For God's sake, man,' Father panted as he stumbled through the shrubberies and across the lawns.

Grampy wheezed and heaved for breath. But he would not give in. Nearer and nearer he got to Father.

He caught him as they were halfway across the old wooden bridge with the thatched roof.

He raised the mallet high above his head once more.

Father pressed himself back into the railings.

They gave way with a sullen, rotting snap and he fell backwards into the clear waters of the River Florey.

He came to the surface with a splutter.

He flapped his arms frantically and struggled to free his feet from the weeds.

'Help!' he shouted. 'Help. I can't swim.'

Grampy looked down on him. He smiled. He sent a great glob of spit arcing into the water.

The weeds sucked Father below the surface again. He struggled desperately, clawing, kicking, thrashing his arms. With a convulsive jerk the weeds released their grip. He came to the surface and slowly the gentle River Florey bore him away from the bridge.

'Help,' he screamed. 'For God's sake, help me.'

Grampy clambered down from the bridge and walked along the bank looking at Father as he bobbed up and down and spun slowly round and round on his back.

'I'm drowning,' cried Father feebly. 'You can't let me drown.'

'Oh, can't I just?' said Grampy softly to himself.

And then he remembered.

The snow-swollen river in the Alps. High crags scratching the clear sky. The platoon exhausted. The platoon sobbing with fatigue. Come on, you bastards, move, move. The men turned their backs on the officer and hung their heads. Move, move, shrieked the officer. Silence. No movement. All right then. We'll take five minutes' rest. Pass me the billy, Ticehurst, and I'll fill it with water from the stream. Clank of metal. Whistle of marmot. And then the scream. Help, help. Help, you bastards. The plunge into the ice-spittled waters. The breath ripped from his lungs. The . . .

Grampy tore off his boots. He stripped himself down to his singlet and his long woollen underpants and he hurled himself into the River Florey.

'Hold on,' he shouted. 'Hold on.'

The powerful crawl stroke of his youth returned to his limbs. He caught up with Father and grasped hold of the back of his collar.

Father spun round and grappled with him.

'For Christ's sake, calm down. You'll have us both under.'

Father heard not a word.

In a red-misted panic he tried to wrap his legs round Grampy and clamp his arms round his neck.

Grampy tried to release his grip, but it was no use.

He pushed back Father's head, raised his fist, struck him on the chin and knocked him unconscious.

It took a long time for them to reach the bank.

It took even longer for Grampy to haul himself and Father out of the river.

They lay on the grass, shivering and groaning, and it was half an hour before they were found by Winston Hayballs.

24

The two old men lay side by side in the same bed.

Grampy's head was swathed in bandages. He had hit it on one of the stone piers at the hatchery. His face was covered with deep gouges. His chest rattled.

On his right-hand side lay Father.

The lids over his closed eye were ice-white. His lips were pale blue. His chest rattled.

Outside a motor mower purred softly.

An army helicopter roared.

Collared doves cooed.

'Can I get you chaps anything?' said the Duke of Wiltshire anxiously.

He mopped Father's brow with his handkerchief.

He rearranged the sheets round Grampy's neck.

They were in the great bedroom at Florey Palace. Winston Hayballs had brought them there as soon as he had found them on the river bank.

'Anyone care for an aniseed ball?' said the Duke of Wiltshire. 'Or perhaps I could tempt you with some readings from *Wisden Cricketers' Almanack*?'

The old bed-bound men did not move.

'Don't go and die on me, chaps,' said the Duke.

The vast coal fire spat. Filbert stood silently by the door. The doctor snapped shut his bag and said:

'There's no danger of them dying, Your Grace. Rest and medication - that's all they need. They're both as tough as nails.'

'Of course they're as tough as nails, you ass,' said the Duke. 'They're my chums, aren't they?'

The doctor bowed and left the room.

The Duke pottered over to his friends' bedside once more. He leaned over them and whispered:

'Fancy all of us chums being under the same roof. I've never been so happy in the whole of my life.'

'The whole thing is ludicrous,' said Nancy.

'What?' said Winston Hayballs.

'Your father and my father incarcerated up there in the palace.'

'Best place for them, missus.'

'It is not the best place for them, Winston. They should be in their own homes being looked after by their nearest and dearest.'

'Grampy? He ain't got no nearest and dearest, missus. All he got is close relatives. You can't get more distant than that, can you?'

'Well, obviously you don't care about the welfare of your own father, Winston. But I care about mine. And I want to look after him here in our own home.'

'No, missus,' said Winston Hayballs. 'He's like a pig in do-dah, is your old dad. He's being looked after by experts look.'

'But I'm an expert,' said Nancy. 'I'm the greatest expert in the world on Father.'

They were in the kitchen of the old Dower House.

Nancy was baking rock buns and marmalade cake for Father. Winston Hayballs was fixing a new plug to the electric toaster.

She glanced at him out of the corner of her eyes.

Broad brown forearms. Tongue sticking out from the side of his mouth. Contented eyes. Secure. Confident.

– We're like an old married couple. I'm baking. He's sitting at the table and the sunlight's streaming in and glowing on his belly.

– I feel easy with him. Secure. God, I'm getting to rely on him for everything. What shall I wear to take afternoon tea with a duke, Winston? Shall I have another gin and tonic, Winston, or should I change to martini? Next thing I'll be getting him to choose the colour of my knickers.

She wiped her hands on the front of her pinny and sat down opposite Winston Hayballs.

'Winston,' she said.

'Yes, missus?'

'I can't cope.'

Winston Hayballs looked up from the plug. He stared at her silently for a moment, and then he said:

'I knows that, missus. I've known it for a long time. I seen it in your eyes.'

He stretched out and rested his hand on her wrist.

'Tell me, Nancy,' he said. 'You tell old Winston what it is you can't cope with.'

'Everything, Winston,' said Nancy. 'Everything.'

'Calm down, Nancy. You're getting a flush to your neck. And when you gets a flush to your neck, old Winston gets a flush in parts what he shouldn't be talking about in front of a lady like you.'

– What's that? What did he say? I've a good mind to . . .

– There's such strength in him. He carried them both back to the palace under his arms. He ran with them. He didn't drop them once.

'Tell me, Nancy,' said Winston Hayballs. 'Pour your heart out to me.'

'Well, take Father for instance. It's awful, but deep down I'm glad he's in the palace. It's wonderful not to have him round, dropping his matches all over the place, demanding food like a demented starling, shouting out for glasses of milk at midnight, forgetting to change his socks, going on and on and on with his ghastly boring stories about India. He's not here, and I'm happy, and I can't cope with it.'

She fidgeted with her pinny. She wanted to stop. She wanted to stand up and go back to her baking. But she could not. She had to speak out to Winston.

'Then there's William,' she said.

'What about William?' said Winston Hayballs.

'Well, he's acting so strangely. He spends all day in the library at the palace. He's made friends with that dreadful little Marquess squirt, which, I might say, Winston, I consider a total act of treachery when he's supposed to be fighting to preserve the village green, about which I might say he did not give one jot until he suddenly started going out at nights and coming back with a great smirk over his face and shouting, "I'm happy. I'm happy." What's he got to be happy about?'

'Don't you know, Nancy?'

'No. Do you?'

'Course I does.'

'Well, tell me then.'

'He's having his bit of nookie with Mrs Godwin.'

'What?'

'That's where he goes at nights. I seen their shadows in her bedroom window when I been out poaching. William have got hisself a bit of fluff look.'

'Oh my God,' said Nancy. 'It'll kill him.'

146

'Why?'

'Because William has never had a . . . well, he hasn't ever . . . William is not very experienced in the ways of the opposite sex, Winston. Do I make myself clear?'

'Well, Mrs Godwin will make up for that right enough, missus. You ask old Wilson Rappaport. She had his kecks off the first time he ever . . .'

'Winston!'

He grinned.

'Don't you worry your head about William, Nancy,' he said. 'He's in good hands with Mrs Godwin when it comes to learning about the finer points of how's your father.'

'But I don't want him to learn about how's your father, Winston. I don't want him to be with Mrs Godwin. I want him to be with me so I can change his typewriter ribbons and correct his spelling and buy him carbon paper and . . . oh, Winston, I can't cope. I just cannot cope with all this change.'

Winston Hayballs stood up. He smiled. He winked at her.

'Right then, missus,' he said. 'That's your toaster fixed.'

And he put on his jacket and went home for his tea.

When William returned from the palace a few minutes later, Nancy was waiting for him at the front door.

'Right, William,' she said. 'In here.'

She pointed to the drawing room and pushed him firmly inside.

She composed herself.

'Right then, William, I want a word with you,' she said. 'I've got something very important to say to you.'

'And I've got something very important to say to you, Nancy,' said William.

'What?' said Nancy, clutching at her throat. 'You've not gone and . . . she's not made you . . . well, come on, man. Spit it out.'

William took out a document from the inside pocket of his jacket, held it up to Nancy and said:

'I know how to save the village green.'

25

And William did indeed know how to save the village green.

He showed Nancy the document which he had discovered in the library at Florey Palace.

It concerned the proposal to build a branch line of the Somerset and Dorset Joint Committee Railway, which was planned to cross the middle of the village green at Winterleaf Gunner.

The incumbent Duke of Wiltshire had agreed readily.

The company were to pay a large sum of money into his coffers and provide him with a saloon carriage for his personal and exclusive use.

And then someone had discovered in the archives a clause in a Bill of Ancient Rights, which asserted that if the village green were to be threatened, and if the villagers opposed the plan, they had the right to challenge the palace to a game of cricket.

If they won, they could stop the destruction of the green.

The villagers had invoked this clause.

The challenge had been delivered to the Duke of Wiltshire by a certain Rufus Hayballs.

A match had been played and Winterleaf Gunner had defeated Florey Palace by seventeen runs.

And so the village green had been saved.

Nancy sprang forward and clasped William in her arms.

She smothered him with kisses.

'I love you, William,' she said. 'I'm so happy. I've never been so happy in the whole of my life.'

William pushed her away and said:

'Yes, that's all very well, but first you've got to win the match, haven't you?'

'Oh, that's no problem,' said Nancy. 'Winston will sort all that out.'

'Winston?' said William.

'But, of course. What would we possibly do without Winston?'

William watched her as she re-read the document, nodding to herself and chuckling.

'Nancy,' he said.

'Yes?' she said without looking up.

'Don't you think you're coming to rely on Winston a little too much?'

'What's that?' said Nancy vaguely.

'Well, all we hear from you these days is Winston this and Winston that. Winston says we should buy a new Volvo. Winston says we should get a new seat for the upstairs loo. Winston says we should . . .'

'William, be a love and move out of the way, will you? You're standing in my light.'

William sighed and shrugged his shoulders.

'So what is it you want to talk to me about, Nancy?' he said.

'Oh that can wait, William,' said Nancy, placing the document in her handbag and walking to the door. 'I'm off to see Winston.'

She threw her Jaeger car coat over her shoulders and made her way quickly through the village to Winston Hayballs' house.

'Hold on,' she said to herself as she reached the entrance to Idle Lane. 'I don't even know which house he lives in.'

– Hold on, Nancy. What are you doing here? People like you don't go visiting their employees. Mother never did. She sent round hand-written notes in beige embossed envelopes. She wouldn't have dreamed of demeaning herself by going to their homes and being jumped at by their Alsatians and gawped at by their snotty-nosed children. And in any case I don't care about the village green. All I care about now is me. All I care about is . . . Good Lord, is that why I'm visiting him? Because I care about me? Because I care about him? No. No, it can't possibly be.

She stopped dead in her tracks, bewildered, her resolve and certainty gushing from her.

'Can I help you, Miss Empson?'

She looked round.

Venetia Hayballs was standing by her side, her basket full of provender from the village shop.

'What's that?'

'I was wondering if you'd lost your way. You must have look or you wouldn't be seen in these parts, would you?'

Nancy wavered. She looked round helplessly. There was no escape. Then she blurted out:

'I've come to see Winston and I don't know where he lives.'

'You wants to see Winston?' said Venetia Hayballs. 'In his own house? It'll take you weeks to get rid of the smell from the kitchen.'

149

'That's a risk I'm prepared to take, Mrs Hayballs,' said Nancy tartly. 'Now perhaps you'd be kind enough to point out to me where he lives.'

'Over yonder,' said Venetia Hayballs, narrowing her eyes as she looked Nancy up and down slowly. 'Number Two. You can't mistake it. It's got a hole in the front door.'

'Thank you,' said Nancy.

She crossed the road.

– No going back now. She's watching me. I can feel curtains twitching. Nancy Empson, what are you doing? It's too ludicrous for words. You're an educated, refined woman. You went on holidays to Switzerland with the school while we were still on rationing in England. You've had lunch with an Air Commodore. If the first bird I see is a sparrow, I won't go to the house.

The first bird she saw was a sparrow.

She knocked on the front door of Number Two. It had a large, jagged hole, head high and slightly off centre. A pair of eyes peered through it at her. A woman's voice said:

'What do you want?'

'I've come to see Winston Hayballs,' said Nancy. 'I have some important business to discuss with him.'

'Oh yes?' said the voice. 'Are you another of his bits of fluff?'

'No, I am not one of his bits of fluff,' snapped Nancy. 'Will you kindly tell him that Nancy Empson wishes to speak to him.'

'Wait there,' said the woman's voice.

After quite a while the door opened and Winston stepped outside.

'What do you want?' he said.

Half a baked bean was stuck to the stubble on his chin and there were blobs of tomato sauce on his chest.

'I want you to take me out in your motor, your car,' said Nancy.

'For a sesh?'

'No, Winston. Not for a sesh. I want to tell you about a fantastic discovery I've just made.'

'What discovery?'

'I can't tell you here, Winston. Take me to the pub and I'll tell you there in private.'

Winston Hayballs sucked deeply through the blue-veined gap in his two front teeth and said:

'Well, it's a bit inconvenient at the moment look. I'm supposed to be cutting my toenails tonight and . . .'

150

'Winston!' said Nancy firmly.

He threw back his head and roared with laughter.

'Yes, Nancy, you looks real tasty, real handsome, when you got your dander up,' he said. 'You get yourself in the car and I'll be with you directly.'

She waited half an hour in the car for him. When he sat in the driving seat alongside her, he was wearing his blue velvet jacket and his canary-yellow cravat with the red fox heads and he smelled of arrowroot biscuits.

'Gridley Miskin?' he said.

'Terrific,' said Nancy.

It was the first day of June.

The fields were plump.

The cattle were plump.

The sun was high and proud.

They established themselves in the snug bar of the pub at Gridley Miskin and Winston Hayballs bought a pint of scrumpy for himself and a gin and tonic for Nancy.

Immediately she launched into her news. She talked rapidly with feeling and animation and excitement and enthusiasm.

She showed him the document triumphantly.

He read it slowly, nodding his head and grunting from time to time.

He refolded it carefully, handed it back to Nancy and said:

'It'll never work out.'

'Why not?'

'The fixture list.'

'What about the fixture list?'

'He'll be all bunged up full for the summer,' said Winston Hayballs.

'Well, unbung it then,' shouted Nancy. 'Oh, Winston, you're the only one who can do it. You're the only one in the village they'll listen to. You're their natural leader, Winston. Well, lead them.'

Winston Hayballs stared at her thoughtfully.

He took a sip from his pint pot and then he said:

'But I thought you didn't care about the village green.'

'I don't.'

'What?'

'I mean, I do. It's just that I . . . it's just that I care about me.'

'And I cares about you, too, Nancy. Old Winston cares about you more than anything else in the whole wide world.'

'Then help me. Stand up and fight.'

Winston Hayballs shook his head slowly.

'Oh, I don't know about that, missus,' he said.

Nancy controlled herself well. She gritted her teeth and said very slowly and very softly:

'I hate you, Winston. I loathe you. I despise you. Take me home.'

'Righto, missus,' said Winston Hayballs. 'I'll just go and buy a packet of pork scratchings for the parrot.'

He drove her home.

They did not speak.

He drew up outside the old Dower House, leaned across her and opened her door.

She shut it firmly.

She turned to him and kissed him full on the lips.

He recoiled, but she drew him into her and kissed him again on his mouth, on his cheeks and on his lips.

'Right then, Winston?' she said, when she had finished.

'Right then, missus,' said Winston Hayballs. 'I'll set things in motion tomorrow morning.'

26

Winston Hayballs was as good as his word.

He arranged a meeting with the Marquess of Sturminster for the following afternoon.

Before their appointment he and Nancy visited Grampy and Father in the great bedroom where the coal fire snoozed and the Duke of Wiltshire offered them liquorice shoelaces.

Grampy lay motionless in bed. His eyes were closed. He did not stir.

Father waved to them weakly and Nancy bent over him and said:

'How are you, Father? How are you feeling today?'

'I've just had this dream,' said Father. 'Fearfully pleasant.'

'What was it about, Father?'

'India.'

'India? How interesting. Do you want to tell us all about it?'

'Not particularly,' said Father. 'It wasn't all that interesting really. Still, if you've got half an hour or so to spare, I don't mind giving you the bare outline.'

'No, Father,' said Nancy. 'Lie back and get some more rest.'

Father closed his eyes and fell asleep.

'I say, this is fun, isn't it?' said the Duke of Wiltshire.

'Is it?' said Winston Hayballs.

'Rather,' said the Duke. 'The old quack let me empty the bedpans this morning.'

'Oh yes?' said Winston Hayballs, raising his eyebrows with interest. 'Anything to write home about?'

'Winston! That's quite enough of that, if you don't mind,' snapped Nancy.

Winston Hayballs chuckled, took a grubby package out of his trouser pocket and handed it to the Duke.

'There we are, me old wingsy bash,' he said. 'Do us a favour and give it to Grampy when he wakes up, will you?'

'Certainly,' said the Duke. 'What is it?'

'A present,' said Winston Hayballs.

'I say, how thoughtful. How touching,' said the Duke. 'What is it?'

'Half a bacon sandwich.'

Instantly the Duke ripped open the paper, extracted the bedraggled, fluff-coated sandwich, and gobbled it back in a series of swift and convulsive gulps.

He smiled sheepishly at Winston Hayballs.

'Not to worry, old boy. He won't find out,' he said. 'Your secret's quite safe with me.'

The coal fire settled itself in the grate with a contented crinkle of cinders.

Father began to snore.

A large spider ambled slowly and hunch-shouldered over the carpet and disappeared into a crack in the skirting board.

'Right then,' said Nancy. 'Time for our appointment.'

'Ah, got an appointment, have you? I love appointments,' said the Duke. 'I once had an appointment with my wine merchant in Fleet Street in London. He showed me a picture of his uncle taken at Bad Ems. Or was it Buxton?'

He smiled wistfully at the memory.

Then he said:

'Is your appointment with your wine merchant?'

'No, it's with your son.'

'Sturminster?' said the Duke. 'Why the devil should you want to have an appointment with him?'

When Nancy told him, his eyes filled with panic. His lips began to tremble, and he took hold of her firmly by the hands and said:

'For pity's sake, madam, I beg of you not to bring my name into it. I want nothing to do with your fight for the village green. It is not my concern. It has long since been taken out of my hands. I have no influence. Do you understand that?'

'Yes, we understands, you old bugger,' said Winston Hayballs. 'Don't you worry. We'll not say nothing that'll land you in the shit.'

The Duke of Wiltshire nodded happily.

'Good,' he said. 'Don't forget to bring another present for your father next time you visit.'

On their way down to the Marquess of Sturminster's study Nancy saw a plump, glowing figure scuttling across the main hall and disappearing into a side room.

She glanced across at Winston Hayballs. He was whistling cheerfully under his breath and sliding his hands over the sensuous curves of the great sweeping marble balustrade. Obviously he had not seen the figure.

Nancy was certain that it was his daughter, Baksi.

The Marquess greeted them coldly in his study.

His deep violet eyes flecked with gold gazed stonily at Winston Hayballs. He could not bring himself to look at Nancy.

– I won't apologize for calling him what I did. I should do, I know. Mother would have done. It's only polite, she would have said. Well, bugger Mother. I'm jiggered if I'll apologize. He's evil. He's shifty. And I'm certain he's been up to no good.

She watched him intently as he shuffled nervously at a stack of papers on his desk.

He coughed sharply and said:

'Well, how can I help you? I'm a busy man, you know.'

'Oh, we knows that right enough, my old wingsy bash,' said Winston Hayballs. 'Got a boozing appointment with your mates at County Hall, has you?'

– He's amazing. No deference at all. He shows more deference to the landlord at the pub at Gridley Miskin than he shows to him. Mother would have kittens, if she could hear him. She'd go bananas if she could see me now standing by his side, revelling in him, enjoying the sight of his body, going all tingly when I . . .

– No I am not revelling in him. No I am not going all tingly. I am here on serious business. And it has to be conducted in the proper manner.

She took the document from her handbag and handed it to the Marquess.

'Perhaps you would do me the courtesy of reading this,' she said.

The Marquess of Sturminster studied the document carefully. He showed no emotion. When he had finished reading, he looked up and said:

'Well? And how does this concern me?'

'You knows bloody well how it concerns you,' said Winston Hayballs. 'We got you in a corner, in a hole look. We're challenging you as is laid down by our rights to a cricket match. And, if I've got anything to do with it, my old matey, we'll knock the living daylights out of you.'

The Marquess of Sturminster stared at him icily for a moment. Then he said:

'Obviously I am unable to make a reaction to your challenge until I

155

have consulted with my legal advisers. I shall, no doubt, be in touch with you directly. I bid you good day, Mr Hayballs, Miss Empson.'

He did not look up as they left the room.

Winston Hayballs sucked deeply through the gap in his front teeth and shook his head.

'I don't like it, missus,' he said.

'What are you talking about?'

'Solicitors,' said Winston Hayballs. 'When they calls in them little two-faced rats with their clean socks and their Irish accents, they got you by the short and curlies. There's no way we can fight the likes of them. We're doomed, missus. We're doomed.'

Nancy spun him round to face her.

'How dare you speak like that, Winston?' she said. 'How dare you give in before we've even started. You're not like that. That's not the real you. You're a man, Winston. You're the first real man I've ever met in my life. Well, act like one and stand up and fight. You can't let me down. You can't.'

They walked home.

The long spikes of rosemary in Mrs Fokine's front garden nodded at them.

Venetia Hayballs rattled her carrier bag and scowled at them.

Nansen Ticehurst smiled at them and said:

'What do you reckon then?'

'Bugger off,' said Winston Hayballs.

They established themselves in the kitchen of the old Dower House. Nancy prepared sandwiches and a pot of tea. Winston Hayballs sat at the table, staring at his thumbnails.

– Yes, we *are* like an old married couple. I'm buzzing around as though I haven't a care in the world. And he's sitting there silent and content and I feel easy with him. I feel secure. I feel . . .

– Good God, I kissed him. The other night I kissed him in his motor, his car. And he's a married man, and I enjoyed it. And he's a village poacher with 'Mild' and 'Bitter' tattooed above his nipples and I kissed him full on the lips. And he hasn't mentioned it once. Not a word. He's started calling me missus again. Well, not all the time, but mostly. What's going on in that mind of his? I know nothing about it. It's like the currents of the river and the shoaling of the salmon and the awful cries of the rabbits at night. I know nothing about it. What's going on in that mind of his? Why has he been so distant with me since I kissed him?

She placed the tray of tea and sandwiches on the table and sat down opposite him.

'Winston?' she said.

'Yes, missus?'

'Will you tell me something?'

'What about, missus?' said Winston Hayballs, still staring at his thumbnails. 'Is it your dado rails what's bothering you?'

'No, Winston,' said Nancy. 'It's your wife.'

'Oh her.'

'No, don't just dismiss it like that, Winston,' said Nancy. 'I want to know all about her. Tell me.'

'Well, it's like this, missus,' said Winston Hayballs. 'My wife is the ugliest woman what I ever set eyes on and that it is the honest truth without a doubt.'

'Then why did you marry her?'

'On the grounds of efficacy.'

'What?'

'Bits of fluff, missus. You marry an ugly woman, and you got every excuse to have your bits of fluff, ain't you? Gives spice to a marriage, do that. Gives it a sparkle look. I wouldn't mind if she had her bits of spare on the side. She wants to, you know. Trouble is she's so bloody ugly, no one'll look at her. More's the pity, eh?'

'Oh, Winston,' said Nancy softly. 'You don't really mean that, do you?'

He looked up from his thumbnails and said:

'I ain't sure now, missus. I been thinking these past few days. I been thinking a lot look. I been thinking it might have been just as efficacious to have married a beautiful woman.'

He pushed back his chair, stood up and made for the garden door.

Nancy called him back.

'Yes, missus?'

'We're going to win this battle, Winston,' she said. 'You and I together. We'll take everyone on. Starting right now with the Marquess of Sturminster.'

'Oh, he ain't no problem, missus. His bark's a damn sight worse than his bite, that it is,' said Winston Hayballs. 'All he needs to make hisself human is a bit of fluff on the side.'

157

Nancy sniffed.

'Is that your cure for all the ills of the world, Winston – a bit of fluff on the side?'

Winston Hayballs looked her up and down slowly.

'I reckons so, missus,' he said. 'Yes, I reckons so.'

He walked out of the kitchen, and he chuckled. But there was no warmth in his laughter.

Nancy went to bed early that night.

She heard William come in. He stumbled against the umbrella stand and giggled.

– Silly man. He's been out with that Mrs Godwin again. He'll have been . . . he'll have been . . . What do I care? He's off my hands now. Let her look after him and his spotty shins and the rash on his elbows and his allergies and his clinking fountain pens and his . . . I'm free of him now. I'm free of Father. I'm free of everyone.

And then the chill came to her body again.

She was being watched.

Eyes were boring into her body, feasting on her body, poking into the innermost secret recesses of her mind.

She was being laughed at.

Two people were laughing at her.

A man and a woman.

They were watching her and laughing at her and whispering to her: 'You're doomed, Nancy. You're doomed.'

27

Three days later Lionel Woodyates delivered a large stiff manilla envelope to the Dower House.

Nancy picked it up, held it to the light, sniffed it, then opened it and read the contents.

A great beam came to her face, and she dashed into the yard where Winston Hayballs was putting the finishing touch to the roof of the stable.

'Winston!' she cried. 'Terrific news. Come down.'

Winston Hayballs clucked grumpily, slid down the drainpipe and came to her, hands deep in his trouser pockets.

'What is it, missus?' he said. 'Discovered a new unwrote string quartet by Béla Bartók, has you?'

'Don't be so ridiculous,' said Nancy. 'I've got a letter from the Marquess's solicitors. They've accepted our challenge. The match is to be played on December thirteenth.'

'But that's in the middle of the bleeding winter, missus,' said Winston Hayballs. 'You can't play cricket in the middle of winter.'

'Course you can,' said Nancy. 'All you've got to do is to remember to wrap up well and make sure you don't stand in draughts.'

Winston Hayballs sighed deeply and shook his head.

'You can't play cricket in winter, missus,' he said. 'It's against the laws of nature look. Write back and tell them it's the first week in September or nothing.'

Nancy brandished the letter under his nostrils.

'They are perfectly within their rights to insist on December, Winston,' she said. 'According to the Bill of Rights they have six months from the issue of the challenge to respond, and it is their prerogative to fix the date of the match.'

'Bloody solicitors,' said Winston Hayballs. 'I told you we was doomed as soon as they poked their shonks into it.'

'We are not doomed, Winston,' said Nancy. 'The match will be played.'

'But I keeps telling you, missus. You can't play cricket in winter.

Ain't you learned nothing since you been in the country? It's all part and parcel of the variations of the seasons. In the summer you plays cricket. In the winter you sits in front of the fire and considers the delights in store for your old Donger.'

'Your old what?' said Nancy.

'Oh, never you mind about that, missus,' said Winston Hayballs. 'It ain't bothered you in the past, and I don't expect he'll bother you in the future neither.'

He turned from her and made his way back to the stables.

'Winston! Where do you think you're going?'

'Back to my roof, missus. You can't play cricket in winter. No one'd ever turn out in a million years.'

'Oh yes, they would, Winston,' said Nancy sternly. 'They would and they will. And you are the man to make them. Winston, I order you to stop work here and now and go out into the village and organize your team for the match.'

And to her intense astonishment he obeyed her.

Meekly and without a word he left the yard.

A spotted flycatcher fluttered from its post in the rose arbour. An army helicopter clattered overhead. She heard the distant, feckless trill of Mrs Fokine's canary.

– He's gone. He did what I said. Just like William. Oh gosh, am I starting all this bullying again? Why have I got to bully people? Why can't they stand up to me? I told him he was the first real man I'd ever met and he just crumpled up in front of me.

– It's just like Geoffrey when I used to tell him off for not being able to reverse in the slow foxtrot. It's just like when I ticked off that drippy medic with the bald patches for stepping on my high heels at Rag Ball. It's just like . . . It's just like all the others. No it isn't, Nancy. No it is not. This is your battle. This is your crusade. And you are going to win it come what may, bully or not.

She turned to retrace her way to the kitchen.

Then she stopped.

– I wonder what an Old Donger is. I'll look it up in my *Reader's Digest Guide to the Countryside.*

She did not see Winston Hayballs for a week.

Neither did she see William.

160

He left the house at sunrise every morning and returned long after the shipping forecast on the radio.

Each day she visited her father at the palace.

He was growing stronger. The colour had returned to his cheeks. But he was still too weak to get out of bed.

Grampy lay by his side, twitching and groaning. Sometimes he opened his eyes, and when he saw Father lying alongside him, he scowled and tried to move away from him. He could not.

Nancy told Father items of gossip she had picked up in the village shop.

Thomas Fitchup had gone to live with his retired cousins in Greater Manchester. Clementine Hayballs was pregnant again. Mrs Fokine's Border terrier had dug up her hebes. There was to be a grand challenge cricket match on 13 December, and the victors would decide on the fate of the village green.

She kissed Father on the forehead, straightened his panama hat, and left.

After a while Grampy's eyes flickered open. He searched for the Duke of Wiltshire. He held out his arms to him. The Duke padded across the room and sat by his side. They held hands.

'So you done it at last, you old sod,' said Grampy.

'Done what?'

'Got off your backside, used your old noddle and fixed up the match.'

'Well, I didn't exactly . . . well, I was involved in a way. I mean, if it hadn't been for me . . . well, yes, I did stand up and . . .'

'You old bastard,' said Grampy happily. 'You old sod. Why couldn't I have thought of that? Why is it always you what ultimate and finally takes the decisions?'

'Powers of leadership, old boy,' said the Duke of Wiltshire, patting his hand. 'Centuries of breeding and blue blood. By Jove, I could murder a dripping sandwich.'

At this Father turned to Grampy and said:

'Now you're back in the land of the living, there's something I have to say to you.'

'Bugger off,' said Grampy.

Father smiled.

'What I have to say to you is this,' he said. 'Thank you for saving my life. It's made all the difference in the world to me. Shake hands?'

'No,' said Grampy. 'Whatever I done for you, we still ain't friends. And we ain't never will be friends. Never, never, ever.'

'Oh yes you will be,' shouted the Duke of Wiltshire. 'I order you to be friends. Do you understand that, you scum? I order you to be friends with Guy. I order you to be chums.'

Grampy closed his eyes and smiled happily.

'You old bastard,' he said. 'You old sod.'

Winston Hayballs reappeared at the Dower House on a Friday morning.

'Well then, missus,' he said. 'You got your team.'

'Winston!' said Nancy. 'How marvellous. How super.'

Then she noticed he had a black eye and an egg-shaped lump on his left temple.

'Winston, whatever's happened to you?' she said.

'I told you, missus,' said Winston Hayballs. 'I been organizing a team for you.'

He marched out to the stables.

Nancy followed him, rubbing her hands on her pinny.

'Winston,' she said. 'I want to know what's happened to your face. I order you to tell me.'

Winston Hayballs turned his back to her and hunched his shoulders. His back tensed. He splayed his feet firmly on the dirt floor. He said quietly:

'No one orders me to do nothing, missus. Just you remember that. You got your bleeding team. Well, be satisfied with that, and don't you push me no further.'

Next morning at half past ten Nancy found William in the drawing room.

He was reading the morning newspaper and drinking a glass of whisky.

'William!' she said. 'Why aren't you at the library in the palace?'

'I've been thrown out,' said William. 'Sturminster's banned me since I showed that cricket match thing to you. He was absolutely livid.'

He smiled cheerfully at her and poured himself another drink.

Nancy sat opposite him.

'Why aren't you writing, William?' she said. 'I haven't heard your typewriter for weeks and weeks and weeks.'

162

'I know,' said William. 'Who cares?'

'I care, William,' Nancy thundered. 'I order you to write. I order you to get back to your study here and now and start writing about your points and your signals.'

She heard the laughter. She felt the eyes probing her. She heard the whispering.

'I haven't spent the best years of my life slaving after you, cosseting you, pampering you, bullying you, choosing your ties, cleaning your shoes, just so you can sit in Father's chair in the middle of the morning guzzling whisky. I've sacrificed my life for you so you can write your so-called books with their silly indexes in black type and all those beastly exclamation marks. Because of me, William, you're well known, you're respected. Well, in the railway world, that is. And I will not have you throwing it all away now just for the sake of . . . for the sake of . . . William I order you to start writing. Now.'

William smiled at her and raised his glass.

'I'm in love, Nancy,' he said.

'You?' said Nancy. 'Who with?'

'Lucy.'

'Who the devil's Lucy?'

'Mrs Godwin,' said William. 'I'm her chum.'

Nancy groaned.

She fled into the kitchen. She sat at the table and buried her head in her arms.

– Why am I doing this? I don't care. I'm free. Terrific. William's in love with Mrs Godwin. Well, let him go and live with her and her black suspenders and her expensive hair-dos, which, I might say, she looks as though she's had done by mail order. And her legs aren't all that long either. And she's got bony knees. My knees aren't bony. My knees are shapely. Geoffrey told me so that night we'd been to the Gilbert and Sullivan and I . . . Go and live with her, William. Set out your stall with her. See how much I care.

July lumbered out with thunderstorms.

August leered in with a brazen sun and young swallows twittering on the telephone wires.

In the great bedroom at Florey Palace Father turned to Grampy and said:

'Did I ever tell you about that houseboat your mother and I once lived on in that lake in Kashmir?'

'No,' said Grampy. 'Was it wet?'

'Oh yes. Frightfully wet,' said Father. 'Well, it was a lake, you see.'

'I'm not talking about the lake, you barmy old bugger,' said Grampy. 'I'm talking about the boat look.'

'All right, all right,' said Father testily. 'There's no need to get all aereated about it.'

'I ain't getting aereated about nothing,' snarled Grampy. 'All I'm saying is get your facts right.'

'What facts?'

'The facts about your bleeding houseboat.'

'Oh that,' said Father sulkily.

The Duke of Wiltshire handed round pontefract cakes and glasses of beer.

He smiled at the two men, glowering at each other in their bed. 'I say,' he said. 'Isn't it fun to be chums?'

Winston Hayballs worked on in a frenzy at the old Dower House.

Nancy watched him from the kitchen window.

She watched him from the window of her drawing room.

She sat in the drawing room and watched him as he ripped out the skirting boards.

– All he does is grunt at me. He never looks at me properly. He takes no notice of me. And I kissed him. And I enjoyed it.

'Winston?' she said.

'What?'

'I've something I want to ask you.'

'What?'

'Have you still got the cricket team intact?'

'Yes,' said Winston Hayballs. 'I told you. It'll be there. Why do you think I just shot three deer? Why do you think I been handing out pheasant's eggs all over the village? Why do you think I got another black eye and a bruise the size of a pillar box on my right backside? You got your cricket team, missus. And all the good in the world may it do you.'

She followed him into the kitchen.

He had stripped down to the waist and he was dousing his chest and his belly in cold water, rubbing vigorously so that his skin glowed and his muscles tautened.

'Winston?' she said.

'What now?'

'What say you take me out in your motor, your car, tonight and we go for a sesh?'

'I can't,' said Winston Hayballs. 'I got a prior arrangement.'

'With a bit of fluff?' said Nancy.

'That's my business, ain't it?' said Winston Hayballs.

– He hasn't got a bit of fluff. I know it. It's just an excuse. I'd know if he'd got a new bit of fluff. He'd be smirking all day. He'd be shaving. He'd be smelling of foot powder and washing-up liquid.

'Winston?' she said.

'Yes?'

'It's a lovely evening, Winston. It's gorgeous. Why don't you show me that wood at the back of your house? You're always talking about it. I'm intrigued by it. I'd love to see it. Take me there now. Go on, Winston, take me to see your wood.'

'I can't,' said Winston Hayballs. 'That's where I got my prior arrangement.'

28

August blistered Winterleaf Gunner.

The village pond dried out. The River Florey rattled in its bed. A heron died in Cuckoo Tree Meadow.

Baksi's stomach swelled and ripened.

'Look at the bloody size of him,' said Winston Hayballs one evening as he went into the kitchen to collect his poacher's pouch.

Baksi smiled at him.

He patted her belly.

'What are you going to give birth to?' he said. 'A bloody wardrobe?'

Baksi smiled again.

'I'm going to give birth to a big bonny bouncing baby,' she said. 'And I'm happy. I ain't never ever been so happy ever.'

Winston Hayballs thrust his shotgun under his arm and growled as he left the kitchen:

'Think yourself bloody lucky then, matey.'

He stepped out into the night.

The moon slivered in the sky. The heat from the day loitered in the shadows and snapped at his heels as he padded softly through the village.

Peace. No voices. No sardines. No stench pipes and dado rails. No demands.

Just the wood where he knew the deer would be waiting. And the meadow where they could graze. And the hedgerow where he would lay himself down, every sense alert and expectant. Damp nose. Soft brown eyes. Twitching flanks. Squeeze the trigger. Bang. Another offering for the cricket team.

Peace. No voices.

There was a light in an upstairs window of the old Dower House. He stopped and looked up at it. He saw the shadow of a woman. Bold features. Handsome curves. Tasty.

The curtains drew.

He could not stop himself. He walked up the lane. He let himself into the garden of the Dower House. He sat in the rose arbour all night, the gun resting on his lap.

Just before dawn he left.

September glowed in Winterleaf Gunner.

'I'm feeling oodles and oodles better,' said Father. 'I think I want to go home.'

'No, don't,' said Grampy.

He was lying in bed propped up by four pillows. In front of him was a tray of canapés, caviare and a half decanter of port.

The Duke of Wiltshire smiled happily.

'No, don't go, Guy,' he said. 'There are so many stories to tell. So many yarns to swap. Did I ever tell you about the time I damn near got drowned in the Alps?'

'I think you did, Herbert, if memory serves me correct,' said Father. 'Weren't you in the Alps at the time?'

'Precisely,' said the Duke. 'Spot on, old boy.'

The great bedroom glowed.

The fire glowed.

Grampy's eyes glowed, too.

'Do you remember the time when you was in India?' he said to Father.

'Oh yes. Rather,' said Father.

'Well, what was the bints like there? I mean, was they tasty and succulent? Or was they all dry and shrivelled with them spots on their forehead?'

Father sat down on the side of his bed and said:

'Well, on the subject of bints, old chap, I have a positive cornucopia of anecdotes.'

Grampy settled himself in his bed. He stretched out his legs, stretched out his arms and said:

'Right then. Fire away, my old wingsy bash.'

'Well, your mother and I once found ourselves in the company of this courtesan in Pondicherry,' said Father.

And the Duke of Wiltshire slapped his thigh, ground his teeth and said:

'Did you by Jove, Guy? Do tell.'

There was a sudden frost on the last day of September.

It did not bother Winston Hayballs.

Nancy watched him as, stripped to the waist, he ripped the tiles off the roof of the Dower House. He worked furiously. He did not pause. There seemed to be anger in his movements.

– Why? Why does he look so angry these days? Why does he ignore me? Where have the smiles and the chuckles gone? What's happened to the foul language and the sly winks?

– Geoffrey used to sulk. He used to pout. So does William. And Father. Why? Why do men have to sulk with me? I'm not an ogre. I always make the effort. Mother taught me that. Always make the effort, Nancy, she used to say. All right then, I'll make another effort.

'Winston,' she called.

'Yes?' he said without turning round.

'I'm giving a dinner party tonight,' she said.

'Oh yes?'

'It's just for you and me.'

'I can't come.'

'Why not?'

'Because.'

'Seven thirty sharp, Winston. On the dot.'

She drove to Sturminster. She bought escalope of veal, celery, celeriac, Paradeisen tomatoes and a case of red Moselwein. She took afternoon tea in the cramped café in the lee of the cathedral close. She bought herself a new blouse and a bottle of expensive French perfume. She renewed her subscription to the RAC in the caravan in the car park at the back of the supermarket.

She soaked herself in her bath.

She washed her hair and conditioned it.

She twirled naked in front of the mirror in her bedroom.

She smoothed the black stockings over her legs.

She put on her new blouse. Her breasts swung free beneath it.

– Me? Not wearing a bra. Me? Showing my cleavage. Wicked, wicked Nancy.

Winston Hayballs appeared at the front door at seven thirty sharp. On the dot.

She ushered him into the drawing room.

He was wearing his blue velvet suit and the canary-yellow cravat with the red fox heads. His hair was slicked back, and there was no stubble on his chin.

168

'May I offer you a drink, Winston?'

'You got a bottle of stout, missus?'

'As a matter of fact I have.'

She handed him a glass and a bottle of stout and mixed herself a gin and tonic.

'What do you want of me, missus?' said Winston Hayballs after he had taken a gulp of his stout.

'A chat,' said Nancy. 'That's all, Winston. A chat.'

'What about?'

'You.'

'Me?'

'Yes. You see, Winston, I'm intrigued about you.'

'Oh yes?'

'Yes.'

She offered him another glass of stout. He declined and asked for rum. She obliged.

'Tell me about the works of Thomas Love Peacock,' she said.

Winston Hayballs shuffled his feet and said:

'Well, he wrote books, didn't he?'

'Yes, Winston, I believe he did.'

She opened a bottle of red Moselwein and gave him a glass. He drank it greedily. She gave him another.

'What other books have you read, Winston?'

'Loads. I read loads and loads of books. Can I have another glass of that wine stuff?'

'Of course.'

She handed him the bottle.

He finished it swiftly, and she opened another bottle for him.

'Who's your favourite author, Winston?' she said.

'Everyone,' said Winston Hayballs. 'Everyone's my favourite author look. You ever heard of Arthur Ransome?'

'Yes,' said Nancy.

'Well then, that just shows what a lot we got in common, don't it, missus?'

She opened another bottle of wine and handed it to him.

– I've never seen a man drink so heartily. Heartily? Nice word. He throws his heart into everything. When he's happy. When he's sad. When he's roguish. When he's angry. Why's he angry? Why are you angry, Winston?

169

She took a sip of her first glass of wine and said:

'You're a man of refinement, Winston.'

'Course I bloody am, missus,' he said. 'I'm a philosopher, too. But I don't practise it look.'

'Why not?'

'Simple, missus. There ain't no money round here being a philosopher. If you wants to earn a living in the country what you got to do is chop down trees and trap rabbits and shoot deer and re-wire houses and turn your hand to anything what people wants. That's the only way to earn money. And you got to have money, if you wants to buy presents for your bits of fluff, ain't you?'

He opened himself another bottle of wine, tugging at the cork savagely.

He drank it from the neck. When he had finished, he said:

'You ain't wearing no bra, missus.'

'I know,' said Nancy. 'Why don't you call me Nancy?'

'It makes you look tasty, missus.'

'Nancy. Call me Nancy.'

He stood up. He began to prowl round the room. His cravat was rumpled. The buttons on the front of his shirt were undone and his belly glistened.

– I'd like to kiss that belly. I would, I would. Honestly.

'I read about it all in books look,' he said. 'Deserts. You know what you get in deserts? In deserts you gets sedimentary strata. And what does you get in cities? I tell you what you gets in cities, missus. You gets lute makers. You gets fog on canals and steam hissing from man-hole covers. You gets symphony concerts and pet shops with macaws on stands and tortoises with chipped shells. You gets mosques and minarets and blokeys sitting cross-legged and hammering at copper trays. You gets boulevards and salons with beautiful women not wearing no bras and ogling you and desiring you and wanting you and making no bones about their lust.'

'Winston,' said Nancy softly. 'Winston.'

He came to her.

He looked down on her. His chest was heaving. His forehead glistened. His lips were moist.

He spoke.

'You're pissed, Nancy. I don't like my bits of fluff the worse for drink.'

'I'm not drunk, Winston,' shouted Nancy. 'I've had one gin and tonic and two glasses of wine and . . . and . . . I am not drunk, Winston.'

She stood up. She opened her arms to him. He shook his head.

'You're pissed, Nancy,' he said. 'Go to bed.'

She fled from the drawing room. She raced upstairs. She flung herself on her bed. She sobbed.

The voices snickered at her. The eyes roved over her greedily.

– I hate him. I loathe him. I despise him. I paid fifty-seven pounds for this blouse. I must be mad. I'm not drunk. I only had one gin and tonic and . . . he had at least three glasses of rum and God knows how many bottles of wine and he just drank it like pop and I haven't had red Moselwein for years and years not since I went to visit Geoffrey at the airfield in Germany when I had to tick him off for driving too fast with one hand and . . . and . . .

There were footsteps on the stairs.

– It's him. He's coming to my bedroom. Thank God I par-cooked the veg. I can easily slip it into the microwave and the escalopes won't take a minute and . . . he's coming to my bedroom and I want him too. I am desirous of it look.

The door of her bedroom opened.

She closed her eyes.

'Yes?' she said. 'Yes?'

'Nancy?'

'Yes?'

'I want to ask you a favour.'

– A favour? Oh yes. He wants to ask me a favour. He wants to . . . Good God, it's William.

She opened her eyes.

William was standing at the foot of her bed. He was reeling. He smelled of strong drink.

'I've come to ask you a favour, Nancy,' he said. 'Mrs Godwin's starting up her parties again. She's giving one tomorrow tonight. She wants you to come. Will you come, Nancy? Please. Please, please.'

171

29

'Please, Nancy,' said William. 'Please, please come to the party.'

It was the following morning.

They were in the kitchen.

Winston Hayballs was sawing timber in the yard.

There were deep bags beneath William's eyes. His cheeks were flushed. His hands trembled.

'And why should I come to the party, William?' said Nancy calmly.

'For moral support.'

'What moral support?'

'I've an announcement to make regarding me and Mrs Godwin.'

'What?'

William hunched his shoulders and clasped his hands in front of his private parts.

'Well, I haven't actually spoken to her in so many words,' he said. 'But . . . well, you know what I mean?'

– He'd better wear his new Van Heusen shirt then. He can borrow father's mauve-blue tie with the green spots. And I'm not having him showing me up in those ghastly socks he bought without my permission on that railway outing to York pulled by Mallard. He'll have to . . . Him? William? Him?

'You?' she said. 'William? You?'

'That's right, Nancy,' said William. 'Please come.'

She began to laugh.

'Oh yes, I'll come, William,' she said. 'I wouldn't miss it for the world.'

She roared with laughter.

She was still laughing when she went out into the cobbled yard. Her shoulders heaved. She bent double and stamped her feet.

'What's to do with you, missus?' said Winston Hayballs, looking up from his saw.

'I'm going to a party, Winston,' she said, and her laughter grew more intense, icier, crueller.

Winston Hayballs put his hands on his hips. He clucked his tongue and he said:

'And where is this party then?'

'At Mrs Godwin's. Tonight.'

'I'll come with you then.'

'What?'

She stopped laughing immediately.

'I'll come with you,' he said.

'But I don't want you to. I hate you. I don't want to be in your company ever again. Do you understand that, Winston? I loathe you.'

'Mebbe, missus,' said Winston Hayballs. 'But old Winston, he ain't going to let you or allow you to go to one of them parties on your own. In the mood what you're in at the present, there ain't no way he won't accompany you. I'll be at your door nine thirty sharp. On the dot.'

That afternoon she visited Father at Florey Palace. She took him a basket of cream crackers, hard-boiled eggs, gentleman's relish, blue Cheshire cheese, radishes, olives, two pork pies and three miniatures of gin.

'Never touch the stuff,' said Father when he saw the bottles.

The Duke of Wiltshire snuffled forlornly through the contents of the basket and said:

'No dripping sandwiches then?'

Grampy, who was sitting in the window seat, wrapped in a blanket, said:

'She makes a handsome picture of a woman, don't she, with them long legs of hers and them shapely ankles on top of her feet.'

Nancy laughed.

'You young blades,' she said. 'You are all the same.'

'I ain't a young blade,' said Grampy. 'I'm an old codger and bloody proud of it. It's been bleeding hard work growing old, missus, and I ain't going to throw it all away now by being young and coming out in spots on my old Donger.'

– I really must look that one up in my *Reader's Digest Guide to the Countryside*.

She turned to Father, who was happily daubing gentleman's relish onto a cream cracker piled high with blue Cheshire cheese, radishes and olives.

173

'Well, Father, I must say you're looking terrific,' she said. 'It won't be long before we have you back home, will it?'

Father dropped his cream cracker onto his lap. He looked anxiously across to the Duke of Wiltshire and then nodded towards Nancy.

The Duke coughed nervously.

'Yes,' he said. 'We seem to have rather a problem there.'

'Problem?' said Nancy.

'It ain't no problem, missus,' said Grampy. 'The old bugger don't want to go home. And neither do I. It's a bloody awful place, home. Full of relations. Bleeding vacuum cleaners going all day long. Bacon rind getting stuck in your teeth. He don't want to go back to all that, do he?'

Nancy looked at the three old men in turn.

Grampy was smiling. The Duke was smiling. Father was fumbling with his cream cracker.

'Well, Father?' she said. 'Is this true?'

'Yes.'

'What?'

'Well, it's nothing personal, old chap, but it is fearfully pleasant here,' said Father. 'What I like about it is its permanence.'

'Permanence?'

'Yes, Nancy. It's what I've missed in my life, you see. All that constant moving houses you subjected me to over the years – well, it's played havoc with my health. Just get used to the water in one place, then off you hoik me to another and I've got to work out how the ablutions work. No wonder I've got such duff sinuses. No wonder my piles don't work and I've never had any chums till now. Fearfully selfish of you, Nancy.'

– The old bugger. The old sod. I'll kill him. I will. I'll disembowel him. I'll run him through with the fruit knife Mother bought me from Scarborough. I'll . . . No, I won't, I'm free. At last I'm free. William's making his announcement tonight. Father's set out his stall. Tremendous. Terrific. Wait a minute. Don't show him what you feel, Nancy. Keep it going to the bitter end. Cool and calm, my dear. Icy and controlled.

She walked to the door coolly and calmly. Her back was straight. Her head was held high.

Then suddenly she turned.

'Well, bugger you, Father,' she shouted. 'Bugger the lot of you.'

174

The door shook on its hinges as she stormed out of the room.

Grampy chuckled.

'By God, I does like a handsome woman when she's got her dander up,' he said.

'Did I ever tell you about the handsome woman I once met on passage out to India?' said Father.

'No,' said the Duke. 'Do tell.'

'Well, your mother was in dock with seasickness owing to the Bay of Biscay, and I was taking a pipe in the forrard smoking saloon, when in walked this bold-looking woman in a sombrero and men's trousers and a whippet under her arm.'

He smiled to himself and began to fill his pipe.

'Well?' said Grampy. 'What happened next?'

'I can't remember,' said Father. 'All I know is it must have been fearfully interesting.'

Winston Hayballs stood in the long September shadows outside the front of the Dower House.

He remembered the parties there in the days of Wilson Rappaport. The women throwing themselves naked into the swimming pool. The splat of vomit.

How he'd hated it.

He remembered the beery men fingering flabby bottoms. Wrinkled suntans. Nutcracker thighs. Predatory eyes. Long fingernails with chipped varnish. Scrawny necks. Teeth biting deep into his neck.

How he'd hated them. How he'd despised and loathed them.

He looked up at Nancy's bedroom window.

She'd be in there now gazing at herself in the mirror. He's seen her doing it when he was working on the roof of the stable. He'd watched her as she'd twirled round and run her hands over her body.

Deserts. A silken tent. Joss sticks. Thick, lustrous carpets. The swish of silk. The sobs. Winston. Oh, Winston, Winston. Cities. A balcony overlooking rain-kissed pantiles. Kaffee mit Schlag. Black opera cloak spread on the floor. Winston. Oh, Winston, Winston.

'Leave her be, Winston,' he said to himself. 'It ain't fair, my old wingsy bash.'

He knocked on the front door at nine thirty sharp. On the dot.

'Oh it's you,' said Nancy.

175

'Course it is, missus,' said Winston Hayballs. 'I told you I was coming with you.'

William stood nervously behind Nancy in the hallway and said:

'Mrs Godwin won't like it, you know, Winston.'

'Oh I knows that,' said Winston Hayballs. 'That's why I'm going. Add a bit of spice to the proceedings, won't it?'

Winston Hayballs led the way as they walked in single file to Mrs Godwin's house.

– God, I can hear the music already. I hate loud music. Even if it's Elgar. I used to like parties once. We danced to Frank Sinatra then. We had buffet suppers. I once danced with a future Member of Parliament. What an awful drip he was. His blazer badge got stuck in my jumper. What am I doing going to a party at Mrs Godwin's? Wife-swapping? Goings-on? I don't go to parties like that. How do they swap? Do they sort of have matching raffle tickets in pink and blue? What happens if the ticket you draw turns out to be your own wife? Nancy, don't be so silly. It won't be like that at all. William wouldn't be seen dead at a party like that. In any case, he hasn't got a wife to swap. And neither have I. It's just another one of Winston's stories. What a liar. I bet he's never read a single word of Thomas Love Peacock. Neither have I, come to that.

Winston Hayballs had snapped a twig off the laburnum tree in Mrs Fokine's front garden and he was swishing it against the stone wall outside the village shop and tapping it against his heel.

– Winston! I offered myself to him like a common little tart. And he refused. And even after he'd refused I wanted him to come up to my bedroom and William came instead and he broke out into hiccups and I heard him being sick in the loo and Father doesn't want to come home and . . . What's going on? What's happening to you, Nancy?

When Mrs Godwin opened her front door to them, she said:

'Winston! What are you doing here?'

'I come as an escort, missus,' he said. 'May I present my companion of this joyous occasion, Miss Nancy Empson, and don't she look a real cracker, too?'

Mrs Godwin smiled at Nancy and whispered to her:

'So it's your turn for the bit of rough tonight, is it?'

– Bit of rough? What on earth can she mean by that? And just look at the skirt on her. It's almost up round her hips. Good Lord, they're all wearing skirts like that. What dreadful legs they've got. And they've got ladders in their stockings, too. Dear oh dear, this isn't my cup of tea at all.

She found herself wedged in a corner next to a plump, bald and perspiring man. His striped shirt was undone to the waist and he had a large gold medallion round his neck. His fingers were encrusted with rings and he had a black moustache.

He smiled at Nancy.

'I don't think I've seen you before at one of Lucy's little dos,' he said.

'That's right,' said Nancy. 'You haven't.'

Loud music. Pumping, throbbing music. Winston surrounded by women. Winston laughing and winking. Winston drinking. He had no eyes for her. He had deserted her.

'You live locally in the village, do you?' said the bald, plump man.

'Yes,' said Nancy.

– Winston, please. Come and rescue me. I hate it here. It's awful.

The smells. Sickly perfume. Wheedling aftershave. Armpits. Feet. Crutches. Strong drink. Bad breath. Cigar smoke. Incense. The heat. The noise. High-pitched voices. Laughter pealing at the eardrums. Coughing. Giggling. The faces. Flushed faces. Florid faces. Saddle-brown faces. Greedy faces. Shifty faces. Rotten apple barrel faces.

'Shall we dance?' said the bald plump man.

And before Nancy could answer he took her by the hand, led her to the centre of the room and clamped himself around her.

– Oh Lord, this is awful. The top of his head only comes up to my chin. I can hardly breathe. What's he trying to do now? What's he saying?

'I'm sorry,' she said. 'I can't hear a word you're saying.'

He steered her to the side of the room, pinned her against a corner of the fireplace and said:

'I was saying that when the fun starts and we toss our keys in the centre of room, mine are the ones with the Aston Martin tag.'

'What?' said Nancy. 'What on earth are you talking about?'

Then suddenly she felt a hand on her right breast. She could not believe it. But it was true. The corner of the pine mantelshelf was digging into the middle of her shoulder blades. He was fondling her buttocks. He was fondling her breasts. She struggled. She could not move. The crowds closed in on her. They began to suffocate her. The

177

hands roamed all over her body. She tried to scream, but no sound came.

– I'm going to faint. I am. I'm going to faint. And I haven't fainted since the afternoon of the RSPCA fete at Whitby. Or was it Southport? I'm going to faint.

She did not faint.

There was a roar and a bellow.

Winston Hayballs grabbed hold of the bald, plump man by the back of his collar, spun him round and smacked him firmly on the nose with the back of his fist.

Blood spurted. Women screamed. The bald, plump man crashed backwards into the record machine.

'Right then,' bellowed Winston Hayballs. 'Who's next?'

He took hold of the minor television personage by the lapels of his jacket and said:

'You'll do. I seen you bloody ogling her all night with your bloodshot eyes.'

And with that he brought his knee up into his groin and hit him on the back of the neck with the side of his hand.

'Any more while I'm at it?' shouted Winston Hayballs.

He stood in the centre of the room, shoulders hunched, fists clenched, rocking lightly on the balls of his feet.

'Take me home, Winston,' said Nancy quietly. 'I want to go home.'

Mrs Godwin screeched at them.

Her face was contorted with fury.

– Ooh, look at her. Now you see her in her true colours. Look at the wrinkles on her neck. Look at the crow's feet at the corners of her eyes. Look at those skinny elbows and those mean, prickly little bosoms.

William stretched out his hand diffidently towards her.

'Now then, Lucy,' he said. 'Calm down.'

'Calm down? Me?' she shouted. 'Get out. The lot of you.'

'You mean me?' said William.

'You most of all,' she said, striking out at him with her feet and her fists. 'You disgusting little man. You pathetic little man. You useless, hopeless, helpless little man. You incurably leadless, limp and slack little man.'

They walked home in the frost.

When they reached the old Dower House, William said:

'I want to be on my own. I'll go into the garden.'

Nancy made to follow him, but Winston Hayballs held her back.

'Leave him be, Nancy,' he said. 'Let him work it out for hisself look.'

They went into the kitchen.

Nancy offered him a drink, but he refused.

He said:

'I'm sorry about what I done, Nancy.'

'There's no need to be, Winston,' she said. 'You were wonderful.'

– He was. He was superb. The squelch when his fist landed on that nose. The terror in the eyes of the minor television personage. The vigour of him. The vitality. The manliness.

'I suppose I better go then,' said Winston Hayballs.

– No. Don't go. Stay. I want you to stay.

He sat down opposite her.

– Stretch our your hands to me, Winston.

He stretched out his hands to her, and then from the garden came a mighty crash.

'William!' shouted Nancy. 'It's William.'

They dashed out into the garden.

There was a light in the shed.

– Oh, my God. Wilson Rappaport. He shot himself in the shed when Mrs Godwin threw him out. He killed himself. Oh, William, William, William.

They raced down the garden, and Nancy threw open the door of the shed.

William was lying on the floor. His face was deathly white. His legs were crumpled. His head was crooked back at a curious angle.

'He's dead,' said Nancy. 'Oh, William, William.'

She went to throw herself at her brother, but Winston Hayballs took hold of her by the hips and pulled her to one side.

'He ain't dead, missus,' he said. 'He's pissed.'

'What?'

'Look.'

He pointed to the floor. A board had been ripped up. And there in the musty, dark, mouse-snuffling recesses was Father's cache of gin.

Winston Hayballs bent down and picked up an empty bottle.

'He's been at the old mother's ruin, missus.'

Without warning Nancy lashed out at the figure lying on the floor. She kicked him in the ribs. She flayed at him with her fists.

William cowered. He grunted. He opened his eyes and said:

179

'Betty Hayballs. Where did you say she lived, Winston?'

Winston Hayballs carried him over his shoulder to his bedroom. He undressed him quickly and covered him up.

'Well then, Nancy,' he said. 'I best be going then.'

Nancy nodded weakly.

She went to bed.

There were no eyes roving over her body, burrowing into the cool, springy attics of her mind. There were no voices, whispering, sniggering. There was no laughter.

She was quite alone.

Outside the old Dower House Winston Hayballs looked up at her bedroom and he said softly to himself:

'Sleep tight then, Nancy. Sleep tight, my love.'

30

Father died peacefully in the third week of October.

It was a serene death.

The circumstances were thus:

The three old men were talking happily in the great bedroom at Florey Palace. Outside the wind bent back the beeches and the cold sliced into the ears of slinking vixens. Inside it was snug and warm and the coal fire exposed its great fat belly.

The three friends were talking about the women of their youth.

'Carletta,' said the Duke of Wiltshire. 'The maid at the old Dower House.'

'Ah, Carletta,' said Grampy. 'There was a choice and rampant young woman for you. Everything a man could desire.'

'Deep, brown smouldering eyes,' said the Duke.

'Nut-brown thighs,' said Grampy. 'Tangled, spicy hair. Thin waist. Great melons of breasts.'

'Juicy melons,' said the Duke.

'How she used to laugh.'

'She was always laughing.'

'It rang out, her laughter look. It was like the flow of the river her laughter. It was like the rush of the spring breezes. It roused you. Made you rampant and strong. She never stopped laughing. Well, only when she cried out look, but then off she'd go again – laughing and tossing back her head and staring at you with them deep brown eyes of hers.'

'Deep brown smouldering eyes,' said the Duke of Wiltshire.

Then he turned to Father and said:

'Were you ever unfaithful, Guy?'

'Yes,' said Father. 'With Mrs Ventris.'

'I say,' said the Duke. 'Do tell.'

'It was in India.'

'I thought it might have been,' said Grampy. 'Who was she then?'

'A half-chat,' said Father.

'Ah,' said Grampy. 'Got a touch of the old tar brush, had she?'

'Yes,' said Father. 'She was the wife of the local station master. In

181

India. She was a very tall woman. She had long legs and a slim body and the most enormous backside. She'd have made the most wonderful fast bowler, if only she'd been a man.'

'Well, that's the tragedy of the whole history of Test Match cricket, isn't it, Guy?' said the Duke of Wiltshire.

Father chuckled. He tapped out his pipe in the grate and sighed deeply.

'Ah, Mrs Ventris,' he said. 'Happy memories. I used to go to the station every morning without fail. I used to like to see the Night Mail to Madras flash by. Or was it the Bombay Mail? Good Lord, I suppose that's where William's got it from.'

'Watching trains?' said the Duke.

'No,' said Father. 'His penchant for tall, slim ladies with long legs.'

Grampy hobbled over to the fire and rattled it with the long poker. The Duke of Wiltshire poured out more raspberry wine and sent Filbert out for another packet of dried dates.

Father filled his pipe slowly. The days of his youth sparkled in his eyes and preened themselves on his lips.

'Yes, I used to go to the station every morning and sit on a bench,' he said. 'Then one morning Mrs Ventris brought me a pot of tea and an egg sandwich, and I suddenly realized what superb ears she'd got. They were very large and pendulous. They had deep cool curves to them. And they quivered.'

'Yes, I knows all about ears like that,' said Grampy. 'Get your tongue in them something chronic, can't you?'

Father nodded.

'Anyway, she brought me this pot of tea and the egg sandwich and something stirred in me,' he said. 'I hadn't felt so roused since I saw Ranji score a "ton" at Canterbury. And she smiled at me and she said: "Mr Ventris is away on business." And she beckoned me. And I followed her through the booking hall into their private quarters. They smelled of patchouli. There was a parakeet on a stand and an old lady in an armchair smoking a cheroot. She took me into the bedroom. There was an alpaca jacket hanging from a hook at the back of the door. It looked so forlorn, so cheated, so humiliated. Yes. Yes. Where was I?'

'In the bedroom with this half-caste bint,' said Grampy eagerly, and he spat wickedly into the fire.

'Ah yes. In the bedroom,' said Father, and he puffed at his pipe.

'Well, to cut a long story short, she took off her togs. And I did likewise. We stood there naked. It was like being in the changing room before the first game of rugger I ever played at the prep school. And then the Night Mail roared through the station. And the buildings shook and rumbled and rattled. And I was unfaithful. Yes. Yes. I was unfaithful twice. On the trot.'

He closed his eyes.

The pipe dropped out of his mouth.

He died with embers of tobacco smouldering gently on the front of his cardigan.

When Winston Hayballs brought her the news, Nancy said:

'Oh dear. Oh dearie me.'

The funeral service was sad and simple.

Nancy wore her severe black suit and William snuffled into his handkerchief and the Duke of Wiltshire wept uncontrollably.

The coffin was borne on the shoulders of Winston Hayballs, his two sons, Tarleton and Woodcock, and Lionel Woodyates, who had a cold.

– Look at that coffin. It's so small. Why are old men's coffins always so small? It's like burying an old tooth.

The Rev. 'Charlie' Barnett committed Father to his final resting place, and William snuffled and the Duke of Wiltshire sobbed.

Winston Hayballs stood at the back of the small gathering and stared at Nancy.

Women in black. He'd always loved women in black. It made their skin glow. It hinted at dark secrets. It promised carnal delicacies he had only read about in books from the public library.

Nancy turned away from the grave.

The Duke of Wiltshire came up to her, leading Grampy by the hand.

He bowed and said:

'My deepest condolences, Miss Empson.'

'Thank you,' said Nancy.

'We were wondering whether we might have a quiet word with you.'

'Certainly,' said Nancy.

They took her to the village pub, where the landlord, Grocott, rubbed his hands together rapidly and bobbed his head.

'It's a great pleasure and honour to welcome you to my premises, Your Grace,' he said. 'My hospitality is at your service and I'll put new paper in the bogs directly.'

'Never mind about that,' said Grampy. 'Piss off and get us three large whiskies. And keep your thumbs out of the glasses while you're at it.'

They settled themselves in a corner beneath the plaque of the Royal and Ancient Order of Buffaloes.

'Don't be sad, Miss Empson,' said the Duke.

'I'm not,' said Nancy.

'He was a good man, your father.'

'Yes.'

'He was my chum,' said Grampy.

'I know.'

She took a sip from her whisky.

– I'm not sad. Really. He died happy. He died in the company of his chums. He never had chums before. Mother didn't approve of chums. Mother didn't approve of Geoffrey. She didn't approve of anyone. Even Father.

She smiled at the Duke.

'Father died when he was telling one of his tales, didn't he?' she said.

'He did indeed, my dear,' said the Duke.

'What tale was he telling you?'

Grampy leaned forward and said:

'Well, it was about this bint with the . . .'

'It was about India,' said the Duke of Wiltshire, scowling ferociously at Grampy. 'He was talking about India.'

'Good,' said Nancy. 'He'd have liked that.'

The Duke smiled at her.

'Don't be lonely, my dear,' he said.

'I shan't.'

'I want you to think of us two as your chums.'

'Too bloody true,' said Grampy.

'Thank you,' said Nancy.

There was a smell of stale hotpot. The fruit machine clattered.

The huntsman, Seymour Bland, dropped a one-penny piece into the lifeboat box on the bar.

'You are a most handsome woman, Miss Empson,' said the Duke.

'Thank you.'

'You are a beautiful woman. Mature. Refined. And what I want to say is . . . well, I know the present circumstances are somewhat delicate,

184

but I have always believed in striking whilst the iron is hot and all that sort of rot. So what I want to say is . . . is . . .'

'Yes?' said Nancy.

– The stones dropped on his coffin just like that money dropping into the lifeboat box. Such a sad, empty sound. Poor Father buried deep in that flinty soil. He always hated gardening.

The Duke of Wiltshire took hold of her hand and said:

'I want to say to you, my dear, with the best possible intentions and with your interests paramount in my mind, that you should seriously consider and indeed contemplate . . .'

He paused and then he said swiftly:

'Getting yourself a husband.'

– Father used to wear an alpaca jacket when he had his school. It had burn marks all down the front. It bulged at the front where he kept his bottle of gin in his inside pocket.

– Remember when the French teacher knocked on your bedroom door, Nancy? He was drunk. You could smell his breath through the keyhole. You screamed. Father came dashing upstairs. He flung open the door and he dragged the French teacher inside by the front of his trousers. He threw him on the floor. He took off his alpaca jacket and he beat him about the head with it. He smelled of gin. He was pissed. He cuddled me and held me close to his chest and he mumbled something about the Night Mail to Madras. Or was it Bombay?

She smiled at the Duke and said:

'Sorry? You were saying?'

'I was saying, my dear, that you should find yourself a husband. And I know the very man.'

'Who?' said Grampy.

'My son.'

'Sturminster?' said Grampy.

'Exactly,' said the Duke.

'Over my dead body,' said Grampy. 'I'm not having her marrying that dried-up old fart with his pot belly and his wet lips and his damp hands and his yellow tongue and his sly eyes and his deceitful feet.'

'How dare you talk about my son like that?' thundered the Duke.

'I'll talk about him any way I likes,' shouted Grampy, slamming his fist on the table and scattering the damp-sodden ashtray.

'Oh no you won't.'

'Oh yes, I bleeding well will.'

185

Nancy stood up.

'I think it's time I left,' she said. 'Thank you for the drink. It was very nice.'

The two old men did not notice her departure. They shook their fists at each other. They cursed. They shouted.

'These bloody hooligans,' said Grocott, the landlord, to Seymour Bland, the huntsman. 'I'd ban them if they weren't all bloody aristocrats.'

Winston Hayballs was waiting for Nancy when she stepped out of the pub.

He walked by her side as she made her way back to the old Dower House. She paused at the front door and said:

'Thank you, Winston. That was very thoughtful of you.'

Before she could put her key in the lock he said:

'I got something to say to you, Nancy.'

'Yes, Winston? What have you got to say to me?'

He did not pause.

'When I saw you stood there at the graveside, Nancy, I fancied you something chronic,' he said. 'I wanted you. I desired you. I desired you like I've never desired no woman before. My whole body wanted you, Nancy. Every fibre of it. Every atom. I wanted to come over and tell you. I wanted to grasp you to my chest, my bosom look, and swirl you away with me.'

This time he paused. He hung his head. He shuffled his feet. He rattled the loose change in his trousers pockets. And then he said softly:

'But it didn't seem appropriate somehow. It never will seem appropriate, Nancy, will it?'

He left her.

She watched him, shuffling away down the rumpled lane, his shoulders drooping, his gait heavy and slow.

She smiled.

– Won't it, Winston? Won't it?

31

The smoke from the bonfires of November rose steeple-straight into the cloudless skies.

William left Winterleaf Gunner to go and live with his sister, Rosie, in Derby.

'It's a terrific place for railways, Nancy,' he said.

'I know,' said Nancy. 'Take good care of yourself.'

'Thank you,' said William. 'When I finish my book on the history of the Midland Railway, I'll dedicate it to you.'

'Thank you,'

She kissed him and waved to him as the train drew out of platform three of the station at Sturminster.

'Don't be cross with me,' shouted William.

– I'm not cross with you, William. I'm not cross with anyone. I'm not even cross with myself.

The life of the village went on as usual.

Thomas Fitchup returned from his stay with his cousins in Greater Manchester. He had found difficulties with the one-man buses. The Marquess of Sturminster made a speech about the perils of extramarital sex. Mrs Fokine bought herself a cordless telephone and Baksi's stomach boomed and billowed.

'I thinks it's disgusting, I do,' said Venetia Hayballs, prodding her with the tip of her umbrella outside the village shop. 'We don't even know who the illegitimate father is.'

'I does,' said Baksi. 'And I ain't telling no one till someone finds out. And I'm happy, too, so there.'

– He's finished at the house. All the work's completed. I paid him by cheque and I haven't seen him since. Not once. That morning in the graveyard. I wanted him, too. I could see him standing at the back of the crowd. I knew he was watching me. I knew what he was thinking. If only he'd asked me then. If only. If only. That's your life, Nancy Empson – if only.

The warmth of autumn slumbered on in the fruit store house.

'I miss Guy most frightfully,' said the Duke of Wiltshire.

187

'Who's Guy?' said Grampy.

'The old bugger from the Dower House,'

'Ah, him. Spent a bit of time in India, didn't he?'

'Yes,' said the Duke. 'Did I ever tell you about the time he lost his attaché case in Karachi?'

'Calcutta,' said Grampy. 'It was bleeding Calcutta.'

– I'm alone. For the first time in my life I'm on my own. It's lovely. If I'd married Geoffrey, I wouldn't have been on my own. I'd have been with him and his awful sister from Sunderland. She's the first person I ever met from Sunderland. She'd got such fat knees and she had hairs on her chin.

– And what if I were to marry the Marquess of Sturminster! Ugh. Imagine him staring at me as I got undressed. Imagine that pot belly wobbling. Mind you, it would be nice to be mistress of a palace. I'd have it redecorated from top to bottom for a start. I'd have the villagers in at Christmas singing carols and I'd give them hot toddies and fudge. I'd join committees. I'd join committees to save the whales and clean up the Mersey. And I most certainly would put my foot down and stop this nonsense about the village green.

– Winston! I haven't seen him for weeks. What's he doing? Has he got his cricket team sorted out? Is he well? Is he happy?

Winston Hayballs lay with his back against the trunk of the great beech tree in the wood at the back of his house. He had shot a fallow deer that morning. He had watched fieldfare and redwing scoffing the autumn berries. He had found himself a new bit of fluff in Gridley Miskin. She had fat legs.

That night when she'd worn the blouse with no bra. That day at the funeral with her springy dark hair and her severe black suit. That night she had kissed him full on the lips.

'Nancy,' he said to the old beech tree. 'Oh, Nancy, I wish you and me could go for a sesh.'

– How he whopped that man at Mrs Godwin's party. And how old she looked. What did she get up to with William? Did they really do it? I can't imagine William getting excited about things like that. When I tried to get him off with Geoffrey's sister, he blushed and locked himself in the loo for ages and ages. I wonder how he's going on in Derby? I don't envy him living with Rosie and her bad temper and her herbal tea.

– I don't envy anyone anything. I'm on my own. I'm free. What do you reckon then, Nancy? Terrific, my old wingsy bash. Shit hot.

Autumn was reluctant to leave Winterleaf Gunner. Blackcaps were still singing in the brambles that skirted Cuckoo Tree Meadow. The consultant obstetrician left his wife, and the minor television personality moved in with Mrs Godwin.

Winston Hayballs sat in the dining room finishing off his mince and cabbage. Baksi came in with a plate of tinned peaches.

He looked at her stomach and said:

'When's that bloody thing going to give birth to itself then?'

'Early next month,' said Baksi with a flounce of her head. 'And I'm going to move in with my Auntie Clementine, because our mum says she can't bear the sight of me no more.'

The Marquess of Sturminster made a speech on family responsibility in the age of the home computer, and Filbert, the footman, got drunk in the village pub three nights running.

– I could run away. I could leave here. I'm a wealthy woman now. Father left me the house and half his bank account. I could go anywhere I want. I could go to Tangiers. I saw it on the television last night with all those awful men wearing Marks and Spencer nightshirts and swatting flies. I could go to Switzerland. I went there on a school visit. I got sick on Toblerone. I could go to Germany. Geoffrey was stationed there and we drank that ghastly fruit beer in a pub in Munster and he tried to do rude things with my stocking tops.

– I could go anywhere I want. Oslo. I wonder what it's like in Oslo? I wonder what it's like in Adelaide? Mother had a pen friend in Adelaide. But I don't think she approved of her.

– I'll go. I'll vamoose.

– Footloose and fancy free. Good old Nancy.

– But first the village green and the cricket match.

– Get your priorities right, Nancy.

– Oh yes, never forget your duties, my dear.

32

Winston Hayballs knocked on the front door of the old Dower House on the morning of the first day in December.

The weather was still mild.

The wind was hushed.

When Nancy opened the door, he said:

'I come about the cricket match, missus.'

'Oh,' said Nancy, and her heart fluttered.

– He looks grubby. He never was a chocolate box, mind you. He was always scruffy. And there's a world of difference between being scruffy and being grubby. You look tired when you're grubby. You look defeated.

She cleared her throat and said:

'What about the cricket match, Winston?'

'We're in the shit,'

'What?'

'We ain't got no team.'

'You'd better come inside, Winston,'

He hesitated. She smiled. She beckoned him. He brushed past her. He smelled of stale perspiration and scrumpy and tiredness.

She led him into the kitchen and offered him a bottle of beer.

He refused. He slumped at the table, shoulders hunched.

– Is it me? Have I done this to him? When I first met him, he was wild and roguish. He was cheeky and chirpy. He was confident, cock-sure, cunning. He was strong. He dominated me. He enchanted me. And now? Good God, is it me who's done this to him?

'Right then, Winston,' she said firmly. 'Tell me about the cricket team.'

'I told you, missus,' said Winston Hayballs. 'It don't exist no more.'

'Why?'

'Well, Ted Cholderton's gone down with mumps. Lionel Woodyates can't get the day off. Wally Shergold's missus have dragged him off on holiday to Majorca in Spain. And the Hopridge brothers are working in Dunoon, and that's in Scotland.'

'Well, find replacements then.'

'There ain't no replacements, missus,' he said wearily.

He took a grubby piece of paper out of his hip pocket and threw it onto the table.

'There's the team list, missus,' he said. 'It's got me beat. I can't do no more, that I can't.'

She read the list carefully and thoughtfully.

'But I don't see your name here, Winston,' she said.

'Course you don't. I can't stand the bleeding game. I'm hopeless at it. You play cricket, missus, and you puts your old Donger in the direst of jeopardy.'

'I don't care about your old Donger, whatever that might be,' said Nancy. 'You're playing. And that is that.'

She wrote his name on the list.

'Now what about those two sons of yours?' she said.

'They don't like it neither.'

'Well, you don't have to like cricket to play it,' said Nancy, writing in their names. 'In my experience people who really like cricket are always totally hopeless at it.'

She paced up and down the kitchen, hands on hips. Then she stopped suddenly and said:

'Nansen Ticehurst.'

'What about him?'

'He can play.'

'But he's an old man.'

'What's that got to do with it? Cricket's an old man's game, isn't it? Look at W.G.Grace and Sir Jack Hobbs. They'd still be playing today if they weren't dead. Right then. We've got to find one more.'

'Why don't you try Grampy?' growled Winston Hayballs.

'Good idea, Winston. We'll have Grampy,' said Nancy.

She wrote down the names on the list, handed it to Winston Hayballs and said:

'There you are. Simple. All fixed up. All you need is a bit of nous. Right then, Winston. On your way and sort it out.'

He stood up. He walked slowly out of the kitchen.

– Why am I speaking to him like this? Why have I always got to be so bossy? Why doesn't he stand up to me like he used to? Why can't I be like other women? Fluttery. Weak. Totally dependent on a man. Winston, I order you to dominate me!

191

She stopped him at the front door and said:

'Why don't we go out for a sesh tonight?'

'What's that?'

'Let's go to that super pub at Gridley Miskin and have a nice long chat . . . and . . . you don't want to, do you?'

'That's right, missus,' he said.

He left her, standing at the door, ruffling her hair and frowning.

He walked to the village green and sat down on the splintered bench beneath the oak tree.

Hopeless. Bloody hopeless. He'd seen the palace team list. It contained two England Test cricketers and one West Indian. They didn't have a chance. Why hadn't he told her there and then? Why hadn't he stood up to her? What the bloody hell was she doing to him? And she was a woman, too.

He looked out over the green.

Mrs Fokine was calling plaintively to her Border terrier, which was yapping in a frenzy at the muscovy ducks.

Black-headed gulls made white gravy boats on the pitch.

They soared up in alarm as a kestrel flew overhead.

Winston Hayballs looked around him with loathing.

If it were left to him, he'd rip it up tomorrow and build a shopping piazza there. He'd build a factory with coal-black chimneys belching smoke out all over the woods and downlands. He'd build skyscraper flats and marshalling yards. He'd build a tank range for the army. A nuclear power station. A missile launching pad. An underground dump for toxic waste. A home for retired wife-swappers.

– No, my old wingsy bash, I tell you what's even better. We'll have an hurricane. An earthquake. A tidal wave look. Let's sweep the whole bleeding place off the face of the earth.

He smiled wanly.

– Funny, ain't it, about earthquakes and all them natural disasters? You never thinks you'll be killed by one. If you was in Bangladesh and there was floods and typhoons and famine and millions of people died all around you, you knows perfectly well that you'd survive. And why? Simple. Because you're English and Englishmen don't ever get killed in natural disasters.

– You're a philosopher, Winston, my old matey. Yeah, you're a one hundred per cent fully paid-up philosopher.

He stood up. He kicked out at Mrs Fokine's Border terrier which had decided to worry his ankles. He spat into the village pond, and meekly he went off to recruit the players for the cricket match.

It was surprisingly easy. He gave his two sons a series of swift and violent cuffs round their respective earholes. He gave Nansen Ticehurst the deer he had shot in the woods that morning down by the hatchery. And to his astonishment Grampy accepted his invitation with intense delight.

'Just what I wanted to perk me up look,' he said. 'I ain't played cricket for a good twenty year or more. As soon as I've scraped the mould off of my box, I'll be fit and ready and raring to go.'

They were in the great bedroom at Florey Palace. Filbert, the footman, was stoking up the fire. The winter sun smiled benignly at the windows.

Grampy practised his bowling run-up and said:

'Did I ever tell you about that time I took six for eighteen on a sticky wicket against Maiden Grovely?'

'It was five for fifty-nine,' said the Duke of Wiltshire.

'What?' said Grampy.

'It was five for fifty-nine and two of them weren't out because our umpire was drunk.'

'He was not drunk,' said Grampy. 'He was merely as inebriated as arseholes, and I will not have you casting aspersions like that on my aspersions.'

He raised his fists and advanced menacingly towards his aged companion.

Winston Hayballs took hold of him by the shoulders and replaced him in his chair.

'That's enough of that,' he said. 'You're going to need all your energy to buckle your box on, ain't you?'

Grampy chuckled.

The Duke chuckled.

'Yes, you're back to form, you old bugger,' he said.

And two hours later the snow began to fall.

It fell softly, relentlessly and without favour.

On the morning of the match the village green was knee deep in it, and the whole of Winterleaf Gunner was cut off from the outside world.

'That's it then,' said Winston Hayballs.

'What do you mean?' snapped Nancy, dressed in ancient gum boots and her mother's best fur coat.

'They'll not be able to get their players in,' said Winston Hayballs. 'So we've won by default.'

'What?' said Nancy.

Winston Hayballs shrugged his shoulders.

'You didn't read the document proper, did you, missus?' he said. 'It stated quite categoric that if one team failed to turn up, then the other would be declared the victors. We can go home now.'

Nancy stepped forward and hugged him. She kissed him. He stood there stiff and motionless.

Nancy began to speak, but her voice was drowned by the clackering engines of three helicopters which hovered above them for a few moments before disappearing behind the banks of beeches and landing in the grounds of Florey Palace.

Within minutes the Marquess of Sturminster presented his team. They had driven from the palace on an open-topped wagon pulled by the home-farm tractor.

The Marquess of Sturminster bowed stiffly to Nancy.

'Good morning to you, madam,' he said. 'A great pity about the state of the pitch, don't you agree?'

'What's that?' said Nancy, glancing nervously across at Winston Hayballs.

The Marquess of Sturminster showed no expression to his face as he continued:

'I have to inform you that by the terms of the Bill it is your obligation as villagers to have the playing surface in a fit state in which to play the game. If you do not, the match is ours by default.'

'Is this true?' said Nancy to Winston Hayballs.

'Oh yes, without a doubt,' said Winston Hayballs. 'And we don't stand a dog's chance of getting the pitch cleared in time to play. No chance.'

'Oh yes there is,' said Grampy. And he turned to the straggle of sullen villagers gazing blank-eyed at the luminaries of the palace cricket team and bellowed: 'You lot. Shift yourselves. Get your brooms. Get your shovels. And get your backs into it now.'

The villagers hesitated.

'You'll not shift this lot with shovels,' said Scott Ticehurst.

'Move,' roared Grampy. 'Bloody well move.'

Shovels were fetched. So were spades and brooms and coal scuttles and hip baths and the ornamental base of the wishing well in Mrs Fokine's front garden.

The villagers warmed to their task. They heaved. They strained. Grocott, the village landlord, appeared with tots of hot rum.

'Don't worry,' he said. 'I ain't paid for them.'

The villagers worked on. They cleared the pitch, but there were still massive drifts in the outfield, and their energies were flagging and the start of the match loomed nearer and nearer.

More tots of rum were passed round, but the villagers' shoulders sagged and their limbs grew leaden.

'We'll never do it,' said Nancy. 'It's hopeless.'

'That it is not, my dear young woman,' said the Duke of Wiltshire. 'We've been in worse situations than this. Alpine passes, sodden trenches, arid deserts and the men of Winterleaf Gunner have never given in. And why? Leadership, my dear.'

He turned to Grampy.

'You,' he barked. 'Unshackle the wagon from the tractor.'

'Yessir,' snapped out Grampy, and he set to on his task instantly.

The Duke of Wiltshire turned to Filbert, the footman.

'You. Onto the tractor and drive us back to the palace.'

'But I can't, Your Grace,' said Filbert. 'I'm supposed to be playing for the palace team look.'

'You snotty-nosed little bastard,' boomed the Duke. 'On the tractor. At the double.'

Filbert scampered onto the seat of the tractor and clinging to his back the Duke and Grampy were driven back to the palace.

'Where to, Your Grace?'

'The old stables.'

The Duke of Wiltshire sprang down nimbly from the tractor and marched into the stables.

A great beam of delight came to his face. He pointed into a gloomy corner.

'There,' he said. 'The old snow plough.'

The three men tugged at it. It would not budge.

'Heave,' shouted the Duke. 'Heave.'

The two old men wheezed and trembled, but Filbert with the aid of a crowbar managed to dislodge the plough from its ancient resting place.

195

'Leave it to me, Your Grace,' he panted. 'I can do it myself.'

'Stout fellow,' said the Duke. 'The spirit of Winterleaf Gunner lives on.'

They shackled the plough to the front of the tractor. They drove at crazy speed back to the village green, sliding, slithering, bumping and bouncing.

The Marquess of Sturminster looked at his father with a sneer.

'You have precisely one half hour to complete your task,' he said. 'Your mission is totally impossible. Why don't you concede now, and we can all repair to our homes.'

'Get out of my way, you miserable little runt,' said the Duke of Wiltshire, sweeping him to one side. 'Filbert. Get cracking. On the double.'

'Yes, sir,' said Filbert.

The tractor ploughed its way up and down the pitch. Slowly the snow was pushed beyond the boundaries.

The villagers looked on, sipping at their tots of rum.

'Come on, come on, Filbert,' shouted Nancy, jumping up and down and clapping her hands.

'Move, Filbert. Move,' shouted the Duke.

And Grampy raised his old warped, splintered bat above his head and waved him on to greater exertions.

Winston Hayballs, swigging shiftily from the bottle of bacardi concealed beneath his poacher's jacket, scowled and said softly to himself:

'Bloody waste of time. I thinks I'll piss off to my bit of fluff in Gridley Miskin.'

He did not get the chance.

With just five minutes remaining before the start of the match Filbert at last cleared the green.

'Well done, Filbert,' said the Duke of Wiltshire, patting the exhausted footman on the back. 'By God, sir, you'll most certainly be mentioned in dispatches for this.'

It was to be a twenty-over-each-side match.

The palace team won the toss and elected to bat.

The two England Test cricketers, opening the innings, scored 217 runs undefeated with elegance and immense disdain.

'Is that a good score, Winston?' said Nancy when the villagers trooped off the field and made for their tots of rum.

'Good score, missus?' said Winston Hayballs. 'It's a bleeding colossus of a score.'

Scott Ticehurst, the village team's number one, was bowled first ball.

He staggered off the pitch, giggling to himself and hiccuping.

The number three was out next ball and in the next over Winterleaf Gunner lost their numbers two and four.

By the time Winston Hayballs came in to bat at number ten the village team's score was 21 for 8.

He glared at his partner, Nansen Ticehurst, who was standing at the wicket, weaving slowly from side to side.

– Why am I bothered? What am I doing here? It's bleeding cold. That darkie bastard what's running in to bowl, he's going flat out for my old Donger.

He stood up and backed away from the wicket. The West Indian fast bowler skidded to a halt and collapsed to the ground, clutching at his ankle.

As he was led off past Winston Hayballs, the poacher grinned at him and said:

'Sorry about that, Sambo. My bottle of bacardi got stuck on the top of my old bat look.'

It was the last ball of the over.

Winston Hayballs crouched down and took another sly swig from his bottle as the bowler prepared himself for his first delivery to Nansen Ticehurst.

– Well, old Nansen won't last. And Grampy's next. So it'll be all over by the end of the over. Plenty of time for Gridley Miskin.

He flexed his arms, looked round at the fielders, winked at them, and then he saw Nancy. She was standing on the distant boundary. She was alone. The dusk was gathering round her. He felt her eyes boring into him. He heard her voice whispering to him. He felt her hands caressing him. He felt her warmth.

He spat on his hands.

'Right then,' he said. 'Right.'

The bowler delivered the ball to Nansen Ticehurst. It struck the side of his motionless bat and streaked away to the boundary.

'Run,' shouted Winston Hayballs. 'Run.'

He galloped down the wicket to Nansen Ticehurst, who was swaying backwards and forwards, smiling and muttering to himself happily.

'Hello,' he said to Winston Hayballs. 'What are you doing here?'

'Run,' screamed Winston Hayballs. 'Run.'

'I can't,' said Nansen Ticehurst.

'Why not?'

'I'm as pissed as a fart.'

Winston Hayballs raised his bat and with all his might thwacked him flush on the backside. Nansen Ticehurst sank to the ground in a heap and began to snore. The fielder returned the ball to the bowler's end and he was run out. He was dragged from the pitch by his snickering son, Scott, and Filbert, the footman.

Grampy hobbled stiffly to the wicket.

'Right then. It's up to us,' he said to his son. 'You know what you got to do?'

'No,' said Winston Hayballs.

'Close your eyes and hit the bleeding thing as far as you can.'

'Right,' said Winston Hayballs.

Grampy prodded him in the ribs with the handle of his bat.

'It's all down to the Hayballs. Just like old times, eh?'

The bowler came up to bowl.

Winston Hayballs clamped his eyes tightly closed and swung out with his bat. He struck the ball right in the meat, and it flew high and handsome for a six.

He repeated the dose with the next three balls.

Grampy hobbled up to him and said:

'It's the last ball now. Whatever you do, just run a single and get the bowling for yourself.'

'What?'

'Do as you're told, you young bugger, or I'll give you the thrashing of your life.'

Winston Hayballs followed his instructions and claimed the next over for himself.

He proceeded to swing lustily and mightily, and the ball hurtled to all corners of the ground.

'Come on, Winston,' shouted Nancy. 'Come on.'

'Hayballs for ever,' shouted the Duke of Wiltshire.

And the villagers drank on.

The score mounted up. The one hundred was reached with a four which streaked to the boundary from the meat of Winston Hayball's forehead.

Up and up went the score.

The two England Test players were forced to retire hurt when they tripped over Grampy's bat and collided with each other.

'Sorry about that,' said Grampy. 'I was just trying to flatten down a molehill look.'

Two more sixes. A four. A single to grab the bowling for himself. Winston Hayballs was a lion. He was a lion rampant, roaring and proud.

Two more bowlers were forced to retire, one with frozen fingers, the other with a broken toe when Grampy stood on his foot.

'Sorry about that,' said Grampy. 'I had to jump out of the way of a dragonfly.'

Another six.

One hundred and sixty scored and four overs left.

Victory was in sight.

'Come on, Winston,' shouted Nancy. 'Oh wonderful, Winston. Wonderful.'

And then Winston Hayballs missed the single at the end of the over.

For the first time it was Grampy's turn to face the bowling.

The Marquess of Sturminster narrowed his eyes and a thin smile came to his lips.

He tossed the ball to the next bowler.

'Right then, Filbert,' he said. 'Do your stuff. Do your duty.'

Filbert looked helplessly at the Marquess.

He looked over to the boundary where the Duke of Wiltshire shouted: 'Do your duty, sir. Do your duty for Winterleaf Gunner.'

Grampy crouched at the wicket.

Filbert ran up slowly.

He stopped and curled a gently looping underarm to the batsman.

Grampy chuckled.

'Good for you, Filbert,' he bellowed.

He swung his bat and was bowled middle wicket.

Filbert began to sob.

Winston Hayballs put his arm tenderly round his old father's shoulder and led him off the pitch.

The villagers had already left for the pub.

The Duke of Wiltshire stepped forward and clasped his old companion to his chest.

For a moment they stood there in silence, locked together.

Then, still in silence, they moved off in the darkness.

'I'm sorry, missus,' said Winston Hayballs. 'I let you down.'

'Oh no, Winston,' said Nancy. 'You didn't let me down. You've never let me down. You never will.'

She rested her hand lightly on his arm.

'You, Hayballs,' she said. 'You were immense. You were noble and brave. You were superb.'

Suddenly she spun round and pointed to the village pub, where the sounds of laughter and clinking glasses spewed out into the night.

'Those were the ones who let us down,' she said.

'Bastards,' said Winston Hayballs softly and savagely.

'What I can't understand is who paid for all that rum.'

'Don't you know?'

'No.'

Winston Hayballs took hold of her hand. She squeezed it.

'It was the Marquess of bleeding Sturminster,' he said.

Nancy hung her head.

'I might have known it,' she said. 'I might have known I could never beat an out and out little shit like him.'

'Come on,' said Winston Hayballs. 'I'll walk you home.'

33

The Duke of Wiltshire and Grampy lay side by side in a chill ditch at the edge of a pinched meadow.

The match was over.

The victorious team had been transported to the palace, and the sounds of their revelry could be heard clawing at the backs of the sombre and aloof beeches.

Louder still was the noise of the revelry from the losing team in the village pub. The singing was hoarse and tuneless. The laughter was sour and cracked with malice. The night shrank away from the blare-lighted windows.

Snow clouds lumbered in again from the west and barn owls hunted and grass snakes did not stir in their deep and leafy winter sleep.

The trench in the foothills. Huddled together. Groans. Moans. Chill eyelids of snow closing in on their senses. Shell shriek. Retreat. Betrayal. The red-capped generals in their mansion supping claret. The men in their trench and there was no fuel to heat their billies.

'Time to move,' said Grampy.

'Yes,' said the Duke of Wiltshire.

The two old men stood up stiffly. They cleaned each other down. They stamped their feet and flapped their arms against their sides. And they set off on their slow, solemn march to the fruit store house in the grounds of Florey Palace.

They crossed the village and stopped in its dead centre.

Shouts from the village pub. Splintering glass. Women's screams.

Boom of music from the palace. Shouting. Laughter. Women's screams.

'All them fights, eh?' said Grampy. 'All them battles.'

'Yes,' said the Duke of Wiltshire.

'We're too old for it now, my friend, my old mate,' said Grampy.

'Yes,' said the Duke of Wiltshire.

Arm in arm they trudged across the green and alongside the high stone wall of the palace and let themselves into the grounds through the old wooden gate.

The music had stopped. The voices had stopped. No laughter. No singing.

'They'll be as pissed as farts,' said Grampy.

'Yes,' said the Duke of Wiltshire. 'Bastards.'

And then they heard a baby's cry.

It came from the fruit store house.

They looked at each other in alarm. They broke into a slithering trot. They threw open the door of the fruit store house. And there before them lying contented and happy and exhausted was Baksi, and she was holding a new-born baby to her bosom.

And crouched at her side was the Marquess of Sturminster.

'Good God Almighty,' bellowed Grampy. 'So you're the bastard what's the father of Baksi's child?'

In the drawing room of the old Dower House Nancy and Winston Hayballs heard the first faint scratchings of the snow.

They sat silently on either side of the empty grate.

Father's chair was empty.

Their minds were empty.

'Nancy,' said Winston Hayballs.

'Yes, Winston?'

'Come to bed, Nancy. Come to bed with old Winston.'

'Righto, Winston.'

He took hold of her hand and led her upstairs to her bedroom. He laid her gently on the bed. He stretched himself out beside her. He put his arms round her.

Silence. No movement.

'Nancy?'

'Yes, Winston?'

'You ain't never had a man before, has you, Nancy?'

'No, Winston.'

He kissed her cheek. He kissed the lobes of her ears. He kissed her neck.

'Oh, Winston, Winston.'

He ran his hands softly over her breasts and along her thighs.

'Oh, Winston, Winston.'

Gently he began to undo the buttons on her blouse. She sighed. She ran her tongue over his lips.

And then there was a violent pounding on the front door.

202

They both sat bolt upright.

'Winston!' gasped Nancy. 'Who is it?'

'Shush, Nancy, shush,' said Winston Hayballs. 'Leave them be, and they'll go away.'

They did not. The pounding grew louder and louder. They heard feet hammering at the door. They heard shouts.

'It's no use, Winston,' said Nancy. 'We'll have to answer it. They'll break the door down, if we don't.'

Hastily they readjusted their dress and hurried downstairs.

'You stand at the door of the drawing room, Winston, and try and pretend we've been . . . we've been . . . oh, Lord, just try and pretend and I'll answer the door.'

She did.

The Duke of Wiltshire and Grampy burst into the hall.

They were wild-eyed and delirious.

They jibbered.

'We've found out,' they cried. 'We know who's done it. We know the culprit. We know. We know.'

They clasped each other and roared with laughter.

Nancy looked back to Winston Hayballs in bewilderment. He stepped forward from the drawing room. He took hold of the two old men by the collars of their jackets and led them into the drawing room. He dumped them side by side on the sofa. He poured them two large measures of whisky. And then he said:

'Right, you two old buggers. Take a good swig, calm down and then tell us what you found out.'

The Duke of Wiltshire spluttered at his whisky.

Grampy drank his back in a single gulp and said:

'We know the name of the father of Baksi's child,' he said.

'Oh. Is that all?' said Winston Hayballs, and he turned away to pour himself a beer from the drinks tray.

'How dare you turn your back on your father, you bastard,' shouted the Duke of Wiltshire. 'Show him some respect, you scum. Stand still, God damn you, and listen to what he has to say.'

Winston Hayballs looked across to Nancy.

She smiled at him and said:

'Do as he says, Winston.'

Winston Hayballs nodded.

'All right then,' he said. 'Tell us your story.'

Grampy told them the story. He told of the baby's cry. He told of the new-born child in Baksi's arms. He told of the Marquess of Sturminster crouching by her side, patting her hand.

'Bloody hell and set light to it,' said Winston Hayballs. 'So it's bleeding Sturminster what's the father.'

'No, you great pudding head,' said Grampy. 'It ain't him.'

'Well, who is it then, Grampy?' said Nancy.

Grampy told him of how he and the Duke had advanced towards the cowering Marquess, fists raised, boot caps at the ready. They told of Baksi's intervention. She had gone into the fruit store house to give birth to the child. The Marquess of Sturminster had heard her cries and moans as he prowled in the grounds away from the drunken excesses of his guests. He had found her and comforted her. He was not the father of her baby.

'Well, who the hell is the father then?' said Winston Hayballs.

'It's Filbert, my footman,' said the Duke of Wiltshire. 'And we've won the battle. We've saved the village green.'

'You're off your beanpoles,' said Winston Hayballs. 'Why have you saved the village green?'

'Tell him,' said Grampy. 'Tell the silly old sod.'

The Duke of Wiltshire smiled and began to speak softly.

'I looked into the baby's eyes. They were deep brown flecked with gold. And I knew instantly.'

'Knew what?' said Nancy gently.

'Well, my dear, many many years ago when I was young and in my prime, there used to be a maidservant here in the old Dower House. Carletta was her name. She had deep brown smouldering eyes and she was eager and she was willing and in the fullness of time she gave birth to my child, who in the fullness of time became my cook, and she in the fullness of time bore a child, who is still to this very day Filbert my footman.'

'I don't understand what you're talking about,' said Winston Hayballs. 'You got me flummoxed.'

'It's simple, Winston,' said Nancy. 'Filbert is the Duke's grandchild and so . . .'

'That's right, my dear,' said the Duke. 'And his son is my great-grandchild.'

The two old men hugged each other again and howled with laughter.

'He's got the golden flecks from my eyes,' spluttered the Duke. 'And he's got the deep brown eyes of his grandmother.'

Winston Hayballs sucked in very deeply between the blue-chipped gap in his two front teeth.

So now he understood it. They had threatened to reveal the skeleton in the family cupboard. All those speeches. Family morality. Sexual probity. Sanctimonious sod. His reputation couldn't stand the scandal. There was no way out for him. He had to give way.

'You clever old bastards,' he shouted. 'You won the battle.'

The celebrations were swift and intense.

The two old men fell exhausted onto the sofa. They cuddled each other. They began to snore softly and contentedly.

Winston Hayballs whispered to Nancy:

'Come on, Nancy. Let's leave them here and go back to bed.'

'No, Winston,' said Nancy. 'Let's go for a sesh in your motor, your car look.'

'Where?'

'Gridley Miskin.'

Winston Hayballs smiled slowly.

'No, Nancy. Not tonight,' he said. 'I knows of a far far better place than that.'

It was not cold in the wood at the rear of the house in Idle Lane.

It was warm and passionate and loving.

It was wild and Nancy cried out.

Winston Hayballs clasped her close to him and whispered into her ear:

'From henceforth and now on, missus, old Winston wants you to consider yourself his number one bit of fluff.'

'Oh, Winston,' sighed Nancy. 'That's the nicest thing anyone's ever said to me in the whole of my life.'

– And it is. It really is.

– And I don't need to refer to my *Reader's Digest Guide to the Countryside* either.